T0196550

Recipe for Love

Recipe for Love

Reva Spiro Luxenberg

Rev. date: 11/22/2016

To order additional copies of this book, contact:
Xlibris
1-888-795-4274
www.Xlibris.com
Orders@Xlibris.com
730013

ACKNOWLEDGMENT

HEARTFELT THANKS TO my husband Dr. Edward R. Levenson for his encouragement, patience, and editing of my book.

Thanks also to Barbara Cronie, Director of the Writers' Colony, and the members of Critique Group I at the Creative Arts School at Old School Square in Delray Beach for their constructive help.

CHAPTER 1

I T WAS THE middle of the night when Sara Solomon, twenty-six years of age, awakened in a sweat and screamed loud enough to bring her father in a mad rush to her bedroom. She had the same repeating nightmare again, only this was the first time she had let out an embarrassing, piercing noise.

Her father turned on the overhead light that revealed a blubbery man in boxer shorts, his chin covered with white whiskers. With eyes as black as a rain cloud he scrutinized Sara with a disapproving look. "What's wrong?"

"Sorry, Dad. I had a nightmare. Go back to sleep."

Mr. Solomon shook his head as he turned off the light and left the room.

Sara switched the light back on. It lit up her antiseptic hospital-white bedroom walls. She had requested black to match her dark moods, but her mother wouldn't hear of it, and her father, as in the majority of times, accepted his wife's wishes. So Sara had to capitulate. She made sure to buy an oil painting of a dark wild sea that she hung over her ebony desk. She covered her twin bed with a sable bedspread and hung raven-colored drapes over her window. Stacked in her dresser neatly were her coal-black bras and panties. Sara, depressed, but a neat freak, had all her possessions in place.

But she wasn't satisfied with her minor acts of rebellion. Often she deliberated about leaving the nest and moving away from Tampa—away from the unhealthy atmosphere in which she was drowning—if she ever expected to mature as an adult and become a published author. Eventually she wanted love and marriage, but so far she had hardly dated and had never even been kissed.

The inertia that stopped her leaving was that it was easier to remain where she was and be waited on by Maria, her parent's cook, and her attachment to the children she was tutoring. She resigned herself to tolerate Maria's opinionated bossiness.

Wearing her gray pajama top, she sat down at her desk, reached into the package of Lay's potato chips in the drawer, and stuffed a handful into her mouth. She turned on her laptop, read the last entry of her mystery, and searched for the right word that would fit the description of a character. She nervously tapped her foot on the carpet. "Adversarial," would do. Striking the keyboard as if mounting a military assault, Sara finished the page she was working on and leaned her chubby body back, satisfied that she had finished the chapter. She fidgeted when the wind picked up and the fronds of the palm tree whacked against the bedroom window.

Her thirty-year-old brother Eric had escaped their mother's exasperating nagging by becoming the chief nutritionist of Davy Foods based in Dublin, Ireland, but he, also, had emotional scars from his upbringing—he wasn't married, wasn't looking, and wasn't interested. Sara's mother was increasing the pressure for both children to marry someone Jewish. "You know," she'd say to Sara, "a boy with a future."

Her father, on the other hand, used to elaborate, "Stop dawdling, Sara. I sent you to an expensive college to find a man. And did you? At twenty-six your biological clock is ticking and now you decide you want to write?"

I know my parents are concerned about our welfare, but they never hugged us or said they loved us, just ordered us around like robots, she thought.

Sara raised her head at the sound of a passing ambulance. Last year she had vowed to recite a silent prayer every time she heard the reverberating whine of the siren. *Dear God, please help that person.* Ambulances saddened her and after she pointed the mouse on her computer to Shut Off, she uneasily began to twirl a strand of her dark wavy shoulder-length hair. Her long eyelashes that curled over brandy-colored eyes and her thick hair were the only features she was proud of. Sara tried to hide her chubbiness under hoodies and extra-large faded jeans. Even though she was overweight, she had small breasts and was ashamed of them. The fattening dishes made by the cook had added inches to her waistline and her hips, but her breasts didn't fill out like her mother's pendulous ones.

Before Eric e-mailed her about how crackers are as bad as potato chips, she used to gnaw on Saltines. He asserted that a typical cracker is made with flavoring and refined grains and filled with sugar, salt, and fats and that unhealthy preservatives are added so the crackers can sit on the shelf for a year. Potato chips were no healthier. Reluctantly she chewed a mouthful of chips and tossed the remainder into the bag in the wastebasket next to her desk. Changing her mind, she took the bag out and, gritting her teeth, she finished what was left. *My lack of willpower is to blame.*

She opened the desk drawer and drew out the package of Hershey's Kisses that she had stowed there. *Life sucks.* She returned the chocolates to the drawer and took out a pen and her journal. As she wrote in her journal about her lack of will power, she stopped and beaver-chewed on her pen. Then she pulled out the drawer and took out a dozen pieces of chocolates. Guilt-ridden, she unwrapped and ate them.

*　　*　　*

The morning brought with it a loud knock at the door, followed momentarily by the turn of the doorknob and the entrance of a middle-aged woman with a mane of dyed burnt-straw hair. Sara grabbed her pen and poked it on the wooden desk in a fit of anger. *My mother barges in. She never waits for me to tell her to come in. To hell with privacy!*

"What are you doing?" her mother asked with great volubility.

"Nothing."

"You call it nothing when you're destroying an expensive desk?" Mrs. Solomon's mouth curved downward with disapproval.

"Sorry," Sara said in a soft voice. She was now dressed in a black hoody and washed-out jeans. Nervously she tapped her foot on the carpet with her loose flip-flops.

Her mother frowned, wrinkles spreading like waves on her forehead. Sara sat still. No movement. No breathing.

"It's time for a special breakfast," her mother said. "Maria prepared cheese blintzes with sour cream. I taught the cook how."

"I'm not hungry," Sara said with a sheepish look.

"If you don't eat her blintzes, Maria will be insulted and she may leave to work for the Williamses. You'll be responsible for my losing the best help I ever had."

"Yes, Mom," Sara said tapping her foot angrily on the carpet. *My mother is always this pushy.*

"Every Sunday you lounge around doing nothing, and you're still in those rags. You should go to the community center like other young women and socialize so that you can meet men. All you do is sit at your laptop and write nonsense."

From the doorway, her father stared into the bedroom with a dark sharp gaze. Secretly Sara thought of him as a walrus. Her mother reminded her of an African lion on the hunt. Between the two Sara imagined she was living in a zoo in which her bedroom was her cage. The recurring nightmare which she kept hidden from her parents reflected deep anger.

Mrs. Solomon took hold of her husband's beefy hand and pulled him in. "What's up?" he said in a booming voice.

"Sara will be the death of me yet."

"You're aggravating your mother again," Mr. Solomon said emphatically.

Oh, how I wish they'd leave me alone. "I don't mean to." Sara began to nibble on the ragged nail edge of her right index finger.

"Stop biting your nails," her mother said with bitterness in her voice. "You're a real mess."

Sara placed her hands under her thighs, hiding the damage she had done. "I'm sorry."

"Let me look at your hands," Mrs. Solomon demanded.

Sara grunted as she pulled her hands out and held them out for her mother's inspection.

Mrs. Solomon looked with distaste at her daughter's nails. Her face twisted into an angry mask. "If you put gloves on your hands, you could stop biting your damaged nails and cuticles. I'm surprised you don't have an infection."

"I can't type with gloves on my hands. I'm sorry."

"They'll help your hands heal. It's your writing which is probably what's getting you so nervous in the first place."

Mr. and Mrs. Solomon exchanged meaningful looks. "Your father," Mrs. Solomon began, ". . . has a suggestion about something we think you need. Tell her, Martin."

Mr. Solomon cleared his throat. "I have worked hard to build up my furniture business, and I have succeeded in putting your brother and you through college. Now I see you can benefit from professional help in sorting out your serious problems. I'm happy to pay for a psychiatrist for you for as long as you need him."

REVA SPIRO LUXENBERG

Mrs. Solomon nodded. "We have in mind a doctor named Dr. Strauss. Mrs. Levine told me Boris no longer has nervous twitches. Your father has offered you help. I want you to take it."

Sara felt her heart pump blood into her reddened face. "I'm not crazy. I don't need a psychiatrist."

"You do, young lady," her father said as he shook his index finger in the air. "Nightmares aren't normal."

Mrs. Solomon stood with her hands on her hips. "You're twenty-six, practically an old maid, not dating, biting your nails, and dressing like a vagrant; and you say you don't need a psychiatrist?"

Sara opened her mouth to repudiate her mother's rebukes, but instead she flew out the door, her eyes overflowing with tears. She returned after an hour in a mood black as night. The rest of the day she remained in her room, a prisoner in a secluded cage.

*   *   *

Later that night Sara tossed fitfully in her bed. Sleep eluded her. She had to do something—to feel better. There in the den was a lure that could change her outlook and pull her out of despondency. It was 3 a.m. when she tiptoed out of her bedroom and stepped into the den quietly closing the door. She turned on the TV, adjusted the volume to low, and inserted the DVD *Now Voyager* she had watched and enjoyed fifteen times. She sat cross-legged on the sofa, her hand in a bowl of jelly beans. Her eyes opened wide with dismay at the dowdy and overweight Bette Davis, who played Charlotte Vale, in the movie. Sara had tears in her eyes when Charlotte's mother cast verbal and emotional abuse at her daughter. Sara wiped her eyes with her hand, grabbed a handful of jelly beans, and stuffed them into her mouth.

Gradually with the help of a psychiatrist, Charlotte changed her appearance from an unattractive woman to a slender beauty. She noted with a smile Charlotte's two-toned, high-heeled shoes. *Someday I'd like to wear a pair like that.* Charlotte wore stockings. *My legs would be sunburned—stockings would be oppressive in the Florida heat, so I'd do without them.* She gazed with pleasure at Charlotte's pretty face and head enhanced by lipstick, plucked eyebrows, and attractive styled hairdo. *I wish I could look like that chic woman. If only...*

Sara watched with increasing interest as Charlotte met Jerry and he called her "darling." Out loud she repeated Charlotte's words. "No one ever called me darling, before." Throughout the picture Jerry lit two cigarettes and handed one to Charlotte who smoked it like the glamorous woman she had become thanks to her psychiatrist. Sara made believe she was smoking a cigarette.

When Jerry and Charlotte shared passionate kisses, Sara fought the urge to bawl. No one had ever asked her out. No one had ever kissed her. *How I wonder what a kiss feels like. I wish I could find true love like Charlotte. How much I wish I could lose weight, but I can't since I'm living in this house.*

Right before the end of the movie when Charlotte said, "Oh Jerry, don't let's ask for the moon. We have the stars," Sara's heart filled with pity for the woman who couldn't marry the man she loved. Her breath whooshed, her pulse raced. She couldn't hold back her keening as the tears tumbled down her cheeks. Her wailing was so loud it woke her mother who turned the knob, opened the door, and rushed in.

Shocked, Sara jumped up and stared at the sight of her mother in her white ruffled dressing gown, her cold eyes hard and unmoved as a predator. With a harsh voice she said, "I saw that ridiculous movie years ago about a stupid woman who falls in love with a married man with children. And you are up in the middle of the night, crying over such trash? And you say you don't need a psychiatrist?"

Sara's jaw became rigid, and her body stiffened. A strange panic left her fighting for breath.

With a fierceness that startled her, her mother gave a derisive smile. Her father appeared—his eyes half-closed. With disdain he said, "Turn off the TV, young lady—go to bed right now."

They gave her no choice. Sara— finally—agreed to meet with the psychiatrist her parents selected for her.

CHAPTER 2

THE NEXT MORNING Sara hurried through her shower, quickly ran a comb through her wet hair, dressed in a loose white cotton blouse and jeans, and skipped breakfast so that she could arrive on time for her job.

Tami Weiss, the seven-year-old boy whom she liked very much, was already seated in the cubicle where Sara used to listen to him read aloud and gently correct his mistakes. Tami not only had Attention Deficit Disorder, but Cystic Fibrosis as well. *Two strikes for the poor distractible child with the diseased lungs.*

Tami read hesitantly, "The house raced around the tree." Cough. Cough. Cough.

Sara wished she could hug the black-haired child with the porcelain skin and huge dark eyes, but the agency frowned on physical touching. With shoulders slumped, Sara corrected the child. "The horse raced around the tree."

Cough. Cough. Cough. "The horse—(cough)—raced around the tree."

"Very good. Wouldn't it be funny if a house raced around a tree?"

Tami gave a weak smile. "That's funny, Miss Sara. Should I go on reading?"

"Of course."

Tami wheezed, hacked, and spit into a tissue. "The old lady led the horse to the barn. Did I read it right, Miss Sara?"

"You did a wonderful job."

"When I grow up, will you marry me?"

Sara blushed just as if a man had proposed to her. "You want me to be your wife?"

"Yes." Tami gasped for breath. "I want to live with you. Then we can read lots of books together."

"That's a lovely idea. All right—I'll wait until you grow up. But I think that by then you may want to marry someone else."

Tami smiled showing off his small pearl-white teeth. "Not a chance. There's no one in the world like you. Can I tell my mother about us?"

"Let it be our secret, but if you have to tell your mother, that's all right," Sara said, wishing with all her heart that Tami could grow up and become healthy and strong.

*　　*　　*

On Wednesday Sara drove to 720 Spring Lane and parked her shabby Mazda at the end of the doctor's curved driveway in front of a pale yellow ranch house. Once inside his office Sara grasped the arms of the black leather armchair and spoke in a low voice, "I don't know why I need a psychiatrist?" She glanced up at the wall where diplomas and licenses were displayed in the attractively furnished modern office with its gray carpeting, filtered overhead lighting, and comforting wood tones.

"Then why are you here?" Dr. Strauss, a man with thin sandy hair and a warm smile, asked in a kindly way. He had crescents under his eyes that reminded Sara of a half-moon.

"My parents insisted."

"Do you always do what your parents want?"

Sara sighed. "Most of the time, it's easier that way."

"How do you feel when they dictate to you?"

"Miserable. I'm angry and I eat to distract myself."

"Are you employed?"

"Yes. I'm saving my salary so someday I'll move out on my own. I work for the Tucker Learning Center. I'm tutoring three elementary school children, and they're doing well."

"What do you see yourself doing five years from now?"

"I'm not sure. Maybe I could be a published writer."

"What about marriage and a family of your own?"

Sara hung her head. "Men don't go for me. I'm shy and I'm fat."

"Who is the closest person to you?"

"My brother Eric, only he's working in Ireland."

"Do you keep in touch with him?" Dr. Strauss doodled the infinity sign on a prescription pad.

"Every day we e-mail each other. He told me he bought a handmade walking stick called a "shillelagh." He hikes in remote areas in County Cork. He sold me his Mazda for a dollar when he left. I took driving lessons, which my parents warned me against, and I passed the driving test the very first time."

"Good for you."

"Driving gives me a chance to get far away from home."

"Do you exercise, Sara?"

"I started to walk a mile after breakfast every day, but I'll never walk off this fat."

"Is your weight a problem for you?"

Sara hung her head. "I would like to lose weight, but sometimes in the middle of the night when I awaken from a nightmare, I eat potato chips and I can't get enough of sweets. And, of course, the cook always prepares fattening foods. It's a lost cause."

$$* \quad * \quad *$$

At the next session, although Dr. Strauss wore a gentle benign expression, Sara felt great anxiety, causing her to press down like a prize fighter on the arms of the armchair. Carefully she scanned her psychiatrist's face. *Had the dark circles and puffiness under his eyes increased since the last appointment? He looks like a man in his fifties, but without the puffiness he would appear much younger.*

"Anything new to tell me?" Dr. Strauss asked as once again he doodled on a prescription pad on his desk.

Sara hesitated. She bit down on the remains of the nail of her left thumb.

"You seem somewhat agitated," Dr. Strauss remarked softly.

"Last night I had a nonsensical dream. No! It wasn't a dream. It was a nightmare. The same nightmare I keep having. I woke up screaming again and scared my father." She crossed her arms over her chest and dropped her head.

"Dreams give us messages. It may be hard for you to talk about something so difficult," Dr. Strauss said, "but Sara, it will help you in the long run."

"All right," Sara took a deep breath. "It took place in my room, but my room didn't look like it usually does. The room had cages, and in the cages were wild animals trying to escape. Lions were roaring, wolves were howling. One lion managed to push open the door of his cage. He sprang out and fell down dead. I was so frightened I woke up in a sweat screaming my head off." Sara wiped perspiration from her upper lip.

"What do you think the dream meant?"

"I don't know. You're the psychiatrist—you tell me."

"Try to figure it out on your own."

"It could be my dream had to do with the anxiety I'm feeling living at home. I do feel like I'm living in a zoo. I want to escape like the lion; but I'm afraid to leave, afraid I'll die if I move out and live on my own."

"You know realistically you won't die if you live away from home. What exactly are you afraid of?"

"Mom and Dad will be furious with me. Suppose I get sick? Who will take care of me? The only time I was away was when I was in the dormitory, and I wasn't alone there." Sara gnawed on her knuckle.

"Were you happy there?"

"I was, and maybe now I need to find a new place with other people. My mother was sick after being hospitalized with pneumonia and I moved back to help her, and ever since I've lived in my parent's home."

"Why do you think your parents want you to live with them?"

"I broke my leg riding my bike when I was sixteen. I think they're afraid I don't know how to take care of myself."

"I see."

Sara hung her head. "I have another problem and it's my weight. Can you help me?"

Dr. Strauss lightly pressed his fingertips together. "Do you have any ideas how to lose weight?"

"I could join a weight club."

"What's preventing you from joining?"

"I don't like groups." Sara sighed, "There is a weight club in the community center. I don't know if I'd like it."

"You won't know until you try."

*   *   *

Charlotte Vale lost weight when her psychiatrist took her away from her domineering mother. I wish Dr. Strauss had a place for me to go, but he doesn't. I don't know if I should join a weight club with a lot of other fatties. Life sucks!

REVA SPIRO LUXENBERG

That night at exactly 3 a.m. Sara woke up in a pool of sweat. She had dreamed she was as huge as an elephant. Bags of flesh surrounded her body—even her face was misshapen and puffy. *I can't lose weight on my own. I hate to be in a group, but it's necessary. I'll go to the community center and find out about it.* Once she made up her mind to go she fell back into a restful sleep.

CHAPTER 3

ON SUNDAY SARA drove to the Ralph Rabinowitz Community Center and parked in the adjacent lot. She sat in the car looking at the brown pancake-shaped building and gnashed her teeth. She entered the building and approached the cheerful-looking white-haired woman at the desk. "Please tell me when the weight group meets?" she asked trying to affect a cordial air.

The woman paused for a moment—put on her tortoiseshell glasses and turned a page in a book on the desk. She explained matter-of-factly, "Fit and Fancy" meets once a week on Wednesdays at 8 p.m. Are you a member of the community center?"

"No—do I have to be?"

"Yes, almost all activities require membership."

Sara paused to let the information sink in. "How do I become a member?"

"You pay $60 a year."

Sara said grimly, "Oh, I didn't know that. I'll have to think about it."

"It's a wonderful group. All the members tell me how much they like it, and they're losing weight and feeling great."

"Thank you," Sara blurted with a sigh of resignation.

The receptionist pointed down a corridor. "We have an indoor pool, a library, a theater, counseling programs, and many meeting rooms. There are art classes and investment programs. The weight group meets in Room 102."

Maybe I can lose weight on my own, Sara thought as she left.

*   *   *

Sara waited two weeks during which time she unsuccessfully tried to lose weight before she had the guts to return to the community center. She approached the same receptionist. "I decided to become a member." Sara placed three twenty dollars bills on the counter.

"It's worth every penny to join," the woman said as she placed the bills in a metal box in the drawer. "I'll make out a receipt and give you a membership card. You have to bring it with you every time you come."

Sara tapped her finger on the counter. In answer to the woman's questions, she supplied her name, address, phone number, and e-mail address. "I'm coming back tonight to join the weight group."

"You'll love it."

I'm not so sure.

*   *   *

When Sara arrived at the community center, it was twilight. She was surprised that she couldn't find a space in the parking lot. It was almost 8 p.m. and she hated to be late. Luckily a car backed out and Sara was able to pull in. She hurried along to the center, showed her membership card to the guard, and didn't pay much attention to the individuals seated in the lobby. Some were conversing, others were knitting, and an older man was reading a book.

She was stopped by a light-haired stout woman with long hair that billowed out from her pretty oval face. It was Tami's mother, Mrs. Weiss. "Hi, Miss Sara," the woman said in a friendly way.

"Good evening, Mrs. Weiss," Sara said breathlessly. "I'm on my way to Room 102."

"Me, too. I started last week and I've already lost two pounds."

They walked briskly down the corridor side-by-side. Mrs. Weiss said with a smile, "I heard you're engaged."

"What?" Sara said, startled. "You're mistaken. I'm not engaged."

"That's not what Tami told me."

"Oh, he asked me to marry him when he grows up. I sort of agreed. I like him a lot. He's a wonderful child."

Mrs. Weiss burst out laughing. "I wouldn't mind having you for a daughter-in-law." When they entered the room, Mrs. Weiss introduced Sara to the leader. "Joyce Mills, this is Sara Solomon, my son's tutor." Joyce had her dark blond hair cut in a mannish style. Her figure was trim.

Sara nodded and took a step back. A muscle flicked in her jaw. The room had four armchairs and six folding bridge chairs spread in a circle. Four stout women were seated in the armchairs and two regular-size women sat in the bridge chairs. Tami's mother sat down on a bridge chair. Joyce held out her hand to Sara and shook Sara's hand strenuously. "Let's get you weighed," Joyce said as she led Sara behind a screen to a scale on the floor.

Sara pulled back. "Do I have to step on the scale?"

Joyce said, "This is a rule we have here. No one need know what you weigh."

Reluctantly Sara stepped on the scale. Joyce recorded her weight and the date on a card and handed it to her. "Bring it next Wednesday when you come back."

There was an empty seat next to a corpulent young woman who appeared to be in her twenties. "Hi," she said. "I'm Joan. I've lost ten pounds in three months." *If Joan lost all that excess weight, she'd be pretty with her even features, short curly dark hair, and lovely violet eyes.*

"Hi. I'm Sara. Does coming here really work?"

"You bet. We discuss nutrition, meal planning, and how to deal with relatives who try to talk us out of losing weight. I'm looking for a partner to jog with. I wouldn't go by myself at 6 a.m. in Green Park. Would you be interested?"

Try new things Dr. Strauss said.

"All right. I've been thinking about exercising."

"That's great. I've need to get away from watching the presidential candidates attacking each other on the TV," Joan whispered.

Sara answered dryly, "I hate when they insult each other. I stopped watching the news. It's too depressing."

Joyce began the meeting by asking how the women were coming along with the program. Two said their husbands had taken them out to dinner, and this week they didn't lose weight.

"It's hard to stick to the program when you go out to restaurants," Joyce explained warmly. "At home you can measure your food before you eat it. Remember our slogan—'It's PC for me.'"

What is she talking about?

"Let's recite it out loud girls, three times. All together now."

Everyone shouted out, "'It's PC for me! It's PC for me! It's PC for me!'"

Sara resolved to raise her hand. Joyce acknowledged her with a nod. "What does PC mean?"

REVA SPIRO LUXENBERG

Joyce said triumphantly, "PC stands for 'Portion Control'. We all measure our food before we eat it. It's the easiest way to lose weight. At the end of the meeting I'll give you a list of foods that need to be measured. You can eat anything as long as it doesn't exceed Portion Control."

The rest of the meeting was devoted to the nutritional content of some foods. Joyce pointed out that some women have triggers and need to stay away from particular foods like potato chips, French fries, candy, soda, nuts, and other foods that they can't stop eating once they start.

The meeting was over in an hour and Sara made up her mind to buy measuring cups in the dollar store the next day. Sara's dark mood had lightened considerably. *I like this weight group. I don't think it will be so hard to lose weight.*

The next day Sara drove to the dollar store. She bought white plastic measuring cups. At 11 a.m. she entered the kitchen where Maria had finished making macaroni and cheese for lunch. She went to the sink and washed the measuring cups preparing to measure the macaroni and cheese dish.

"What you do?" Maria asked.

"I need to lose weight," Sara said. "I'll eat just one cup of the macaroni and cheese."

"This is *mi cocina*. Mrs. Solomon, *ven aquí*," Maria shouted.

Sara's mother rushed in. "Why are you in the kitchen?" she asked her daughter, raising her plucked eyebrows.

Sara's chin shot out grimly as she became very uneasy. "I went to the community center and joined a weight group and I have to measure what I eat."

"You can do that when you live on your own, but in my house Maria is in charge of the kitchen and there will be no measuring."

Sara grasped that her mother and Maria would be in charge of food preparation and disbursement. Discouraged about succeeding in weight loss, she stopped going to meetings.

*　　*　　*

The following week at sunrise Sara met Joan in Green Park. Both wore shorts, white T-shirts, and athletic sneakers appropriate for the asphalt walking trail. The one-mile scenic trail was lined with divine bright red dogwood trees. "Let's go," Joan said her violet eyes shining as she spotted a great blue heron. As Sara walked briskly, her spirits rose when she saw a pearl-white ibis pecking at the grass alongside the trail.

When they finished their walk, both of them exhausted, they dropped down on a bench and rested. "I missed you at the last meeting. I'm so glad you'll be coming to the weight club," Joan said breathlessly as a lazy iguana passed in front of them.

"I can't come," Sara said in a flat voice.

"Why not?"

"It's a long story." Sara bent down to tie her shoelaces.

"I like long stories."

"My mother is very bossy. She won't let me measure the food. We have a cook and she gets upset if anyone enters her kitchen."

"You're compelled to follow the rules in your house, but really, not letting you in the kitchen is not only control-freaky, it's stupid." Joan smiled sardonically. "I have an idea. Cut down on your portions without measuring them."

"I don't think I can. My mother watches me like a hawk."

"How old are you?"

"Twenty-six."

"It's time for you to move out on your own. Your home environment is bad for you."

"I'm thinking about it."

REVA SPIRO LUXENBERG

CHAPTER 4

D R. STRAUSS COUNSELED Sara on a weekly basis for four more months. At one session in the spring she sat hunched over in the chair across from Dr. Strauss's desk clenching her teeth. "How are you?" he asked.

"Uneasy. I sleep with the light on in my bedroom. I still have frequent nightmares that my parents don't know about, and the light gives me a modicum of security. Last night at two a.m., I awakened in the middle of the night by another nightmare similar to all the ones about animals in cages. I stumbled my way to the kitchen and drank a cup of strong black coffee. I returned to my room, switched on my computer, and, as I watched the screen brighten, my pulse quickened and I had a creeping uneasiness. I wrote some caffeine-sharpened dialogue that wasn't any good so I erased it. Dr. Strauss, I'm not a writer, just a pretender and a fraud."

"There is no virtue in self-flagellation. You write, therefore, you are a writer. As you continue to write, you'll improve. You need to relax. Do you have any hobbies?"

"Yes. I have a box turtle, and I enjoy feeding her and watching her walk around."

Dr. Strauss cleared his throat. "That's unusual. How did you decide to get a turtle?"

"My mother forbade me to have a dog. She said I wasn't capable of taking a dog out walking, and besides if I went out too much it was dangerous. You never knew who could be stalking you."

"I see. What about a cat? There are cats that are homebound."

"My mother told me cats will cause a house to smell from urine, but she let me have a turtle that doesn't bark or leave an odor—and I have a feeling of affection for my pet."

"Having a turtle isn't exactly what I had in mind as a hobby, Sara. Is there anything else you like to do?"

"I like to read and write. I've read most of the classics—but my scribbling doesn't compare with the writings of Jane Austen and Charles Dickens."

"You're hurting yourself by contrasting your ability with other writers."

*   *   *

The following day Sara took the pages of the mystery she was writing and tucked them into a file drawer. *What do I know about mysteries? I'll write about a young woman like me.* She began to plot a completely new novel about the life of a single woman. *It's exciting to start anew. I'll call my novel BETSY MOSS.*

*   *   *

The summer arrived bringing with it the heat, the humidity, and the threat of hurricanes that Florida is known for. The weather didn't prevent Sara and Joan from their walks every morning. Sara had lost two pounds during this time; but Joan, who had continued with the weight club, had lost thirty pounds and looked gorgeous.

Sara was still plagued by nightmares and anxiety, and she kept all her weekly appointments always arriving a little ahead of time. One Friday when Sara parked in front of the psychiatrist's door, a storm broke. Thunder roared and lightning burst from the sky, and the rain came plunging down like bullets. Sara threw her raincoat over her head and raced to Dr. Strauss's reception area. The doctor opened his door and beckoned to Sara to enter his office. *It's his inner sanctum, a place where I'm expected to reveal my dark secrets.*

"I had a dream," she said without hesitating. "It was a long dream, but I remember part of it."

"That's good, Sara. Most dreams are quickly forgotten. Dreams are a connection to the unconscious mind. What was your dream about?"

Sara touched a finger to her forehead. "I was in the chemistry lab in college, and a boy asked me out on a date. He took me to the movies and afterwards in his car he kissed me." That's all I remember."

"How did you feel when you woke up?"

"Very happy."

Dr. Strauss made some notes on a yellow legal pad. "Your dream is a manifestation of a hidden desire."

Sara perked up. "Yes, I think so. I've never been kissed and I yearn for a man to take me in his arms and kiss me. I wish to love and be loved."

"That's a healthy desire."

How I wish I could meet some guy who will love me.

"That wasn't a nightmare, but every once in a while I still have a frightening nightmare. Is there anything I can do to stop them?"

"First of all you must stop eating before you go to sleep. Food triggers an increase in metabolism and brain activity and is a potential stimulus for nightmares. Secondly, if possible when you are having a nightmare, if you can recognize that it is a nightmare you can try to change its outcome. Try to ride it out from within. It's not easy to do, but you may be able to succeed."

"I'll try anything. Doctor Strauss, I'm still anxious when my parents hound me about marrying."

"You need to take the first step to meet men, and then afterwards the steps get easier."

I hope it's true. Walt Whitman wrote, "Now, voyager, sail thou forth, to seek and find." I have to take the first step, but it's so frightening.

*   *   *

After seeing Dr. Strauss for eight months, Sara plopped down on the leather armchair and immediately started to talk. "My mother is impossible. She doesn't let up. Now she keeps nagging me about biting my nails. She's driving me up a wall. I don't know what to do. I'm depressed and I sleep more than I should."

"I had a patient with the same fingernail biting habit," Dr. Strauss gave a slow thoughtful nod. "The young woman went to the beauty parlor and had her nails painted in a color she liked, and she stopped biting them."

"I never thought of that," Sara said. "Maybe it'll help me. "You know Doctor, I'm still writing my novel, and it's shaping up."

"Glad to hear that."

Fifty minutes flew by. Dr. Strauss looked at his watch. "Time's up."

When Sara left the psychiatrist's office, she didn't go home but parked her car in front of a beauty salon. She sat in the car with her index finger tapping on the steering wheel. Dr. Strauss was encouraging her to strike out on her own and become a more independent person. She wasn't sure about changing her hair style. *What good will it do when I'm so fat? It's so hot I have to wear shorts and my thighs look like tree stumps. I know I need to lose a lot but Maria and Mom insist upon serving dishes with sauces and rich desserts like pies, and if I refuse to eat everything, they both get that look in their eyes that means you better do as we wish or else. Mom pours ketchup on French fried potatoes and insists that ketchup is a vegetable. I have to try to take a stand or I'll go down the drain.*

Sara marched into the salon. *If I look different, maybe I'll feel different, and just maybe I'll feel better about myself.*

Sara noticed the sign over the hair dresser's station that read BRENDA.

"Cut my hair short, Brenda," she said with a confidence she didn't feel.

"Are you sure? Once off, you can't put it back."

"Do it." Afterwards she peered in the mirror and found the look, a halo of curls, flattering for her oval face. She remembered what Dr. Strauss suggested, a manicure but she decided to wait until her nails grew out—if ever they would.

Without warning Brenda picked up Sara's hand and examined her nails. "Sweetie, why don't you treat yourself to a manicure? It'll help you to stop biting your nails."

Sara hesitated for just a few seconds. "Okay. What do I have to lose? I'll do it."

At the manicuring station a young Asian woman thoroughly examined Sara's hands before she dipped them in a solution.

"Velly bad. I fix—to your nails I add acrylic nails. What color?"

There were about fifty nail polish bottles on three shelves on the wall. Sara studied the shades. Immediately she rejected green, silver, gold, and copper. After two minutes she chose black to reflect her dark mood. *What will my mother's reaction be? Maybe she'll praise me for my effort at looking more feminine, like a young woman who's interested in attracting a male for marriage.*

It took two hours before Sara left for home, one hour later than when lunch had been served. When she entered the house, Mrs. Solomon looked scornfully at her daughter and shrieked, "What did you do to yourself? You look cheap."

Sara's chest tightened. *Oh, no. I should've known my mother would be her critical self.* She shrunk back, her shoulders hunched like a turtle pulling into its shell. "I thought you'd be pleased."

"Your long hair suited you, and now you're out of style. Women your age wear their hair long."

"But Mom…"

"And as far as those phony nails, they'll ruin your own nails that you should stop biting. A young woman, who is deeply depressed, selects black nail polish. You should be feeling better about yourself after so many hours of therapy. I'm terribly disappointed in you and your doctor. And not only disappointed, but disgusted."

"But Mom…"

"And young lady, you missed lunch and will have to wait to have dinner before you put anything in your mouth."

I can't eat dinner. Ohhh, I'm getting cramps. Why, oh why, can't she stop the oral diarrhea? I can't take this anymore.

"I don't think Dr. Strauss is doing you any good. I'll tell your father to stop paying him. You've been going for eight months without results. It's a waste of thousands of dollars. I don't want you to go to any more appointments."

CHAPTER 5

MRS. SOLOMON, WITH a determined expression, sat down next to the desk in the library, picked up the landline phone, and called Dr. Strauss.

"I want to talk to Dr. Strauss right now," Mrs. Solomon said to the receptionist. "It's an emergency."

After a minute Dr. Strauss picked up. "Hello, Mrs. Solomon. What's the emergency?"

"Let me be frank," Mrs. Solomon said in a strained voice. "Sara is changing and not only not improving, but she's a whole lot worse since she started the so-called therapy with you. My husband and I agree we want Sara to discontinue seeing you and we won't pay for any additional sessions."

"I see," Dr. Strauss replied in a calm manner. "I would like to know what Sara is doing and saying that is upsetting you and your husband."

"All right, I'll tell you. First, she's not going out with any men. I believe she has no intention to marry and make us grandparents. She absolutely refuses to meet any of the suitable men that we suggest."

"Mrs. Solomon, Sara will date when she's ready and it's usual for young women in this day and age to select who they will consider. Is there anything else that disturbs you?"

"Yes. Secondly, Sara stays in her room and continues on the useless path of writing a novel. My husband and I didn't send her to an upscale university to become a struggling author. Our hope was that in college she would find a wealthy Jewish man to marry, but she didn't. Something is very wrong with her. Other women her age are married and have children."

Dr. Strauss cleared his throat. "Mmm. Is there anything else that upsets you about Sara?"

Mrs. Solomon clutched the phone tightly. Her voice rose an octave. "Sara came home with her long hair cut off. 'I thought you'd be pleased,' she said. Pleased? I was horrified. She had lovely long hair that's in fashion nowadays, and now she looks like a man."

"I'm taking your concerns seriously. I think Sara needs more time with me to sort out her feelings about marriage and a career, and if I were you as a caring parent, I would let your daughter have at least six more months of therapy, and if the results don't please you, then you may stop it."

"There is another concern I have, Dr. Strauss. I happen to know that one of your patients has improved since he is on medication. Why haven't you given my daughter medication for her nervousness?"

"I prescribe medication where it's needed, and in Sara's case I don't believe she needs anything more than therapy."

"Okay—all right—I'll go along with your recommendation for six more months. It's not that we're trying to save money or that we can't afford your fee, which, by the way, is tax deductible as a medical expense, and if you think you can help Sara improve her life and get married, then go ahead."

*   *   *

As it turned out it was fortunate that Sara continued seeing Dr. Strauss since she suffered a loss that hit her like a Mack truck. Her favorite student, Tami Weiss, was stricken with pneumonia. His immune system failed due to his cystic fibrosis and in two days he died. Sara needed to see her psychiatrist three times a week. She took a leave of absence from her job at the learning center as she was too depressed to work. Gradually she recovered and needed only one session of therapy a week. She began writing her novel again, and joined Joan every morning for their walk in Green Park.

The weekly appointments with Dr. Strauss continued for another six months. Meanwhile Sara's confidence in making her own decisions strengthened with each fifty-minute session. She knew she had to move out on her own. Every time Sara met Joan when they ran together Joan would ask, "Are you ready to move out?"

One morning Sara asked, "Where should I go?"

Joan said, "I heard the people in Palm Oasis on the east coast of Florida are pleased with their city. They're crazy about the amenities there and the availability of inexpensive lovely rentals with an ocean view. You could get a job there. Of course, I'd miss you terribly, but I'm thinking of how much you would benefit by leaving the nest and striking out on your own. I'm staying put because my parents don't lecture me and it's rent free, and to be perfectly truthful I started dating a terrific guy."

*   *   *

One evening Sara's parents caught her watching TV in the living room. "We arranged for you to visit a matchmaker," Mr. Solomon said. "I'm paying and there's no reason for you to complain. It's time for you to get married."

Mrs. Solomon added, "We see no progress that you've made since you've been going to that psychiatrist, and I agree with your father that you have to make an effort to meet and marry one of the men who the matchmaker will send you. What do you say?"

Sara's hands clenched at her sides. A dark, bubbling rage geysered up from the pit of her stomach until she tasted the vileness of it in her throat. "I need time to think over your offer."

As soon as her parents heard that she didn't outright refuse them, they left the room. Sara raced to her room and began to pack her belongings. *I can't stay here any longer.*

She decided she'd sneak out when her parents were sleeping and call them once she was away. She'd stay in a motel for a night or two and start looking for a permanent place and a job. She knew she was a coward and that Dr. Strauss wouldn't approve of her leaving without telling her parents, but at all costs she had to avoid a heated confrontation or she would melt and accede to their demands.

*   *   *

At 5 a.m., when her parents and the cook were sleeping, Sara loaded the Mazda with suitcases, books, and her cherished laptop. She went back to her room and picked up the aquarium that housed her pet box turtle, Daisy. She gathered Daisy's powdered vitamins, powdered calcium, and her water dish and placed them in a shopping bag.

In three hours she would arrive at Palm Oasis in time to eat breakfast and look around town. With her hair cut and layered with tousled waves she felt a bit more confident about her appearance. She'd have to diet and lose the fat that filled her chunky body. Renting a room and eventually finding a roommate might be difficult. Her finances were limited, but perhaps she could be a nanny or work as a companion to a senior citizen. She was strong and capable of cleaning houses.

An hour later as Sara was driving her car, her cell phone rang. She checked and it was her parents who had learned that she had skipped out. Sara shivered. *I can't talk to them yet. I'm not strong enough. My mother would surely yell at me and call me names and my father would back her up. I'll phone them when I get settled.*

As Sara drove her car, the orange ball of sun began to bake down, but the air-conditioning kept her cool. She couldn't concentrate on the scenery as she kept wondering about her parents' reaction. If she gave them her address they might even come and insist she return. *I have to put them out of my mind and think about how I'm going to find a place to live and a job.*

Instead of dwelling on the present predicament, Sara's mind turned to dating. *I may meet some interesting men. I'm free and since Mom and Dad live clear across Florida, I won't be having them dictate to me.*

*   *   *

Sara drove on autopilot almost like a person in a hypnotic state. Before realizing that her journey was over, she was in the midst of Palm Oasis. Bistros. Art galleries. Boutiques. There, on the corner, was a gas station; and luckily it had a stand with local papers. She parked the Mazda, stepped out, bought the Palm Oasis Tribune, and turned to the section on rentals.

Attractive room for rent. Ideal for a single person. Female preferred. Sprawling ranch house on the beach. Utilities included. Affordable. Call owner for details. 561-247-5555.

Maybe instead of checking into a motel, Sara thought she could at least inspect the advertised room for rent. Her stomach growled. She had skipped breakfast, and driven across Florida and she had to get a bite that would tide her over before she called about the room. Across the street was a luncheonette that looked clean. After a breakfast of scrambled eggs, an onion bagel, and coffee, Sara took out her cell phone and dialed.

"Hello," a man's voice said.

Sara hesitated. *Should I hang up or ask about the room? I'll take a chance.* "My name is Sara Solomon and I read the ad about the room for rent and I'm interested in looking at it."

"Okay. My aunt owns the house and she would like to rent it to a female. Drop by at 10 a.m. and I'll show it to you."

What should I say? Is it safe? Is this man a thief, a rapist, a killer? My fears are taking over. Can't let that happen. "All right. What's the address? I'll be there."

"It's 5446 Pine Tree Road. Bye. See you at 10."

The house was on a block of similar Florida ranch houses, surrounded by hedges with purple bougainvillea flowers. Sara parked her car and, although she had the air-conditioner on high, her face was coated with perspiration. This was a scary move. *Who was that man who answered the phone?* She gazed at the driveway where two cars were parked. One wreck of a filthy black car had duct tape holding a rusted fender together. The other tan car was clean, but it looked like it was at least fifteen years old.

Sara wiped her face, finger-brushed her hair, left her wallet under the seat just in case the man intended to rob her. She stepped out and approached the house with her head high, trying to look confident.

The door opened before she had the guts to ring the bell. A man about her age and her height looked her up and down in what she thought was a threatening way. He had thick brown hair that spilled over his broad forehead, and on his face he sported a straggly beard. In his left hand was a giant cup of Coca Cola. Sara shivered with disgust. Ever since she was frightened by bearded Uncle Lou when she was a baby, she recoiled at the sight of bearded men. Obviously, this man had no idea of the harmful effects of soda. In Eric's last e-mail he had written that soda with its high sugar content was a no-no and she stopped drinking it. But she needed a room and forced herself to talk to him.

"Hi, I called about the room for rent," she said. Her stomach churned as the taste of the onion bagel lingered in her mouth.

"Come in." His voice was smooth as a lullaby.

"I'm Elliott Morse."

"How do you do." Sara stood glued to the doorway.

"I do fine," Elliott said. "I'll tell you about the setup. All three bedrooms face the ocean. I live in one room and Tracy lives in the other one. The owner, my aunt, Helen Roth, would love for me to move out because my room is a mess, but I'm making a huge effort to clean it up. Aunt Helen lives two blocks away. She's been looking for a new tenant for a month."

Elliott held the door open, and Sara had no option but to follow him into a large room that contained two folding chairs, a table, an exercise bike and dumbbells. He motioned her to one folding chair next to the table that was piled high with tabloids.

Sara sat down and modestly pulled her sundress over her knees, while Elliott stood over her casually sipping his soda. Unexpectedly, a few drops of sticky liquid fell from his beard onto her hand. "Oh my, goodness!" she cried.

"Sorry," Elliott said as he drew a handkerchief from the pocket of his jeans and wiped the drops from Sara's hand. "The rent is $650 a month and my aunt expects a month's security deposit."

My knees are shaking. What should I do?

"I'll show you the room," Elliott said.

Following meekly along, Sara wondered if it was a good idea to share a house with a soda-sipping bearded male.

He held the door open and Sara stepped into a bedroom. It was a room that Sara had dreamed about—sky-blue coverlet on the queen-sized bed, blinds that overlooked a spacious private beach and a calm ocean, and a desk in the corner next to a white bureau. A door opened on to an adjacent luxurious bathroom with gold fixtures.

"The bathroom is shared by Tracy and the young woman who takes this room," Elliott said with his smooth-talking voice.

Sara looked at the tiled floor that was covered with clumps of long blond hair. She inspected the sink and found more hair to her dismay.

"Tracy doesn't always clean up after herself," Elliott said. "I'm sure she will when she shares the bathroom with you."

"I'm not sure about living here," Sara said perplexed by Tracy's lack of neatness and the fact of sharing a house with a man.

"You'll love it," Elliott said. "Let's go back to the living room and I'll fill you in."

In the living room, Sara sat down on the folding chair. Elliott opened a closet and pushed the exercise equipment in. He sat backward on the other folding chair and faced Sara. "Every Saturday night we have dances here. Singles come from miles around. This is a hot spot. We charge only for refreshments. Do you like to dance?"

"Yes. It's good exercise." *I sat on the sidelines at the last dance I went to. Not one guy asked a chubby female like me to dance. Why would they?*

"It's also fun."

"Of course it is." *It's also noisy and I'd lose my privacy and no one would ask me to dance. I'll leave before it's too late.*

"You'll quickly adapt to the routine in this house. My aunt is waiting to meet you. I'll call and tell her you'll be over in a few minutes."

I'm getting out of here and driving to the next town.

*   *   *

Back in her car, Sara pondered about her next stop. The room was gorgeous, the rent affordable, but she was wary of the occupants. She should try other places where everything might be more conventional. Sara's heart began to hammer at a terrible pace. *A new life is frightening. Maybe I should talk to Mrs. Roth. Maybe not.*

CHAPTER 6

WHEN SARA PARKED the car in front of Mrs. Roth's house, her hands gripped the steering wheel tightly as if it would fly away if she let go. She had a package of Marlboros in the glove compartment. When, at eighteen, she had tried smoking, her mother had laid a guilt trip on her so severe that she never put a cigarette in her mouth again. But at twenty-six she determined to smoke just one cigarette, one and only one—maybe, perhaps, could be it would relieve her anxiety about meeting the landlady who she imagined might be like her controlling mother.

Opening the glove compartment, she removed the package of Marlboros, tore open the box with shaking hands, and took out a cigarette. She pressed the car's cigarette lighter in and in a few seconds it popped out. She pulled it free and as her hand shook even more, she pressed the coil to the tobacco at the end of the cigarette. She drew in smoke, and released it in a burst. Her eyes watered and she began to cough wildly. She opened the window and not only threw the cigarette out, but tossed out the whole package. A teenage bicyclist, who happened to be riding by, saw the cigarettes, stopped and picked them up. He grinned at Sara as he waved to her. She frowned. *I'm an idiot. I shouldn't have done that. Sometimes I'm just too impulsive.*

In the deepest recesses of her mind she recognized that now was not the day to start a destructive habit—besides her brother would be horrified. According to Eric, taking a drag on a cigarette was equivalent to shooting a bullet down your throat. She had bought the Marlboros in an effort to be rebellious and assert her independence, but she realized that smoking was foolish. She squeezed her hands together, and dug in her fingers below her knuckles so strongly that she caused indentations on her hands from the tips of her acrylic nails.

Through the windshield Sara looked with concern at the gray sky dotted with patches of black, but she wasn't sure that it meant rain. There were times the clouds teemed and times they blew over. Florida's weather was unpredictable. Sara frowned as she remembered she had left her umbrella back in Tampa. *I'll take a chance and go in. Qué sera sera. Whatever will be, will be.*

Stepping out of the car, she didn't make it to the door. Lightning flashed, thunder rumbled, and the rain drops turned into a deluge. Sara sprinted down the path lined with cobblestones like she was being chased by a monster. When she reached Mrs. Roth's door, her hair was as limp as her old stuffed Raggedy Ann doll. Her sandals sloshed with every step. She pressed the doorbell, genuinely dismayed by her appearance. *I look awful. Am I doing the right thing?*

The door opened to reveal a stout older woman with silky silver hair fashioned in a bun. She leaned on a walker, her face contorted as if she were in pain. *This woman is in such bad shape she can never be an effective landlady.*

"Elliott called me about your wanting to rent the room. He said to trust you. Come in," Mrs. Roth said weakly as she led Sara to a cozy library with bookcases crammed from top to bottom. Sara looked with interest at the books. Mrs. Roth lowered herself to a sofa that caved-in under her weight.

"I saw you looking at my books. I read a lot," she said warmly. "Please sit down."

"I'm soaked," Sara said. "I can't sit on your armchair. I'll ruin it."

"Sorry, let's go to the kitchen where there are towels you can use to dry off. We can sit at the table and talk." Mrs. Roth leaned on the handles of the aluminum walker and pushed. Sara noticed the half-circle tennis balls on the feet of the walker. She concluded they made it easier for this poor woman who looked absolutely exhausted—to move the walker. Sara trailed behind her, wetting the tile floor with pools of water.

"Tell me about yourself," Mrs. Roth said as she handed Sara a yellow Turkish hand towel. Sara took a seat at the table opposite Mrs. Roth. She dried her hair and then removed her sandals and ran the towel over her feet. She slipped her right foot under the chair, ashamed that Mrs. Roth might see the discoloration on her big toe. It had happened last year when she hit her foot against the bedframe after her mother had rebuked her harshly. The mark still hadn't disappeared.

Swiftly she dried her head and then ran her fingers through her hair where soft curls appeared. Then she dried her cheeks. *If only I didn't have eruptions on my face. If only I could look fairly decent, not so plain.*

Sara spoke softly. "My name is Sara Solomon. I'm single. I moved away from my parent's home in Tampa to be more independent. They don't approve of my new writing career."

"That's too bad. I think being a writer is admirable." Mrs. Roth's face lit up as she smiled warmly. "What are you writing?"

"I was writing a mystery; but I dropped it and began a story about a girl who suffers from her bossy mother. In the end she overcomes her problems and becomes an English teacher in a high school and eventually marries the principal."

"Interesting. I'd like to read the whole thing. Would you care for a piece of apple pie that my aide left in the fridge?"

"No, thank you. I made up my mind to lose weight and I'm starting today, although I know I shouldn't have eaten a bagel for breakfast." *I hate to be so chubby.*

"That's all right, dear. You can start your diet right now. By the way how are you planning to pay the rent?"

"I'm young and healthy and I can be a saleslady, a maid, or a nanny."

Mrs. Roth adjusted the silk shawl on her shoulders. She looked thoughtful. "I have an idea. My second cousin, Susan, has been taking care of me four hours a day, but she's getting married next week and she's moving to Colorado. You don't have to pay me rent if you'd be interested in taking her place. I'll pay you $100 a week as an aide. Your duties would be to shop, help me dress, and get into the shower safely, also light cooking—but no cleaning as I have a girl who cleans."

Sara fidgeted with her fingers. "You're very generous. I'd like the job and I thank you for the offer, but frankly I'm not sure about sharing the house with Tracy and Elliott."

Mrs. Roth's frail body shook as she laughed. "Don't concern yourself with them. Elliott and Tracy are playing in a modern version of *Othello*—and Tracy is Desdemona, his wife."

"Really?" *Wow, that sounds fascinating.*

"I believe Tracy has fallen for Elliott, but that's their business."

That's a relief—then he won't bother me.

"Usually Elliott is clean shaven, but for the part of Othello he has elected to be bearded. Did I tell you he's my nephew? He's the son of my dead brother."

"It's nice that you have a relative close by."

Mrs. Roth nodded. "Yes, it's convenient. He's too busy to come over often, but I understand and I forgive him. Elliott is a talented and fluent writer. Someday his plays will be featured on Broadway. I'm proud of him."

"Oh, so he writes plays."

"Yes, he's an excellent writer and has a great sense of humor. I'd like to see this play performed, but somehow I've not been able to make it to the show."

"Why not?" *She seems like such a nice lady. It's a shame she hasn't seen the play.*

"I've asked the cousin of mine who is taking care to bring me to the show, but she never has. I don't know why."

"Maybe she has other commitments." *Poor lady. I'll take her.*

"What do you say about moving in?"

"I say okay." *But I have reservations. I guess if things go wrong I can move out.*

Mrs. Roth extended her hand. Sara shook it tenderly, afraid to squeeze and inadvertently hurt the woman. When she withdrew her hand, Sara felt a nudge on her calf. She looked down and laughed as she saw a fluffy gray-haired cat rubbing against her leg. She petted the cat and it purred with delight.

"Her name is Emeralda because her eyes are the color of emeralds. She's a treasure," Mrs. Roth said. "If she ever disappeared, I'd be devastated."

"Oh, I'm sure she'll never leave you."

"Yes, I agree. She's a house cat, never been out the front door. She's wonderful company for me and no trouble at all. She even sleeps next to me and never wakes me up."

When Sara left to go back to the rental room, the shiny orange basketball sun had reappeared. *Am I lucky? What would Dr. Strauss say? Maybe he'd approve, or is this the start of something I'll regret.*

CHAPTER 7

SARA SCHLEPPED HER heavy suitcase to the front door of her new home. She put down the suitcase, put the key in the lock, and opened the door to find Elliott passionately kissing a young blond female in the living room.

When they parted the blond said, "I love living with you, my Moor."

"This is the time I hit you on stage," Elliott said, "but not now." When he spotted Sara standing at the door he wiped his mouth with his handkerchief erasing all trace of Tracy's lavender lipstick. "Sara Solomon, may I present a young aspiring actress? This is Tracy North. We were rehearsing the last act of my play."

"Pleased to meet you," Sara said. *It didn't look like a rehearsal to me, more like a sizzling scene.*

Tracy cast a scornful look at Sara as if a barrel of trash had walked in. Then she turned back to Elliott and looked at him with bright blue flirtatious eyes. He stood silently looking at the ceiling.

Tracy was dressed in a revealing bikini that showed an endowment that Sara suspected was artificial. No woman was built like that—even Dolly Parton had to have help. Her stomach roiled, and she felt a rising antipathy to Tracy like repeating onions.

"Don't mind me," Sara said. "Mrs. Roth okayed me and I'm moving in. Just go on with what you were doing."

"We've rehearsed enough," Elliott said as he took hold of Sara's suitcase like it was made of feathers and brought it into her room.

He seems pleasant enough, but I don't know about that woman. She was kissing him like she was swallowing a goldfish.

Elliott plopped down on the bed in Sara's room. "I knew that my aunt was going to rent to you."

"How did you know that?" Sara said with a questioning look.

"Instinct. I can tell a lot about people just by looking at them."

"Well then, did you know that your aunt hired me to look after her?"

"It makes sense. She needs a younger person she can rely on. My aunt is one sick lady."

Sara snapped open the lock on the suitcase, drew out the laptop that she placed on the desk.

"Do you write?" Elliott asked, tipping his head to the right side.

"A little."

"Like what?"

"A drama about a young woman with parental problems."

"Show it to me sometime. Do you need help bringing in more stuff?"

Sara's muscles ached. "Thanks. I'd appreciate a hand."

After they made their way to the car, Elliott looked surprised when he found a turtle in an aquarium. "What's this?"

"That's Daisy, my pet box turtle," Sara said with pride.

"What's it good for?"

"She eats small portions of raw chopped meat and cantaloupe, and she's sets a good example for me to lose some weight—and besides I enjoy watching her eat."

Elliott stared at Sara's girth. He put his hand on his bulging stomach. "Let me know if you have a diet that works. I need to lose a few pounds."

After bringing in the aquarium, Elliott went back for the remainder of Sara's belongings and left her alone. After she filled the water dish and placed Daisy in it, Sara lay down, stretched out on the bed, and quickly fell into a deep sleep.

It was dinner time when she awoke with a pang of hunger. She would have to drive to a supermarket and buy some provisions. Meanwhile she made her way to the kitchen and peeked in the large stainless steel refrigerator to see how much space was left for fruits and vegetables. Every shelf was loaded with foods she knew were bad for a person's health. Two shelves were loaded with beer and soda. The rest were packed with meats of all kinds. There was no produce at all. This was a problem she hadn't anticipated. Maybe she could find space in Mrs. Roth's refrigerator, but that was probably filled with medications.

As Sara stood in front of the open refrigerator, Tracy entered the kitchen.

"Why are you standing in front of the fridge with the door open? Are you stupid or something?" Tracy said with a sneer.

"I was looking for an empty shelf where I could put my food," Sara answered meekly.

"You need glasses if you can't see that there is no empty shelf," Tracy said, giving Sara a look of frosty annoyance.

"I live here now and I'm entitled to at least one shelf."

"And what do you intend to put on that shelf?" Tracy asked with a smirk.

"Fresh fruits, vegetables, eggs, fish, and chicken."

"Are you nuts?" Tracy said as she curled a strand of her long blond hair around one finger. "Fish will stink up the refrigerator."

"I'll bake it, and if it's wrapped in aluminum foil it doesn't have an odor."

"That's enough bellyaching, girls," Elliott said as he came in and casually leaned against the kitchen door. "Let's have peace in this house. I'll take out one of my shelves with the soda and the beer and make space for you."

"Don't be so self-sacrificing." Tracy stood erect, her chin tilted up. "We need that cold soda and beer for our next party."

"We can buy more when we run out. A bag of ice is cheap enough if we need it," Elliott said as he began removing the soda and beer cans.

"Thank you," Sara said, and as an afterthought added, "You know soda and beer are packed with sugar and they're not good for you." *I remember when Eric told me that sugar raises the insulin levels depressing the immune system.* "I advise you to keep away from sugar."

Elliott shot a scathing look at her. "Thank you for your advice. When I feel I need it, I'll ask you for it."

Tracy winked to Elliott as she said, "Don't pay attention to her. She doesn't know anything and spits out advice like she's an authority."

"I'm not an authority, but my brother is and I've learned a lot from him."

"Listen tubby, you're the last person Elliott and I will listen to about health," Tracy said as she took hold of Elliott's hand and pulled him out of the room.

*   *   *

A week later as Sara was working at her computer and concentrating on her novel, she wasn't paying attention to Daisy who was crawling around on the floor. She always took her out of her aquarium to let her exercise. Most times the turtle wound up in one corner of the room or another, but today she disappeared. Sara peered under the bed. She wasn't there. She thoroughly examined every inch of her bedroom, and noticed that she had forgotten to lock the door which was slightly open—enough for the turtle to squeeze through.

Unexpectedly, Sara heard a woman's scream. She ran to the kitchen where she found a frightened Tracy holding a rolling pin ready to attack Daisy who was looking up at her. "Get this miserable creature out of my presence," Tracy shouted. "She almost bit me."

"I'm sorry you're scared. She wouldn't hurt a fly," Sara said as she bent down and picked up Daisy. *What a coward, afraid of her own shadow; or maybe she's doing this for effect?*

Elliott rushed into the kitchen, and grabbed the rolling pin out of Tracy's hand. Tracy flung herself into Elliott's arms and hugged him for protection as if Daisy had been a lion ready to pounce on her.

"Mrs. Roth doesn't allow pets in this house," Tracy said, spitting out the words.

"I'm sorry Daisy got out of my room—it won't happen again," Sara said apologetically. "I promise to keep the door closed. Mrs. Roth never told me I couldn't have a turtle. It's not like she's a dog, or cat, or a parrot."

"I don't care," Tracy shot back icily. "Get rid of it. Put it in the garbage."

"I won't."

"It's an ugly green animal," Tracy said turning to Elliott. "Get me a glass of rum and coke. I need a stiff drink."

"Boy, she's bossy," Sara thought as she watched Elliott leave the room.

As soon as Elliott disappeared, Tracy turned to Sara with another complaint, "I'm going to report you to Mrs. Roth, and she'll make you throw that creature out. It really should be cooked and made into turtle soup. Just boil it and I'll be happy to eat it."

"Why are you so cruel to me?" Sara asked, shaking.

"Cruel? Keeping a reptile is cruel. It belongs in a jungle. If you think I'm cruel, then you don't know what cruel is. Just keep out of my way and I'll ignore you when I see you—then you won't unjustly accuse me of being cruel."

Sara knew that anything she would say to Tracy would fall on deaf ears. She took Daisy and went back to her room. *If I ever thought my parents are hard on me, I take that back. I have never met a worse person than Tracy.*

CHAPTER 8

SARA WENT ONLINE, and an e-mail from Eric telling her of an easy way to exercise was waiting. She read it carefully and then moved her chair away from the desk. She planted her feet wide and firmly on the floor, placed her hands on her thighs, and hinged forward at her hips, rolling her torso parallel to the floor, hands dangling toward her ankles. It felt good, and she held the position for ten breaths. Her loving brother was always thinking about her and giving her good health tips. She answered him, thanking him and telling him she missed him terribly. The simple exercise eased her away from the discomfort of dealing with the pretentious Tracy who was becoming her nemesis.

Every day for a month Eric e-mailed her with details of both healthy foods for her to eat and of more easy exercises. The first week Sara ate just salads and fish and she lost five pounds. Then she added three fruits and in subsequent weeks lost an additional one or two pounds a week.

*   *   *

A week later Sara's arms were filled with grocery bags making it difficult for her to use her front door key. She rang Mrs. Roth's bell and gasped as she looked at her landlady-employer whose hair was blond and curled. On top of that she had on makeup that made her look at least ten years younger. Furthermore, Mrs. Roth stood straight without the aid of a walker.

Sara pressed her fingers into her eye sockets. "Oh, my God!" It was enough for her to go pale.

Sara looked again and another Mrs. Roth stood in back of the first one. This one had silver hair and leaned weakly on a walker. "I owe you an explanation, Sara," Mrs. Roth said. "I'd like you to meet my identical twin, Mrs. Alice Lefkowitz."

Mrs. Lefkowitz held out her hand. Sara shook it and feeling relieved, she smiled.

"Pleased to meet you," Mrs. Lefkowitz said kindly.

"How do you do," Sara answered. "I didn't know Mrs. Roth had a twin sister."

"I'm older by fifteen minutes," Mrs. Lefkowitz replied as she led the way into the living room.

Sara noticed that Mrs. Lefkowitz's right eye twitched as she spoke. *She looks great for her age, but she isn't perfect. Who is?*

Mrs. Roth moved her walker to the left of her favorite arm chair and slowly lowered herself. Sara and Mrs. Lefkowitz sat on the sofa.

"Well," Mrs. Roth said addressing her sister, ". . . how's the bride?"

"Wonderful. Lenny and I had a great honeymoon. Hawaii is gorgeous, but expensive. My husband likes the best of everything. He loves to gamble, but he's a terrible poker player." Mrs. Lefkowitz hesitated before she added with a grin, "But he's a great kisser."

"My husband was a good kisser, too," Mrs. Roth said as she looked thoughtful. "I sure miss him, and I'm glad for you."

When the conversation lagged, Sara turned her head from one sister to the other and peered at both of them. She tried to sort out the features of their faces that must have been very pretty years ago. It was a shame that Mrs. Roth's health had deteriorated. Sara wondered what the secret was that was making Mrs. Lefkowitz look at least a decade younger than the other twin. *Could the reason be that Mrs. Lefkowitz has love in her life and a youthful attitude?*

Mrs. Roth spoke up. "Lenny is Alice's third husband. He's twenty years younger than she, but both of them don't care. Once you're an adult the difference in age doesn't matter. What do you think, Sara?"

Wow, what should I say? Twenty years is big time. "I agree. As long they love, respect, and trust each other, the age difference is minor." *I hope I got out of that one all right.* "Do you need me to do anything for you right now?"

"No, dear," Mrs. Roth said. "You run along and work on your novel."

*   *   *

After three months of working for Mrs. Roth, the woman noticed Sara's drop in weight. "You look fabulous," Mrs. Roth said kindly.

"I'm eating mostly veggies, eggs, fish, and salads."

"That's a great idea. I think I'll do the same. I could lose a few pounds, too."

Sara wondered if Mrs. Roth lost about forty pounds would she be able to lose the walker and all the medications she was on. *I won't push her to lose weight. She'll have to be motivated on her own. I hate when people tell me what to do, and so I'll keep my thoughts to myself.*

Sara led Mrs. Roth out to the screened front porch. They sat on white plastic chairs, letting the perfume of the garden flow over them. Sara felt a new kind of peace. Her novel was progressing. She was losing weight and exercising, and keeping away from the contemptible Tracy.

Later that afternoon Sara heard a light knock on her bedroom door. "Who is it?"

"It's Elliott. I'd like to talk to you."

Sara slipped on her sandals and opened the door. Elliott held out tickets. "The last performance of my play in the Palm Oasis Community Theatre is tonight and I'm inviting you to see it."

"I was planning to write another scene in my novel." *I wonder if I should get involved with Elliott and Tracy, a female with an IQ in single digits.*

"You can write another time. I'd really like you to come."

Should I go? Sara tapped her foot.

"Please come. I invited my aunt and she has agreed to go if you'll accompany her."

It's something I wanted to do all along and just never got around to. Sara reached for the tickets.

Elliott smiled and handed them to her. "I'm glad you're coming. They're front row seats. Be there at 8 p.m.—afterwards we're having an informal party with big band music and liquor to drown in. There'll be agents from Broadway in the audience. Anything can happen. Wear what you like."

When Elliott left, Sara went to her closet to look for a becoming outfit. She had a light blue dress with a V-neck. She tried it on, but it was too large and hung on her. She opened a bureau drawer and took out a white leather belt that she put around her waist. The dress would do. She'd put on a gold necklace and matching gold earrings. Her beautician had once told her, "Matchy-matchy is boring. Girl, you must mix silver and gold for a stylish look." But Sara stuck with her traditional upbringing. When you wear a gold necklace, you wear gold earrings, and when you wear a dangling silver necklace, you wear silver earrings.

In the front row of the small theatre, Mrs. Roth sat on Sara's right. Two teenaged girls were on her left. Both girls chewed bubble gum with a vengeance and annoyed Sara with loud popping sounds as they blew huge bubbles. One of the bubbles burst and shocked a stout lady who cried out, and only then did the girls take the gum out of their mouths and fasten it under their seats. *How disgusting!*

Sara read the program that gave a brief description of the scenes and featured the biographies of the actors of *OTHELLO, THE LOVER.*

When the lights dimmed in the Palm Oasis Community Theatre, a spotlight bathed the stage in bright illumination. It focused on the Master of Ceremonies in a navy suit who stood in front of the curtain and in a booming voice announced, "Ladies and Gentlemen, Elliott Morse has revised Shakespeare's play by bringing it into the 21st Century. This tragedy has been turned into a musical comedy, also starring the writer Elliott Morse, who plays Othello, and Tracy North, a gorgeous gal who plays the part of Desdemona. Sit back and enjoy."

Sara gritted her teeth. *She's no gorgeous gal, just a domineering, arrogant shrew. She twists my guts like macaroni.*

After the announcer left the stage, a narrator stepped in front of the curtain and began to sing.

"This is the tale of Othello,
A hale and hearty fellow
Who lived in Venice city,
Wed a gal so very pretty.
He listened to a bad guy,
Caused his poor wife to cry,
Now the curtain will rise,
And you'll hear all the lies,
The question you see,
Is to be or not to be."

The curtain rose with a thump and a thwack to reveal a bedroom scene. Sara was surprised to see Elliott as Othello, in blackface with a beard, wearing pajamas. And there was the moron Tracy appearing as Desdemona. She wore a revealing diaphanous nightgown. *What a slut!*

REVA SPIRO LUXENBERG

The two lovers were on a double bed kissing ardently. When Othello turned away from Desdemona, he strode to a corner of the stage. Desdemona jumped up and followed him, and drew him into another passionate embrace. *I don't think it's funny even though the audience is laughing softly.*

When the couple finally broke apart Desdemona, who now had some of the black dye on her face, began to sing:

"My Othello, my toy,
My soul's sweet joy,
I, so very chaste,
Married in haste,
Daddy displeased,
His mind diseased,
I bid him adieu,
For my love it is true."

Sara screwed up her face. *I had no idea that Tracy had such a good voice. She sings like an angel and looks like a Hollywood star, but she has the character of a charging rhinoceros.*

Othello took Desdemona's hand, and with an exaggerated flourish brought it to his lips and kissed it.

Sara's stomach churned. *How disgusting.*

The curtain closed with a sound like a squeaking shoe, and it opened soon after on a scene with an actor who held a crooked cane. He spoke nonsense to a bumpkin, whose toga kept falling off his shoulder, and slipping to the stage, revealing a long pair of boxer shorts decorated with hearts. It was so funny that Sara laughed loudly. *Elliott has a great sense of humor, but his taste in women leaves much to be desired.*

When the lights flickered, the audience emptied out during the fifteen minute intermission.

Sara and Mrs. Roth stayed seated. "Isn't the play amusing?" Mrs. Roth said.

"Yes, Elliott is really talented."

"What did you think of Tracy's acting?" Mrs. Roth asked.

"Her acting is a bit overdone." *The less I see of Tracy the better I feel.*

After the lights flickered, the audience took their seats.

The curtain lifted on a scene inside a building where Othello faced Iago. Othello grabbed his beard and tugged on it as a nervous gesture. Unexpectedly, it fell to the floor, Othello bent down, picked it up, and put it on his face lopsided.

Sara laughed again. *I wish I had a sense of humor like Elliott.* Othello sings:

> "I don't believe my dear wife
> Would ever dare to ruin my life,
> For me she surely does care,
> She'd never have an affair,
> Her love it is pure and true,
> Our recent marriage is new,
> Cassio, I think is a good fellow,
> Loyal, true, kind, and mellow."

Othello's beard fell off, and as he attempted to retrieve it, he accidently kicked it with his shoe and it landed on a woman's lap in the audience. She picked it up and hurled it like a baseball back on the stage. *I wonder if this is part of the play or if it happened accidentally.*

Sara, with concentrated interest, watched the next scene that took place in a courtyard. Six men were dueling. One man parried and thrust his sword into another man. Ketchup, which represented blood, covered part of the stage where the man fell. A young player came from behind the curtain with a mop and cleaned off the ketchup. *Another hilarious scene. Elliott is a gifted playwright.*

Sara gritted her teeth as Tracy, acting as Desdemona, sang:

> "Men are not gods, methinks they're nuts,
> They do not use their brains, only their guts,
> I offer my soul and my heart
> Begging you not to part
> From your wife who loves you so,
> Othello, my dearest, don't go,
> Another wife you will never get
> Don't rue the day that we met."

REVA SPIRO LUXENBERG

Sara watched with interest as the curtain rose on a bedroom scene. Desdemona reclined in bed with a pillow under the small of her back. Othello stood over her and tried to snatch the pillow. Desdemona hit Othello's hand, whereupon Othello smacked her face. *It warms my heart to see Elliott hitting Tracy.*

Othello sings:

> "Here is my journey's end.
> This rift will never mend,
> This act with heavy heart I relate,
> For I am through with my mate."

Finally the play is over. *I didn't want to come but it did me good to see Elliott slap Tracy.*

The curtain calls lasted for three minutes. The play was a smash hit.

*   *   *

Driving back to the house, Sara and Mrs. Roth agreed that the play was a great comedy. "Shakespeare wouldn't rest in his grave if he knew how Elliott gave a humorous twist to the bard's serious play with the theme about the harm of unfounded jealousy," Sara said.

"But it was so funny, wasn't it, dear?" Mrs. Roth said.

"You bet." *I would have enjoyed it more if Tracy hadn't been in it.*

That night, after both women had gone to bed and were asleep, Sara was awakened by a pounding on her bedroom door. "Who is it?"

"It's Tracy. Open up. I have news."

Sara stumbled to the door and opened it to find Tracy grinning. "There was an agent in the audience. He loved my performance. He's getting me a part in an off-Broadway play."

"Oh!"

"Is that all you can say?"

"When are you leaving?"

"Tomorrow."

Oh, boy, I'm sure glad to see Tracy go. Now there will be peace in the house. Or maybe not.

CHAPTER 9

TWO DAYS LATER when Sara was working on her novel, Elliott knocked on her bedroom door with his distinctive knock.

It's him again. "What is it, Elliott?"

"Open the door and I'll tell you."

"Tell me before I open the door." *He's Tracy's guy. I don't want to get involved.*

"It's a surprise."

"What's the surprise?" *I need a surprise like peanut butter needs ketchup.*

"Open up."

When Sara opened the door her heart skipped a beat. Elliott had shaved and he looked as handsome as Brad Pitt. "I had no idea you looked so..."

"So what?"

"I don't know. So clean-shaven."

"Do you like the change?"

"I suppose I do."

"Then let's sit on the back porch and watch the rhythmic waves of the Atlantic Ocean."

"Tracy wouldn't like that."

Elliott grinned. "Tracy isn't here and I don't give a hoot."

Should I go with him? I think he's a womanizer—but he does look cute, and Tracy may never come back.

Elliott took her hand in his, and Sara moved with him to the back porch. They sat on two beach chairs and scanned the broad expanse of the beach, watched the moon-spangled water, and listened to the gently lapping surf. After two minutes Elliott put his arm around Sara's shoulder. She trembled but allowed the intimate touch until she questioned his motives and moved away. In a second Elliot moved closer so that their bodies brushed against each other. Remembering how Elliott had kissed Tracy, Sara pulled away again. He took her hand and kissed the center of her palm. She closed her eyes, and once again he slipped his arm around her. *This is happening too fast.* She leaned back against his shoulder and tried not to think, just feel— and it did feel right.

After a minute Elliott angled his head and with his arm still around her he asked, "How is your turtle doing?"

Wow, he's interested in my pet. "Daisy hasn't eaten for a week after she laid one egg."

"What did you do with the egg?"

Sara sighed. "It has to be fertilized and Daisy hasn't had the opportunity to meet another turtle, so I put the egg in the garbage and she stopped eating."

Elliott patted her arm. "Could be Daisy is mourning the loss of her egg."

"Maybe. Who knows what's in the mind of a turtle?"

"A friend of mine has an assortment of reptiles and every year he takes them to a reptile doctor in Boca Raton. I'll ask him for the phone number if you want to take Daisy for a professional opinion."

"Thanks. I think she should be examined. I have to go in now," Sara said squirming. *He's a thoughtful guy, but I don't trust him where women are concerned. When and if Tracy comes back, he'll dump me for her.*

*   *   *

After Elliott provided Sara with the vet's number, she made an appointment for the following morning after breakfast. She put Daisy in a shoe box and carried the box to the car putting it down on the passenger's side. Sara hoped that the vet would bring Daisy back to good health. Daisy tried to get out—but she couldn't reach the top of the box, although she kept clawing the cardboard.

Sara drove carefully to Boca Raton, parked the car in the parking lot next to FLACK REPTILE REFUGE, and took the shoe box with her as she entered. She stopped at the reception desk where an older woman with marble lines on her face smiled and gave Sara a form to fill out.

Twenty minutes later a youngish vet came out and shook hands with Sara.

"What do we have here?" Dr. Flack asked as he peered into the shoe box. He had kind gray eyes and a mass of ebony hair.

"Her name is Daisy, and she's a box turtle who hasn't been eating for ten days," Sara said with a chill.

"I'll examine her and let you know what I find."

Sara fidgeted with her fingers as she sat waiting for the diagnosis. The box turtle was part of the life she had brought with her when she moved out of her parent's home and she was attached to her.

A half-hour later, Dr. Flack entered the waiting room and sat down next to Sara.

"Is Daisy sick?" she asked, her face flushed.

"She has a prolapsed uterus, which has to be removed surgically."

"Oh no!" Sara cried.

"She'll be all right," Dr. Flack said. "We'll start her on the antibiotic Oxytetracycline. Her stitches are absorbable and will be inside her."

"Oh!" Sara's heart fluttered fast.

Dr. Flack tried reassurance. "She needs this operation. What do you say?"

"Will she feel pain?"

"No, we'll sedate her."

"Then go ahead, doctor," Sara said reluctantly.

Back at the house Sara met Elliott on his way out. "What's up?" Elliott asked. "How's Daisy?"

"She needs an operation."

"You're kidding."

"No. She's being operated on early tomorrow morning." Sara's eyes filled with tears.

"I didn't know a turtle could be operated on. What's the operation for?"

Sara hung her head. "It's embarrassing. It's a female thing."

"Come on, out with it. You don't have to be embarrassed. Just tell me what's wrong."

"Well—it's like this. After she laid an egg, her uterus became prolapsed."

"I don't believe it."

"I'll be devastated if she dies under the knife." Sara hung her head.

"If you need me for comfort, just call."

That night Sara tossed in her bed. After she fell asleep, she had a nightmare. She watched the operation in horror and saw Daisy lose her shell. Sara awoke in a sweat in twisted sheets. She showered, dressed quickly, and drove to the vet. Dr. Flack met her in the waiting room.

"Daisy is still under sedation. The operation went well and she'll need shots every third day. A radiograph reveals an irregular-shaped egg still inside her and it may be that she's been having trouble laying eggs."

"Oh my," Sara said in a low voice.

"An egg here and there is abnormal for box turtles. Yours has been straining partly due to a low-calcium intake."

"I'll give her plenty of calcium when I take her home," Sara assured the vet.

"I want you to know she has two uterine tracts which female box turtles have, and we have removed one, and we cannot tell if the egg inside the other tract is still okay. I hope she'll be able to pass it. If she's back eating well, acting okay, and hasn't laid within thirty days, it may need to be removed surgically."

Sara bit down on her lips. *My poor animal. See what sex has done to her. I'm inexperienced. I better be careful. I don't trust Elliott after the way I saw him with Tracy. I'd like to marry a decent man.*

For the next month Sara watched Daisy carefully. She hadn't laid the egg. Reluctantly Sara brought Daisy back to the vet.

"I'll operate early tomorrow morning," Dr. Flack said with an authoritative tone.

"I guess you have no choice," Sara answered, her breath tight.

The next morning Sara arrived early. She waited an hour until Dr. Flack, in his scrubs, entered the waiting room. "I'm so sorry, Sara. Daisy died under the knife. There's no charge. Do you want us to bury her?"

Sara pressed her hands together. She shivered. Tears welled up in her eyes. "Yes, please. I had no idea how dangerous a second operation would be."

"This shouldn't have happened, but sometimes a reptile is weaker than we thought." Dr. Flack stared at Sara a long, painful moment.

A lump lodged in her throat. She gathered her things and went out the door.

Sara drove back automatically, her heart filled with sadness. She looked in her mirror when she heard the shrill sound of a siren behind her. She pulled the car over to the side, opened her window, and saw a female police officer leave her car and move next to her.

"What did I do?" Sara asked sadly.

"You went through a stop sign two blocks back. License and registration."

Sara fumbled through her purse and came up with the documents. "I'm sorry officer. I guess I wasn't thinking. My box turtle was operated on this morning and died under the knife. Are you giving me a ticket?"

"Not this time. I'm giving you a warning. Next time you'll get a ticket."

Sara drove away and parked in front of the house. When she entered her room she threw herself on her bed and began to sob. Elliott knocked at her door, peeked in, and saw Sara weeping. He didn't utter a word, but took Sara in his arms. She put her head on his shoulder, and they stayed like that until Sara had no more tears left.

"I'm sorry," Elliott said looking ruffled. "I once had a cat that got run over, and I understand how hard it is when you get attached to an animal."

"I'm being silly," Sara protested.

"It's not being silly. It's being human."

He had awakened some feeling in her that she had never felt. Was it love? No.

It was just physical attraction. It couldn't be love. Elliott was attached to Tracy and if she ever came back he'd go back to her. The feeling was just a liking for a man who had a tender heart.

CHAPTER 10

ON SATURDAY SARA was off from work. Sad thoughts about the loss of her pet box turtle, Daisy, filled her mind to such a degree that she couldn't write the next chapter in her novel. A hollow feeling swept over her. *Am I lazy or depressed?*

Sara hoped that talking with Elliott would relieve some of her sadness, so she stood with her fist at his door ready to knock, when she was taken aback by a sign, DO NOT DISTURB, PLAYWRIGHT AT WORK. That does it, Sara fretted, as she returned to her room and slipped into a one-piece bathing suit. She grabbed a blanket, left the house by the back door, and started down the beach steps, crossing the hot sand. She spread the blanket on the sand near the ocean, lay down and fell into a troubled sleep under a sun that shone with harmful rays. An hour later she woke up looking like the inside of a watermelon. Her mind had been so filled with thoughts of Daisy she had forgotten to put on sunscreen. The severe sunburn caused her to shiver uncontrollably.

Elliott had taken his laptop to the back porch when he glanced up and noticed Sara dragging herself along the beach. He raced down and helped her up the stairs and into her room. With her permission, he applied witch hazel to her burning skin. For three days Elliott took care of Sara, who suffered and brooded silently.

Elliott is not for me. I better watch out before it's too late. Mom and Dad would be horrified if they knew I was living in the same house with a man. I told them I'm working for an elderly woman and am renting a room from her. What will I say if they drive here and learn the truth?

On the fourth day Elliott said, "Turn over, I'll try some aloe cream on your legs and arms."

Sara, still in pain, did as she was told. Elliott dabbed the cream on as many body parts that he could reach and still act in a gentlemanly fashion. "Does it burn?"

"Yes, it does. I'll never do this again for the rest of my life. Mrs. Roth had to hire a temporary aide. I hope she doesn't fire me."

"She won't. She's very fond of you." Elliott unscrewed the cover of the cream and gently put more cream on Sara's neck.

*   *   *

The following week at 11:15 p.m. Sara was awakened by the ringing of her cell phone. "Hello," she muttered, annoyed that anyone would call her so late.

"Sara," her mother said in a sad voice. "I'm calling you from Tampa General Hospital where your father was admitted to Emergency with severe chest pains. He's being evaluated for a possible heart attack. I'm falling apart and I need you to come here right now."

Sara bolted to an upright position. "Mom, let's wait until we get the results of the test. If it's serious, then of course I'll come. I'll wait for a call back from you."

She heard her mother weeping. "You better come right now. Your father may die, and you must see him before he passes away."

It's no use arguing with a mother who knows how to dish out guilt, and maybe Dad is in bad shape. I better get up, get dressed, and drive across Florida.

The darkness of the night was scary black even though the ivory moon appeared. Sara's heart hammered as she sped up, and halfway there she began to sneeze. *Oh, of all things I'm coming down with a miserable cold. I hope it's not the flu. My whole body aches.*

By the time Sara reached the hospital she had used up all her tissues, and her nose was running like a water spout. She opened her moist eyes wide when she found her father sitting in a wheelchair in the lobby of the hospital. Her mother's hair was disheveled, and she had no makeup on; but she was smiling. "Your father is discharged. It turned out he had bad indigestion. It may have been from the fatty chicken soup our cook made." Mrs. Solomon looked at her daughter, genuinely dismayed. "What's wrong with you?"

Sara's face was flushed, her eyes were tearing, and she wiped her eyes with her hand. "I have a cold." *I'm so angry that I drove here for nothing—but I'm too sick to argue. I just want to leave and go home.*

Mrs. Solomon stepped away. "Keep your distance. We don't need to catch your germs. You can stay in your room and convalesce."

"No thanks, Mom. I'd rather drive back." *I don't care how sick I feel. I won't have my mother dictating to me.*

Sara felt a weight had been lifted from her heart when she learned her father was okay. "I was so worried about you, Dad. I'm glad you're better. Take care of yourself. Bye now."

The aide pushed Mr. Solomon's wheelchair out the front door of the hospital to a waiting taxi. He called to Sara, "Young lady you're in no position to drive. You look like you have fever. Come home and we'll take care of you."

Sara sneezed ten times in a row before she said in a thin voice, "Thanks. I think I will stay with you until I feel better."

*   *   *

Once in her old room Sara called Elliott, "Hi, I'm in my parent's home," she croaked.

"You sound awful."

"I feel awful. I think I have the flu, and I won't leave here until I feel better. I need to ask a favor."

"Ask away."

"Please call your aunt and tell her I'm sick and can't take care of her."

"Done. I'll hire someone else until you get back. By the way Tracy was fired from her acting job and has come back. She's in a bad mood and I have to console her."

"I understand." *When it rains, it pours—Tracy and the flu. She'll be horrible to live with again.*

It took two weeks for Sara to recuperate, two weeks of being nagged by her mother to stay in bed and keep away from everyone.

"Only get up to go to the bathroom," her mother warned repeatedly. Sara reverted to feeling like a helpless child—especially when her father brought her quarts of sugary orange juice to drink and waited in her room until she finished. Afterward she heard her mother scold him for coming close to her and being exposed to her germs.

Every day during the time she was there her mother called to her from the closed door. "Make sure you move your bowels."

Sara felt miserable, and often she blinked her tears back. *I can't wait to leave Tampa and return to Palm Oasis. I don't feel like seeing Tracy again and being the butt of vicious attacks.* She reluctantly stayed in her parents' home a month even after she was physically able to leave. The best thing about being in Tampa was that Joan visited her. Joan was excited about how much weight both of them had lost.

"Remember when I said that after you leave your parents' home you'll be able to lose weight. I was right," Joan said with her calm, luminous smile.

"I don't need a weight club," Sara said, "all I did need was to live on my own."

"I have good news," Joan said with a superior sniff.

"What?" Sara said glancing at her friend.

"I'm going steady with a guy that comes to our weight club. He's also losing weight, and he's a gorgeous hunk."

"I'm so glad for you," Sara said as she covered Joan's hand with hers. *I wish I could meet some guy.*

*   *   *

Finally the day came when Sara said goodbye to her parents and—against their strong objections left. During the drive back Sara enjoyed listening to the CD's of Barbra Streisand, Anne Murray, and Jimmy Buffett, her favorite singers.

After Sara reached the house, she parked the Mazda and hurriedly walked to the front door. When she opened the door, she smelled an unfamiliar odor of something burning. In the living room Tracy and Elliott sat on the couch kissing. Smoke was rising from a dish on a small glass table. "What's going on?" Sara said loudly.

Tracy and Elliott parted quickly. "Hi, so you're back," Elliott said.

"What's burning?" Sara asked grimly.

Elliott bounced up, grabbed some sand from a container, and threw it on the dish to extinguish the flame. "Don't worry. We don't do drugs. I lived with Native Americans for two years. For centuries they practiced 'smudging', actually burning aromatic herbs to purify locations. What you smell is White Sage, which we hope will remove negative energy from this house."

"It stinks," Sara said, her eyes blazing.

"I think you stink," Tracy sneered. "You have the nerve to leave here for a month, and then you think you can come back and criticize a perfectly harmless practice."

Sara backed off. "I thought it was marijuana. I never heard of 'smudging'."

Tracy's lips curled. "You never heard of a lot of things. This herb enhances memory. My memory of you has faded, and I'd like to keep it that way—when and if you move out."

"I'll stay out of your way, Tracy," Sara said. She turned to Elliott, "How is Mrs. Roth doing? Who did you hire to take care of her?"

Tracy tugged at the top of her halter dress with a décolleté that reached down to China. "I've been taking care of Mrs. Roth and doing a great job. You've been fired!"

All the color drained out of Sara's face.

CHAPTER 11

SARA STOOD PENSIVELY for a few seconds, digesting Tracy's information. "I don't believe that Mrs. Roth fired me."

"Well, she did," Tracy said in her usual arrogant tone.

Elliott piped up. "Stop your teasing, Tracy. Sara, believe me, my aunt is waiting for you to come back. Tracy filled in while you were absent."

"What a crock," Tracy said. "I'm glad to get away from that old witch. By the way, it's too bad you missed last night's supper. We ravenously ate the best turtle soup ever."

Sara groaned. *Why does Tracy torment me like this. She knows I love turtles.*

Elliott jumped in. "We had tomato soup, not turtle soup—and Tracy is trying to get your goat, Sara. Pay no attention to her lies."

"Just kidding," Tracy said as she ran her fingers through her long hair.

"Why did you come back?" Sara asked upwardly tilting her chin. "I thought you were acting in an off-Broadway play."

Tracy pursed her lips. "The humor was trite. I put some teeth marks into it and the director got peeved, so here I am. Make the best of it."

"I'll try," Sara said. *No matter how hard I try to make peace Tracy really wants war.*

*   *   *

It was the middle of the night when Sara rose to go to the bathroom. Just as she was ready to go back to bed, in the adjacent bedroom, she heard Tracy moan, "Oh… Elliott,

Oh… Elliott. That was fireworks. You truly are the best lover ever."

Sara's mouth went dry. *I can't stay here any longer. This place is poison for my mental health. But where will I go? What should I do?* She sat up in bed, her fingers drumming on the coverlet—the pulse in her temple throbbing.

In the morning, after being awake half the night, Sara left the house to go to work. In Mrs. Roth's kitchen Sara poured Cheerios into two bowls, spilled some of the miniature donuts on the counter, and was adding cashew milk when her employer/landlady entered and looked with concern at Sara's bloodshot eyes and the uncharacteristic mess she made.

"I see something has upset you, my dear."

"It's really nothing for you to worry about," Sara said in a breathy manner.

"Stop what you're doing. I insist you tell me what's bothering you." Mrs. Roth pointed to a kitchen chair. "Sit," she ordered.

Sara sat down. "It's embarrassing."

"I'm an old lady, and I've heard embarrassing things before. Just trust me to keep your secret and tell me what it is."

Leaning toward her employer, Sara spoke in a low voice. "It was the middle of the night when I happened to overhear Tracy talk to Elliott in her bedroom. It made me uncomfortable to hear what she said and how she said it."

"So the slut is making you uncomfortable. I warned Elliott about her, but he's a man, if you know what I mean. There's an easy solution for this problem."

"There is?" Sara grimaced.

With a triumphant smile, Mrs. Roth announced, "There are two empty bedrooms besides mine in this house. The house, as you know, is two blocks away from Tracy. Move in with me."

The offer was appealing, but doubt filled Sara's mind. "I don't know. You're used to living alone. I'll get on your nerves." *Maybe she'll get on my nerves.*

"Nonsense. You're the most considerate person I've met in a long time. I promise you we'll get along like we always have. I'll pay you the going rate for a live-in-aide, and you don't have to pay rent. Of course, you'll have to prepare most of my meals, and we can eat out in restaurants sometimes." Mrs. Roth glanced at Sara with a hopeful expression as she smoothed down the tablecloth with her hands.

"Thank you, but I have to decline. Being an aide will prevent me from writing my novel, and that is important to me."

"Don't worry about your free time, Sara. You can have afternoons off from noon to five. You don't have to cook dinner. We'll eat out."

To her astonishment, Mrs. Roth had said the exact words Sara wanted to hear. *Restaurants. More money. Freedom from Tracy and Elliott. Time for writing,* "All right, I'll go back right now and get my things. You're an angel to take me in. I can't thank you enough."

*　　*　　*

After two weeks Sara felt tremendous relief from the pressure from Tracy and Elliott that she had been suffering. There had been a hot iron on her chest—and now, thanks to Mrs. Roth, it was removed. At night as she lay in bed, Sara wondered why Mrs. Roth had to use a walker. It was obvious that her employer's twin sister was the same age at sixty-five and was healthy and active. What was causing Mrs. Roth to age before her time?

At lunch time, when they sat together, Sara raised the question that was bothering her. "How come you use a walker, Mrs. Roth? There are times I've seen you get around without it."

"It's a long story."

Sara eyed her a moment. "I like long stories."

Mrs. Roth put her Swiss cheese sandwich down. "A year ago I ate in a restaurant with my cousin. I think that the cod fish was contaminated. That night, when I was alone, I had cramps and awful diarrhea. Are you sure you want to hear the rest?"

"Yes, go ahead."

"I guess I got dehydrated and fell down on the tile in the bathroom. I couldn't get up. After a couple of hours I realized that if I wouldn't get help, I would faint and die. I forced myself to crawl to the bedroom. I couldn't stand up to reach the phone, but I remembered that my purse was on the floor in the closet and my cell phone was in it. I reached it and called for an ambulance."

"You must've been scared."

"I was plenty scared. I had injured my leg and my back. I had to go to rehab and they gave me a walker there. I'm afraid to walk without one now—besides my back hurts me a lot."

Sara's voice was calm. "How long is it since you've seen your doctor about the pain in your back?"

"I don't like doctors. Mine is really nice, but I haven't seen him for nine months."

By the time they finished lunch, Sara had convinced Mrs. Roth to make an appointment with her doctor.

The following week Sara accompanied her employer to the doctor's office where they waited three-quarters of an hour before Mrs. Roth was called in. Sara remained in the waiting room with the other patients. Most of them, it seemed groaned, coughed, and sneezed. She picked up a copy of the *Reader's Digest* and was three-quarters through it when Mrs. Roth appeared, a dark cloud seeming to pass over her face as she sat down on the chair next to Sara.

"What did the doctor say?" Sara asked as she placed a comforting hand on Mrs. Roth's arm.

"He bawled me out for not coming to see him sooner. He said he is referring me for an MRI of my back. He asked if I had claustrophobia; and honest me, I had to tell him I wasn't afraid of closed spaces. My husband and I had a small plane and I was never afraid to sit next to him in the cockpit."

"What's an MRI?"

"It's short for Magnetic Resonance Imaging. They put you in a tunnel with noise like a jet plane, and the machine reads your insides. I don't think I'll go."

"Don't be frightened. It's best to find out just what's wrong. I'll go with you."

Mrs. Roth grimaced. "You don't understand. My back hurts a lot, and I may have bone cancer."

"What makes you think so?"

"My husband died from bone cancer."

"You can't catch cancer. I doubt very much if your ailment is that serious. Besides, it's better to learn what's causing the pain, and then something can be done to relieve it."

It took a lot of urging on Sara's part to convince Mrs. Roth to go for the test.

*   *   *

Mrs. Roth had to fill out a three-page health history before she was taken in for the MRI. Sara noticed that her hand trembled while she was writing. Nothing she said was able to calm Mrs. Roth's nerves. Sara waited an hour before Mrs. Roth came out and sat down next to her.

"It was horrible," Mrs. Roth said. "I had to lie down on a hard surface and they put a cushion under my knees, and it didn't help. During the procedure my back hurt even worse than before. A technician covered my ears with padded earphones to protect them, and they sent some music through the earphones, but it didn't sooth me. Then I moved into a narrow tunnel. I'm roly-poly, and my hips were crushed against the sides. I can't understand why they don't make it larger for fat people like me."

"I guess because it's an expensive device," Sara said as she patted Mrs. Roth's hand.

"Then the problems started for real. The noise was like a jet plane taking off. Every few minutes there was banging like a hammer, changing to peeping like a bird, and then tapping like a pen on iron. I'm sure my hearing is affected. I had to lie still, and believe me it wasn't easy for me not to move. Afterwards they told me that I have to wait a week until I see my doctor and get the results. I don't know if I can last that long."

"The worst part is over. Now let's go out and have a good lunch."

"Do you think I can have a hot fudge sundae with whipped cream and a cherry on top for dessert?" Mrs. Roth licked her lips.

"You bet, and I'll have one, too. I have an intuition the report will change the rest of your life."

CHAPTER 12

A LTHOUGH IT WAS pouring, the sun shone brightly through the translucent rain drops the day that Sara drove Mrs. Roth to her 11 a.m. appointment with Dr. Miller. When the nurse called Mrs. Roth into the examination room, she grabbed Sara's hand. "Please, come with me. I have no idea what the MRI showed and I'm scared."

Sara nodded in agreement, and they entered the examination room hand in hand. The nurse, Marylou, a pretty young woman with a swarthy complexion and long straight black hair said, "Please sit here," indicating two stools. She passed a thermometer over Mrs. Roth's forehead, took her oxygen level, and put a cuff on her arm to measure her blood pressure.

"Everything is normal, Helen," the nurse announced enthusiastically. "Your vital signs are the same as those of a thirty-year old."

Mrs. Roth offered a weak smile.

Dr. Miller entered the room, greeted the women, and sat down on a stool in front of the computer. He looked at the report on the monitor, his expression one of deep concentration. At last as Sara and Mrs. Roth waited, both women concerned about the results of the MRI, the doctor swung around. "Helen, you have nothing to worry about. I'll read the impression aloud. 'Mild to moderate multilevel lumbar spondylosis with multilevel neural encroachment.'"

"What does it mean?" Mrs. Roth turned pale.

"It means that you need to take Tylenol for the pain of arthritis. I will schedule you for physical therapy, and I predict shortly you can dispose of that walker. I want you to walk in the pool every day to strengthen your muscles. Now, Helen, go to a restaurant and a movie with this lovely girl, have a good time, and laugh a lot."

Sara drove Mrs. Roth to HEAVENLY EGGS, a restaurant that featured all varieties of egg dishes. The ambience was warm and inviting. Artistic china plates and platters decorated with colorful roosters and chickens were jauntily displayed on high shelves around the room. Wired baskets of faux brown and white eggs hung from the ceiling.

Sara and Mrs. Roth were led to a booth where a pitcher of ice water and lemon slices awaited them. A middle-aged waitress greeted them with a big smile. She wore a uniform with a badge that read Sandy. Sara was amused as she spotted an embroidered chicken on the pocket of the waitress's uniform. Sandy handed them oversized menus listing so many foods containing eggs that they began to chuckle.

Five minutes later Sandy returned. "Have you ladies decided on what you want?"

"I'll have a cheese omelet and decaf coffee," Mrs. Roth said.

"Same for me," Sara chimed.

While they waited for their lunch, Mrs. Roth said, "Please call me Helen. Mrs. Roth makes me feel like I'm one hundred."

"Of course, I'll be happy to call you Helen. That's an appealing name. Is there a special reason your mother gave you a Greek name?"

"You bet—she knew that Helen of Troy was the cause of the Trojan War, but my mother didn't name me after that Helen. She liked the actress Helen Hayes and she named me after her."

"How nice," Sara said. "Helen, Dr. Miller advised you to go to the pool. How about it?"

"Forget it. I won't go."

"Why not?"

Mrs. Roth choked on her words. "I'll look like Dumbo the elephant. It's just too embarrassing to appear in public in a bathing suit with all this flab hanging out."

Sara gave Helen a raised-brow look. "When I first worked for you, I was chubby and miserable, but then I followed my brother Eric's advice about eating in a healthful way. Now I'm trim and I feel like a new person."

"I don't know if I can follow a diet. When I'm hungry, I need to eat."

"Helen, I'll guide you, and believe me you'll lose weight. I promise you for certain that you'll never be hungry."

*   *   *

Sara sat on the front porch next to a round white plastic table. She bent over her laptop and sent her brother an e-mail.

Dear Eric,

                I hope you're fine and dandy. All
              is well with my employer, Helen Roth,
              and me. Helen, now I call her Helen—
                  is a darling woman who needs to
                     lose a great deal of weight. I
                  followed your advice, and it wasn't
                 hard for me; but this older woman
                   succumbs to hunger pangs and
                    then reaches for sugary, salty,
                 fatty snacks. I'd appreciate if you
                 could send me a diet for her that
                     includes restaurant meals.
                    Helen has been kind to me
                     and I want to help her.

                                    All my love, Sara."

                        *   *   *

The doctor's prescription indicated that Mrs. Helen Roth was to receive physical therapy three times a week, Monday, Wednesday, and Friday. The first time Mrs. Roth went to physical therapy she came out smiling and told Sarah it was a breeze. The chief therapist, Harry, a young handsome muscular fellow, had measured her, tested her arms and legs, examined her back, and declared that he would devise an individual program for her that would strengthen her muscles.

When Helen Roth left after the thorough exam, she told Sara, "I think I'm going to enjoy coming here."

The second time she complained bitterly. "I had to go on a stationary bicycle for ten minutes. I was exhausted—but Rhonda, my personal therapist, kept saying, 'Keep going. It'll get easier.'

Then she had me walking up and down steps ten times until my legs hurt. But at the end she massaged my back and my legs—oh, that felt so good. And then she put a hot pad on my back and I loved it." Helen smiled—then frowned when she added, "But all in all I didn't like the exercises."

"Remember what your doctor said about your not needing a walker. Just keep going and you can toss the walker," Sara said encouragingly.

The times that Sara took Helen for therapy she made sure to bring her laptop so she could continue writing her novel *Betsy Moss*. It was taking shape—about a freshman in college struggling to overcome her shyness—trying to cope with her difficult scholastic and social life. Not only was Sara writing mornings after breakfast, but when Helen didn't need her, she took advantage of every free moment.

*   *   *

Week after week Helen took off one or two, or more, pounds by following the diet that Eric had e-mailed Sara. By the time half-a-year had passed she had dropped thirty pounds, didn't need a walker, and was not embarrassed to go into the neighborhood pool. Meanwhile Sara had also flourished as she jogged two miles a day and also continued writing—struggling with all the problems that she heaped on her protagonist.

One sunny morning as the two women sat at a booth in HEAVENLY EGGS munching on spinach omelets with sides of tomatoes, Helen raised a disturbing question. "You're a pretty young woman, talented, honest, and kind—but why aren't you dating with an eye to marriage?"

Sara swallowed a mouthful. "I can ask you the same question. Why aren't you dating? You're a pretty older woman. You are honest and kind and haven't gone out with a man since your husband passed away fifteen years ago."

"You answer a question with a question. That's unfair."

"All right. No one has asked me out." Sara twirled a slice of tomato in the air.

Helen took a sip of black coffee, no cream, no sugar. "You don't go anywhere you could meet single men. How do you expect to ever get married?"

"It will happen when it happens."

"Excuse my French. Bullshit!"

"Now you're resorting to vulgarity? How shameful." Sara laughed so loud that a couple in a table across from their booth stared at her.

She lowered her voice. "What do you suggest?"

Helen pursed her lips. "I watch a Jewish station on TV, and they advertise a dating service called MATCHMAKING FOR LOVE. You write in all about who you are and the kind of person you're looking for. They search their data banks and match you up. Molly, a woman I met in Physical Therapy told me all about it. She met her fourth husband like this. They don't charge too much. It's worth a try."

"It sounds like someone desperate is looking for someone desperate, almost like picking out groceries at Publix."

The red-headed woman across the aisle leaned over in an attempt to eavesdrop. Helen noticed her and spoke softly. "You know if you try this, you can use your experience in your novel. An author should broaden her horizons."

"Mmm—okay, Helen, I agree but on one condition."

"What's that?"

"You have to sign on the same as I will."

CHAPTER 13

L ONG LINES OF people at the entrance of HEAVENLY EGGS waited for customers to leave and free tables. Inside the restaurant loud conversations echoed through rooms in which all the tables and booths were occupied.

"Don't be ridiculous," Helen said to Sara as she picked up her second cup of coffee. "I don't need an online dating service. Dave was good to me—he was both a husband and the child I couldn't have. I'll never marry again. But you're young and strong and deserve to have a husband and children. You should sign up. I'm all washed up at the age of sixty-five."

Sara slid over to the edge of the booth and stood up. "No, I beg to differ with you. You're far from being washed up. Please excuse me. I'm off to the restroom."

When Sara returned, she explained matter-of-factly, "I see how dead set you are about registering for the matchmaking service, and since you won't do it, I won't either—but since I'm interested in dating, I just put my name and phone number on the bathroom wall and added a little message, 'Looking for Prince Charming.'" Sara smiled devilishly.

Helen squared her shoulders and laughed. "Did anyone ever tell you, you're a stubborn mule and not a convincing liar?"

"Me? A liar? Never."

"You're trying to make me change my mind. I'm a washed-out woman with not a chance in hell that any man worth having will accept me—so please drop this idea of my reaching out to a dating service."

"You're not washed out—but you are a woman alone, so give it a try. Just look at it as another adventure in your life."

Helen squirmed in her seat. "I suppose I can register. But you should understand that I definitely won't go on dates. Just take a good look at me." She pointed to her silver hair and out-of-style outfit. "No decent man will be interested in a wreck like me."

Smiling sweetly Sara said, "Now you look like Cinderella, the tattered stepdaughter, before she met the prince—but let's leave right now, make room for the crowd of hungry customers, and go straight to a beauty parlor I noticed a block away. There's no reason you have to be gray and dowdy."

*　　*　　*

It looked like it was a slow day for pink-themed Sally's Full Service Salon with its pink-striped wallpaper, and pink tile. There was a pink plastic cape draped around the neck of the lone female customer who was having her hair dyed. An unoccupied male stylist sat at his station reading *People* magazine.

Helen definitely did not appreciate the pungent odor of the hair dye that wafted through the air-conditioned air. She made no bones about it and got ready to walk out.

"I like my silver hair, and I changed my mind about dyeing it. The hair dye stinks, and I'm sure it will burn my scalp and my hair will fall out."

Sara held her back. "It won't burn your scalp." She pointed to the woman in the midst of having her hair dyed. "Just look at this lady. Do you think that if the dye burned she would go through with it?"

Helen nodded in grudging agreement. "It's true that a woman will put up with pain to look better. You never had your hair dyed, did you?"

"No, but my mother has done it many, many times without bad results."

"Okay, smarty pants, I'll have my hair dyed blond if you'll have your hair dyed too."

"I have no silver hair. What's the purpose of my doing this?"

Helen smirked. "The purpose is for you to get firsthand knowledge. You're pressuring me, and I'm turning the tables on you."

"Have it your way," Sara said. "Who knows? I may like a change."

The flamboyant male stylist put down his magazine and approached the women. "My name is Carlos, and please to follow me. I take you lovely ladies to stations next to each other." Carlos wore black slacks, flip-flops minus socks, and a black shirt draped over which was a long orange-, purple-, and white-striped scarf.

Helen and Sara sat on chairs facing a mirror with pictures of two cats tucked into the corner of the mirror.

"Are these your cats?" Helen asked with interest.

"Yass," Carlos said proudly. "They love me. I love them."

"I have an indoor cat," Helen said.

"Yass, madam—good for you. And now what shall I do for your hair?"

"Cut it short—not too short—it should cover my ears. Color it blond and style it any way you wish."

"Leave it to me." Carlos fingered Helen's hair. "Good texture." Then he turned to Sara. "And you? You want what?"

Sara grimaced. "I don't need a haircut, but I want it dyed."

"Ah!" Carlos ran his hands through Sara's hair. "Good healthy hair with natural curls. I give you blond highlights. Yass?"

"Yass," Sara said—then caught herself off guard. *I didn't mean to imitate him. I hope he doesn't take offense.* "I mean yes. Sounds good."

As Carlos slipped into the coloring room, he flung his scarf around his neck.

*   *   *

The two women left the beauty salon just as it was closing. Helen had shorter golden blond hair. Sara sported a flattering new glamorous look with chestnut hair adorned with blond streaks.

Helen and Sara cast admiring glances at each other. "Let's go to the mall tomorrow and get new outfits and makeup," Sara suggested.

"I feel like a new woman." Helen smiled. "Wait till my sister sees me. Why I think I look younger than she does."

"You look fabulous," Sara said as they both got into the car. At red lights on the drive home Sara couldn't stop looking at herself in the rear-view mirror. She just couldn't believe the marvelous change in her appearance. *I wish my brother could see me now. I'll take a picture of myself and e-mail it to him. I won't send a picture to my mother. She'd probably say I look cheap.*

*   *   *

The next day at 10 a.m. when the mall opened, Sara and Helen entered Macy's. They came out with new outfits. Then they stopped for a lunch of salads and iced tea. After that they went back to Macy's and had makeovers from an Esteé Lauder representative who worked with both women and applied foundations, blush, lipsticks, mascara, eyebrow pencils, and eyeliners on their faces. They loved what they looked like—Helen bought everything, but Sara could afford only the eyeliner.

At home Sara looked in the hall mirror. "Someone strange is looking at me. I've disappeared and a new person has taken my place. Now is the time to take pictures. I already charged my battery, and the camera is good to go."

Sara and Helen took photos of each other. Sara saved them on Picasa and edited them. "We have to fill out the dating application, namely about our personalities, hobbies, and interests and about what kind of man we'd be interested in."

"I feel wonderful without a man. I don't want to meet men," Helen said.

"Just meet them. You don't have to marry them." Sara looked in the hall mirror and a pretty girl looked back at her. She had blond highlights, glowing skin, and wore brand new white palazzo slacks topped with a designer blouse of red taffeta with a sweetheart neckline, jeweled buttons, and three-quarter sleeves.

"First impressions count," Sara said. "Now we submit our photos on-line to the dating service."

Helen plopped down on the couch. "Don't you dare. I came this far, but I won't go any further."

Oh, yes you will, if I have any say in the matter.

CHAPTER 14

HELEN SAT NEXT to Sara watching closely as Sara went online on MATCHMAKING FOR LOVE.com. Sara paid the fee with her credit card; and when she was asked for a user name she took the name of the protagonist in her novel, Betsy Moss. Then she supplied the pertinent information, such as name, address, age, and sex; but she was stuck when she had to describe herself and what she was looking for in a man. *Do I tell the truth? If so, should I say I'm basically a hermit attempting to write a novel and all I want in a man is for him to be truthful and dependable, not critical or controlling like my parents?*

She answered the questions quickly, afraid that if she took too long she wouldn't have the guts to proceed.

"I'm a college graduate who is writing her first novel.
I would like to meet a man with a good heart,
a good sense of humor, and someone who is dependable and honest.
I'm an independent woman who doesn't take well to orders.
Betsy Moss."

Sara cocked her head to one side looking at Helen, "Now it's your turn."

"I decline."

"But you promised," Sara said anxiously, tapping her finger on the desk pad.

"I changed my mind. I wouldn't know what to say on a date. What would I talk about? My MRI? How I make a noodle pudding? How I just dyed my silver hair? How I haven't made love for fifteen years?"

"No—all you have to do is smile and listen to the man talk about himself. My friend, Joan, in Tampa, told me this."

"Suppose he asks about me, what should I say?"

"Tell him you're a widow interested in male companionship and that you like to go to restaurants, concerts, and romantic movies."

"Really?"

"Of course you meet him in a public place so it's safe." *I wouldn't want Helen to get into trouble.*

"Oh—I never thought that a man who would answer might be a crook, a nogoodnik, maybe a murderer." Helen nervously twisted a few strands of her dyed blond hair around her index finger.

I need to encourage her. "You'll be able to tell. Your judgment is good, and that's why you don't let him take you home in the beginning."

Helen's face paled. "What do I say if he wants to drive me home?"

Sara thought for a moment. "Say NO."

"This is too complicated. I won't remember it all."

Sara rose and paced around her bedroom. Then she dropped down on her bed. "All right. We'll rehearse. I'll be the man. I approach you and say, 'You're an attractive woman. I bet you've gone out with hundreds of men.' "What do you say?"

Helen hesitated. "No. I haven't."

"That's it?" Sara wrinkled her forehead.

Helen threw up her hands in desperation. "I told you I don't know what to say."

"You say, 'Many men have been after me, but I have always kept my distance!' Can you remember this, Helen?"

"I suppose." Helen shrugged her shoulders. "But what if he asks how I spend my time; what should I tell him?"

"That's easy. You say, 'I read a lot. I go to the movies. I watch TV programs like the news on CNN, I cook, and I enjoy shopping.'"

"Should I say I go to doctor and dentist's appointments?"

Sara answered quickly. "Certainly not. That's not his business."

"What about going to the beauty salon?"

"Not his business."

"I don't think this dating is for me. I never dated anyone in my whole life, just my husband who I met in high school."

"It's time you started. It will definitely make you feel much younger. What user name do you want?"

Helen cocked her head. "Helen the cook."

Sara's eyes opened wide. "You shouldn't use your real name since a stalker may be looking for you."

"Forget it." Helen started to walk toward the door.

"Come back, you coward. Just pick an easy name like Cookie Gal."

"Okay, already. I'll go with Cookie Gal."

"Sit down next to me. I'm filling out the application for the dating service."

"I didn't say I will go on any dates."

Sara rested her fingers on her laptop. "Will you at least go on one date?"

Helen hung her head.

"Well?"

"One date and only one date."

Sara suspended her hands six inches above the keyboard. "What picture should I send?"

Helen thumbed through all the photos Sara took of her. "Here's a good one."

Sara glanced at the picture. "Not that one. Pick one of you where you're smiling."

"I don't think so. He'll think I'm an easy mark. I'd rather come across as a serious woman."

"You know, you're exasperating. All right I'll send the picture you chose." Sara selected it from Picasa and sent it out. She answered the questions for Helen, because Helen couldn't describe herself or what she was looking for in a man. *I hope Helen gets at least one answer.*

* * *

That night Sara dreamed about a starry sky with a full moon that lit up a desert. A handsome sheik left his camel outside her tent, entered, and planted a kiss on her lips. She woke up smiling, and immediately went online to see how many men had answered her. Sara's smile faded when she learned that no one had replied. *What's wrong with me?*

Helen also had a dream. Her dead husband came down from heaven to warn her of the dangers of dating men she knew nothing about. She woke up with tears in her eyes.

* * *

Before breakfast Helen, who wasn't computer savvy, asked Sara to go online to see if anyone had corresponded with her. To Sara's delight and surprise she learned that a man of seventy had answered Helen. George Washington was a recent widower, a retired chef, and had moved from Brooklyn, New York to Boynton Beach; and he was looking for companionship with a woman who liked cooking.

"I don't want to meet him," Helen said as she entered the kitchen and sat down at the table.

"Why not?" Sara asked, disappointment evident in her tone.

"My husband warned me against dating strangers."

"You told me your husband died fifteen years ago."

"Well he did die, but he came to me in a dream—and I believe the soul of the departed comes down from heaven to help the loved one."

Sara replied with a sigh of resignation, "If I was your age, and a man answered me telling me all about himself, I would be happy to meet him. So far no one has communicated with me. You don't know how lucky you are."

"I can't ignore my husband's warning."

"Don't you think that your husband is looking down at you and might be jealous and that is the reason he told you not to date?"

"Jealous?—Oh, I forgot when we were married he watched me like a hawk. He did have a strong streak of jealousy in him— why I remember that once when we were in a restaurant and the waiter complimented me on being a beautiful woman, my husband didn't leave him a tip."

"Come on, Helen, take a chance. You have nothing to lose and you may very well like this gentleman. Meet him in HEAVENLY EGGS. Tell him to wear a striped tie and a blue short-sleeved shirt. See if he'll do this."

"I'll go if you go with me. I'll say you're an acquaintance and just happened to pass by and you noticed me. If I don't like what he looks like, we'll walk away—who knows, he may be covered in tattoos, or have a beard down to his belly button? He might not be clean and he might have small eyes—I'm suspicious of men with small eyes."

In the kitchen Sara began making breakfast. She set a plate with scrambled eggs in front of Helen. "You know that you just enumerated all negative traits. He could be handsome, clean, and well-dressed; and he might not have a single tattoo."

Helen started eating. "I'll try it once, not because you urge me to, but because I have an adventuresome spirit," she said sarcastically. "Remember, my husband and I used to own a small plane and we flew all over the United States. Actually I was scared stiff, but I went along with what he wanted."

Sara brought in her laptop and began typing an e-mail to George Washington.

"I would like to meet you tomorrow at noon
at HEAVENLY EGGS. In order for me to recognize you,
please wear a striped tie
and wear a short-sleeved blue shirt, Cookie Gal."

It took only five minutes for the man to answer.

"I have a striped tie and a blue shirt.
I'm looking forward to meeting you tomorrow.
See you then, George Washington."

CHAPTER 15

I T WAS THE warmest October in Florida's history; even in November the temperature was in the high eighties. The evening sky, aglow with twinkling stars over Palm Oasis, was cloudless for a change; and there was no rain in sight. In the afternoon good-natured Helen had baked an apple pie, left the house, and taken it as a gift to Ann Wilson, her next door neighbor, whose husband had passed away on Labor Day.

Sara sat at her laptop in her bedroom, checking the progress of her online dating service. She took a deep breath and pulled up MATCHMAKING FOR LOVE.com, hoping that at least one guy had answered. *Helen had good luck and maybe it will carry over to me.* No one had responded in the morning, but this was evening and the results might be different.

Sara's eyes widened as she looked at nine responses. Quickly she read through all of them and inspected their pictures. As she leaned closer to the laptop, the pulse in her temple throbbed. Almost every male looked appealing with the exception of one who sported a long dark beard. Sara preferred clean-shaven men.

The first man, B29, an accountant, was searching for a woman who was trim and good-natured—liked hiking, restaurants, movies, and classical music. Sara went through the list. *Since I lost weight, I'm trim.*

"Sara?" Helen called through the bedroom door, "I'm back. Do you want to go for a walk?"

Sara rose and opened the door. "Not right now. I'm on line with MATCHMAKING FOR LOVE.com."

"Did any men answer yet?"

"Yes. Nine. I eliminated one, but eight look promising. The first one, B29, is an accountant; and he likes hiking, restaurants, movies, and classical music."

"Sounds all right to me." Helen's eyes sparkled. "I made a date for tomorrow with George Washington, the seventy-year old man."

"Good luck. I was just about to answer B29."

"Good luck to you too," Helen said on her way out the door.

Sara typed,

"Hi B29, I do jog,
but I would be interested in hiking.
I like movies, going to restaurants, and classical music.
Betsy Moss."

Sara decided she wouldn't answer the other men just in case they all wanted to go out with her. She'd be overwhelmed. *One at a time is enough for now.*

B29 answered her e-mail the next morning. He suggested they meet at Orient House, an exclusive Chinese restaurant on Willow and 5th Streets. Sara agreed, even though she wasn't particularly entranced by Chinese food.

The next day Sara took extra pain with her makeup, wore a new yellow dress with a round neckline and three-quarter sleeves, and carried a yellow leather clutch bag. She drove her car to Orient House and found a parking spot across the street. She reached for the door handle to exit the Mazda, and then froze. *Who is B29? What do I know about him?* She felt by remaining in the car, she would somehow feel more confident. It didn't work. Her fingers tightened on the steering wheel. She tried to calm herself by taking a few deep breaths and remembered how Dr. Strauss used to say, "Be brave. Meet new people." She steeled herself, opened the door, and crossed the street.

After walking up the path lined with rosebushes, Sara entered the restaurant that was lit dimly with Chinese lanterns. She waited near the entrance with her hands clasped tightly together. In front of her was a small bridge over a pond with green lotus flowers where large fish darted around—some orange fish with white spots, others white with orange spots. Sara thought they looked like goldfish. She should have felt peaceful, but her heart was racing.

A good-looking man with bushy dark brows came up to her. "Hi, Betsy. I'm B29, although my real name is Bernie. I see you're admiring the koi that are a lucky charm for prosperity. I love this restaurant for its tranquil setting, elegant ambiance, and superb food."

Sara stood speechless, at attention, overwhelmed by Bernie's ease and charm. Finally she managed to say, "Hello. Pleased to meet you."

"I have reserved a private booth for us." Bernie pointed to the back of the restaurant. A waiter led the way.

Sara wiped the perspiration from her upper lip. *He looks nice.* She liked that he wore a Hawaiian shirt and pressed slacks. He had brown hair parted on the left side. His voice was velvety smooth. Sara had devised a scale for men. Ten was the highest. Bernie had ten points for neatness and cleanliness, ten for dressing well, ten for voice, and ten for looks.

They sat down in the booth opposite each other. A Chinese waiter in a black uniform approached them with the menus. Sara knew what she wanted right away, but kept her eyes glued to the menu anyway. Bernie took a couple of minutes to decide.

"What will you have?" Bernie asked.

"I'd like tofu with spinach and brown rice, please."

"Anything else?"

"Tea."

"Hot or cold?" Bernie asked.

"Hot, please."

The Chinese waiter stood poised with a pen and pad. Bernie said in an authoritative tone, "Gan-chaoww nyoh her." The waiter nodded, wrote the order down, and left.

Bernie cleared his throat. "I ordered dry-fried beef and noodles, a Cantonese dish that I prefer."

All that Sara could come up with, after hearing such a revelation, was, "Oh."

"I was in China two years ago. Chinese cuisine is one of the three grand cuisines in the world, together with Turkish, and, of course, French."

"Really?"

"Did you know that egg rolls aren't eaten in China?"

"No, I didn't know that." *Is this guy for real?*

"Why did you order tofu?" Bernie asked.

"I don't eat meat."

Bernie frowned. "Why not? There must be something wrong with you if you don't eat strengthening food."

This guy's not for real. "My brother is a food expert and connoisseur, and he says meat is harmful."

Bernie laughed. "Ridiculous. I'm as healthy as a bull. You look emaciated. I like girls who like meat. Cantonese dishes surprise foreigners, so the saying goes that the Chinese eat everything with four legs except tables and everything that flies except airplanes. Cantonese dishes may contain cats, dogs, sea life, and snakes, but so what?"

Sara's face lost all color.

The waiter returned pushing a side table on wheels that had a gas burner. He cooked the dishes on the table and added sauce. Bernie smiled warmly, "This side table service is one of the most elegant food services, and this is why I always frequent this restaurant when I look for the best."

After the waiter served the dishes without comment, Bernie put his hand in his pants pocket and drew out chopsticks. "I always take my own personalized chopsticks with me." He held the chopsticks out for Sara's perusal. They read, "Bernard L. Garner." *Whoa, he thinks the world of himself.*

"Chopsticks, invented in China, have been used for over four thousand years. Do you know how to use them?"

"No."

"I'll teach you—that is if you want to learn."

"I like to learn new things." *But one of those things is not how to use chopsticks.*

"Hold your dominant hand out. Place the chopstick between your thumb and index finger and try to pick up a noodle."

Sara tried again and again. *I can't seem to get the hang of it.*

"Maybe next time you'll eat meat," Bernie said taking for granted that Sara will date him in the future.

There won't be a next time.

Sara picked at her food with a fork. Bernie, on the other hand, finished every morsel with the expert use of chopsticks. When the waiter returned, he dropped off the check along with two fortune cookies. Bernie read his aloud, "You will soon travel to a faraway land."

"Are you planning on traveling?" Sara asked.

"Yes, I'm returning to China in two months. My company is sending me there to do the books for a Chinese toy manufacturing concern. What does your fortune cookie say?"

Sara drew out the small piece of paper from her cookie. "It says, 'Don't trust everyone you meet.'" *How true!*

"That's evident with most people, but I'm a trustworthy soul," Bernie said with a huge smile that revealed some food between his front teeth. He put his hand in his pocket and drew out a silver toothpick and began picking at his teeth.

How gross can one be!

"Will you see me next week?" he asked.

Sara didn't hesitate answering him. "Since we don't like the same kind of foods, I don't think we should see each other again."

"From the moment I saw how thin you looked, I knew we weren't destined for each other."

Oh well, there are seven more guys for me to date. They can't all be a disaster, and probably a few at least will be better than Bernie. He's a minus one.

CHAPTER 16

ELEN, NERVOUS AS a wet cat in a bathtub, opened her closet door. "Sara," she shouted, "I need you."

Sara came scurrying into Helen's bedroom. "What's the matter?"

"I can't make up my mind what I should wear on my date with George Washington."

"How about the emerald dress with the white collar?" Sara reached in and drew out the dress.

"No, I don't think so. He'll think I'm trying to show off my green eyes."

"Don't be silly. You'll look great." Sara held the dress up, and Helen hesitantly reached for it.

"Mmm—Okay —I'll try it on, but if I don't like it, I'll try another one."

"You called me in for advice," Sara said, her hands on her hips. "My advice is to wear this dress."

After Helen put the dress on, she looked in the mirror. "I look kinda nice, don't I?"

"You look scrumptious."

Ten-thirty a.m. the following day, Helen tried to be stoic about her date. She put on the green dress, and wore matching sandals and a sun hat.

"You don't need a hat," Sara said.

Helen put it aside, listening to her.

"You need a touch of mascara," Sara said as she pulled a tube of mascara from the pocket of her shorts.

"I have never worn mascara. I'm too old to put it on. If he rejects me because of no mascara, I'll live with that," Helen said stubbornly.

Sara smiled ruefully. "Alice, your twin, wears mascara, and she obviously is exactly your age. Women of ninety wear mascara. It will emphasize your lovely eyes. Sit down on this chair and I'll apply it."

"Will it hurt?"

"Not a bit; just open your eyes wide—that's right—now look in the mirror."

Helen jutted out her chin as she looked at her eyelashes. "Oh, nice."

"You didn't have your nails done," Sara said.

"I feel like a pig when the polish chips off."

Sara came out of the bathroom with two bottles of nail polish—a light pink shade, and a pearl white. "Sit down at the kitchen table, and I'll put polish on your nails. What color do you prefer?"

Helen knew when Sara meant business, and she selected the pearl white. Sara applied the polish and covered it with a top coat.

"Now don't touch anything for fifteen minutes," Sara said.

Helen sat in front of the TV watching the news on CNN and wondering if all this fuss was going to pay off.

* * *

Helen entered HEAVENLY EGGS accompanied by Sara. *Nothing can happen in a restaurant and if I feel uncomfortable, I'll just leave with Sara.* She spotted George Washington immediately. He had a full head of silver hair and a pleasant expression. He wore a blue-striped tie and a short-sleeved shirt navy shirt. Helen turned to Sara and held her thumb up, and Sara took the hint and walked out the door.

"Hi, I'm Cookie Gal, only my real name is Helen."

"I'm George Washington, only my real name is George. You're prettier than your picture," George said, as he led her to a booth next to a window overlooking the sidewalk. A garden dotted with flowering bushes was under the window. Royal Palms lined the street.

Helen bit down on her lips. She said in a soft voice, "I've been here before."

"A pretty woman like you must have dated many men," George replied.

"Not really. I guess I've had a few admirers."

"Shall we order?" George asked, and called over a waitress with a frilly apron.

"I'd like a spinach omelet, please," Helen said.

"I'll have the same," George said to the waitress.

"That's a good choice," Helen said. "Their spinach omelets are delicious. They're made with Feta cheese."

"Tell me about yourself," George said wide-eyed.

"Not much to tell. I'm an old senior who likes to cook."

George said, "You're not old, you're like a vintage wine. I'm sure you've had an exciting life."

"Not any more than other people."

"You know a prune is an experienced plum."

"You're funny," Helen said smiling.

"Here's another one. 'Youth is a gift of nature, but age is a work of art.'"

As the time passed and George told more jokes, Helen began to feel more and more at ease. George told Helen about some of the recipes he created, and Helen told him about the favorite dishes she liked to cook.

When they were having coffee, George leaned over and put his hand on Helen's hand. She drew back, thought better of it, and allowed his hand to remain on hers.

Just then Helen was startled when her sister Alice stood at the edge of the table and said, "Lenny and I were passing by, on our way to the Crystal Casino, when I looked in the window and saw you. You look great."

Helen stammered, "G-George, this is my twin sister, Alice, and her husband, Lenny."

"Pleased to meet Helen's closest relatives," George said. "Would you care to join us? We're almost finished, but we could have another cup of coffee and we could talk."

Lenny spoke in his brash voice, "Nah. We're going to the casino. I'm down a couple of thousand, and I need to win my dough back."

"What do you play?" George asked as he moved closer to the wall to make room for Lenny.

"Blackjack," Lenny said as he sat down next to George in the booth.

"I like roulette myself," George said.

"Helen and I play the slots," Alice said as she sat next to her sister. A nervous twitch in her eye was evident.

Helen looked down at her sister's left hand. She wore only her plain gold wedding band. "Where is your large diamond engagement ring?"

Alice's face fell.

"I needed cash so I brought it to the pawn shop," Lenny said. "But I'll buy Alice a bigger and shinier diamond when I win big at the tables today."

Helen's face paled. *I knew Alice was a darn fool when she married a man twenty years younger, and a gambler to boot.*

George wiped his mouth with a napkin and didn't offer a comment. Once again he covered Helen's hand with his and she felt comforted.

"Material things fade away," Alice said. "It's love that really counts. Isn't that true, Lenny?"

"You better believe it," Lenny replied. "I woke up feeling great, like this is my lucky day. I'm going to be a big winner. I don't count cards, folks, but most of the time I have a sixth sense. Why you know, I've won hundreds of thousands playing all over the world. Remember, Alice, when I won real big on the cruise ship to Alaska? I bought you a Russian hand-painted pin in Sitka. Yeah, it's love that counts."

"I'd like some blueberry pancakes," Alice said sounding childlike.

"Let's not get started eating now," Lenny remarked. "We'll eat later in the casino. They have some great dishes that I love."

"But I'm hungry now," Alice said softly as she breathed deeply and her left eye twitched.

"You've been putting on too much weight ever since we got married," Lenny complained as he looked with scorn at Alice's puffy cheeks.

"I have to eat when I'm hungry or I'll faint," Alice said weakly.

"I gotta go," Lenny said, ignoring Alice's wish. "Say, why don't you folks come with us to the casino? I bet we'll have some real good fun."

CHAPTER 17

SARA PACED THE living room, looking out the window every few minutes. Helen had been out for eight hours. *I hope she's all right. You never know what can happen when you meet a stranger.*

She took a few minutes to go to the bathroom, and when she came back Helen had come home and was standing in the living room. "How was it?" Sara asked frowning.

"Good and bad," Helen answered as she plopped down on a gray tweed wingback.

"Tell me everything. Don't hold back a thing."

"George turned out to be a very nice man, and he asked me out again for next Tuesday. That's the good news—but, and it's a big but, my sister Alice has dug herself into a ditch with the worm she married. I warned her not to marry a man twenty years younger than her. I knew he was after her money—but Alice didn't heed my advice—and now she's suffering."

Helen bit down on the thumbnail of her right hand. "When I was with George in the restaurant, Alice spotted me through the window and she and Lenny came in, and reluctantly we went with them to the casino. Lenny dropped another three thousand and cursed. He flew off the handle, and Alice had to sign a note for him. He's gambling away all the money she had inherited from her last husband."

"I'm sorry to hear that," Sara said. "Do you think she'll divorce him?"

"I wish I knew, but Alice has always kept her problems to herself. She suffered with her first husband for a dozen years before she divorced him. I'm afraid for her as she seems really nervous with that twitch of hers going a mile a minute."

"Gee, Helen, she's walking a tough road; but she's traveled this road before—and all you can do for her is to be there for her when she needs you." Sara put her hand on Helen's shoulder.

"Thanks for listening to me. You're a good friend."

"So are you."

* * *

Sara waited a week to answer HaHa123's e-mail from MATCHMAKING FOR LOVE. Her experience with pompous Bernie had left a sour taste in her mouth, but what the man wrote looked promising. He liked to jog, loved nature and animals, including turtles. He owned a chain of hardware stores and liked to read science fiction.

He proposed that Sara meet him at the entrance of Palm Oasis Wetlands and Nature Center. He wrote they could meet informally, sit on a bench, and then jog on the boardwalk. Sara thought it was an enchanting place to meet a new guy. Her new lilac shorts set would show off her shapely legs and she could wear her purple sneakers. Helen had been out again with George, and she had a wonderful time with him when they took a long drive in his Lincoln on A1A, a picturesque road with millionaires' homes to gape at. *I have nothing to lose. If this one's a jerk, I don't have to see him again.*

Sara waited a half-hour until HaHa123 showed up, waving his hands about and apologizing profusely. He looked about 5'9", stocky, but without visible body fat. He had a tan, short blond hair, broad shoulders. When he removed his sunglasses, his eyes were gray. He wore white shorts, a white Lacoste polo shirt, and white deck shoes. *So far, so good.*

They walked the boardwalk until they found a bench to sit down on.

"My name is Hal. What's yours?

"Sara."

"Look in the water, Sara," Hal said as he pointed to a flock of large wading birds. "They're roseate spoonbills with beautiful pink plumage. Aren't they beautiful?"

"Nice," Sara said. "The last time I visited here I saw young herons. The variety of wildlife in their natural habitat is amazing. Shall we jog and look for the alligators and the turtles?"

"I'm wasted. I had an argument with one of my employees, and I had to fire him. I'd rather sit and talk with you. Do you mind if I smoke?" Hal didn't wait for Sara to answer. He drew a pack of cigarettes from one of his short's pockets and lit up.

Sara coughed from the irritation of the smoke.

"Sorry—the breeze is blowing the smoke in your direction. I'll turn my head away. Most girls don't mind my smoking. I tried to stop, used those 'e-cigarettes', but it's not the same as the real thing. Tell me about yourself."

"I tried smoking, but it didn't last long. The smoke got into my eyes and burned them."

"When the women learn that I am the owner of a chain of hardware stores, they go after me for my money. The gold diggers expect me to take them out on the town, and I resent it. I want a woman who will love me for myself. That's why I picked this place to meet a new woman."

He's good looking, but kind of cheap and narcissistic.

"Have you ever been married?" Hal asked.

"No."

"You're a pretty girl. Why not?"

"I haven't met anyone I'm interested in. Have you ever been married?"

"Yeah, once. I have a kid. She's nine months old. My ex-wife is the daughter of a manufacturing magnate. I don't have to give her alimony, but the child support is killing me."

"You didn't reveal anything about your ex or having a child," Sara said as she took a deep breath. *I'm relieved I didn't tell him my full name or where I live.*

"Who would meet me if I told the truth about my life? It's just a deception of omission. I'm really a nice honest fellow. I'm lonesome, and I guess you are, too."

"Let's walk around." Sara rose from the bench and stretched. "It's peaceful here, but for some reason I feel agitated."

Hal stood. "Yeah, I guess we can walk to the nature center. Would you like some ice cream?"

"I expected to jog. Thank you, but I'll skip the ice cream." *I'll skip him too.*

"From your expression it seems like you aren't interested in me. Am I right?"

"I don't think we'd hit it off as a couple, nothing personal of course."

"Oh, well, nothing ventured, nothing gained. It wouldn't be the first time a woman turned me off."

Sara winced. "You're turned off? Why the nerve of you? I'm not interested in a man with an ex-wife and a child."

"So be it," Hal said as he strutted away toward the exit.

Two down and six to go.

Sara drove home with a bitter taste in her mouth after her meeting with Hal. As she stepped out of the car, her cell phone rang.

"Hello Sara. This is your mother. You haven't called in eight days."

Sara turned the key in the front door lock. *Next time you want to talk to me, try calling me instead of complaining that I don't call you.* "Wait a minute, Mom. I'm just getting home."

"From where?"

Sara plopped down on the sofa. "I met a guy from a dating service, but he told me he was married and had a kid."

"If you would come home, like you should, I can introduce you to single, comfortable Jewish men. A dating service is the worst idea I ever heard."

"I'm not coming home."

"Why is a single helpless young woman not living with her parents?"

Sara rose from the sofa and began pacing the living room. "Dr. Strauss thought it's best for me to live by myself and not depend on my parents."

"Tell me, does Dr. Strauss have a single daughter? I bet he doesn't, or he wouldn't give you advice that could get you into hot water."

"Mom, this conversation is going nowhere. How are things with you and Dad?"

Sara heard a cough on the phone. "The cook left and I'm looking for another who will follow orders."

With the cell phone to her ear, Sara got up and walked to the kitchen, and peeked into the refrigerator. "That's the third cook who has quit," her mother said. Sara closed the refrigerator door. *I don't feel like eating. Talking with my mother causes me to lose my appetite.*

"These maids are impossible. They spend a couple of hours cooking and when I ask them to do the wash or vacuum the house they have the *chutzpah*, the nerve, to say that their job description doesn't cover housework."

"Mom, did you ever consider hiring a maid to clean and a cook to prepare your meals?"

"Sometimes I wonder why we paid for your college tuition. Two servants cost double what one servant can do if she's flexible. I'll just keep looking until I find the right one."

"That's what I'm doing with the dating service."

"You never told me what to do before. I don't think we should have sent you to that psychiatrist. He put weird ideas in your head."

"Goodbye, Mom. Have a good day."

She won't have a good day. She likes to wallow in misery and dictate to me.

CHAPTER 18

S ARA AND HELEN sat on the sofa watching the evening news on Fox.

"I feel sorry for those poor people," Sara said pointing her finger at the TV, ". . . five thousand of them who lost their homes due to flooding in Mississippi and Louisiana."

"I feel sorry for them too," Helen said, ". . . but I feel sorry for you that you seem to have given up on meeting more men."

"My dates have been awful. I need a break."

"Not all men are like the ones you met. You have to brace yourself and try again."

Sara got up and turned the TV off. "That last one was a brute. There we sat eating dinner. He had a fat face with puffed out cheeks. He ate like food was going out of style, and then when I had just started my key lime pie, he had the gall to put his knife in my pie and said he wanted to try mine."

"Okay, the man was a pig. But the next man on the dating site looks like a gentlemen. He says his partner has died and he's looking for a new partner. He loves wide open spaces and he owns land. He could be a catch."

"Helen, dear Helen—do I need a man who is widowed. Maybe he has ten children all under the age of twelve. I'd have diapers to change and meals to cook—for a tribe."

"Don't be ridiculous. A partner doesn't mean a wife. He wrote he was single. Try only one date."

"Do you know you're a pest?"

"So get some bug killer and spray me, but go out. You may like him."

*   *   *

"I'm through with all these jerks," Sara said, pounding on the kitchen table. "I don't think there's a decent man out there. I won't waste my time looking for a man on MATCHMAKING FOR LOVE. I need to devote myself to my writing."

"Try again, Sara," Helen said. "If at first you don't succeed, try, try, again."

"Those horrible men are making me nervous." Sara paced the kitchen.

"Once more—please—for me."

"All right. I'll answer the next one, his user name is Friendly175."

*   *   *

Sara met Friendly175 next to the fountain with the cherubs in Blueberry Park. He was tall, muscular, and although he had a scar on his cheek he wasn't bad-looking. The day was sunny and there was no breeze as they sat on a bench under a palm tree and exchanged background information. His name was Seymour and he was searching for a woman with a big heart.

"What do you do with yourself?" Seymour asked as he gazed into Sara's hazel eyes.

"I'm writing a novel about a college girl. What interests you?"

Seymour began talking about his favorite subject—himself. "I love to hunt. I'm looking for a partner who will take part in hunting."

"I don't hunt," Sara said—disappointed that this man liked hunting, killing animals for sport.

"That's all right. I'll teach you. I have a retreat of twenty thousand acres of flat scrub land that is well-stocked with deer, wild turkey, and wild boar."

"Oh…"

"I had a regular hunting partner, Sam Gilbert, but he passed away from congestive heart failure. I think it might be fun to have a female hunting partner. We could sit in a blind waiting patiently to sight a turkey. What do you say?"

Sara's face turned red. "I don't think I'd like to kill an animal."

"You'd soon get used to it. I crave the release. It's like an addictive drug."

"Doesn't it bother you to take an animal's life?"

"Hell, no. My previous partner and me used to sit in the blind waiting for an animal to approach the mechanical feeder or the corn we threw on the ground as bait. I can teach you how to use a Weatherby rifle. I always get the animal locked in the scope of the rifle as it comes to feed. I can bring it down with just one shot before it picks up my scent."

"You really get a charge out of this, don't you?" *This guy's a murderer. Poor animals. They don't have a chance.*

"It's a feeling like no other. I once spotted two bucks through my binoculars. One was an eight-pointer and the other was a real large ten-pointer approaching me dead on. Ever so slowly, so as not to rustle my camouflage of crackling dry palmetto, I lifted my rifle to my shoulder and aimed at the ten-pointer. As I pulled the trigger the cross hair in the gunsight was straight with the stag's chest. The shot rang out as I fired. It felled the ten-pointer and scared off the smaller deer." His eyes widened and lit up with pride.

"I don't want to shoot anything. I don't feel well," Sara said as she jumped up and moved quickly away. *What a jerk. Maybe it's me who's the jerk for meeting these awful men.*

*   *   *

"Sara, you can't stop meeting men. It's not good for you to stay home all the time. You have to get out and socialize. Just follow my example," Helen said as they sat on the back porch after dinner. "I met George online, and he's such a wonderfully gentle man. Please keep trying."

Encouraged by both Helen and Dr. Strauss, Sara made up her mind to try MATCHMAKING FOR LOVE once more—but definitely that would be the last time. She sat at her computer and went online. It didn't take long for a picture of a good-looking man to pop up. Seeing the picture of a cop was discouraging, even though he was unmarried, but somehow he had an engaging smile. She read about Alex The Cop and it intrigued her. He wrote he had a good sense of humor and loved animals; and he offered to take his date to a theme park where she would be enchanted by exotic animals.

Their date was all Alex promised it would be—intriguing. He called for her at 8 a.m., and it took a couple of hours to reach the park. Sara wasn't sure if she was mesmerized by the exotic animals there or by Alex, the policeman.

"Look at me," Alex called out. "I'm on the back of a tortoise who is hundreds of years old, and I'm riding it like a horse. It's a grass eater, but he's as strong as a bull. Are you having a good time?"

"Wonderful," Sara said with a big grin. She opened her hands filled with nuts, and lemurs ate their fill of them. She was bewitched watching a parrot ride a miniature bicycle.

"Have you ever had a pet bird?" Alex asked.

"No, but I did have a box turtle, It died after an operation."

"That's a shame," Alex said.

They spent the day in the theme park, had dinner in an Italian restaurant, and when Sara came home Helen asked about her date.

"He seems to be a good guy."

"Will you see him again?"

"You bet."

CHAPTER 19

A MONTH LATER THE sun shone brightly, the weather was flawless, and the gentle breeze kissed the palms making them sway in a rhythmic undulation. Sara couldn't have wished for better weather on this very special day that she had secretly planned. The only detriment would be that she had to be civil to Tracy. She would make sure to keep her distance from that witch.

It was a Sunday afternoon, and Sara had prepared her neighbor, Ann Wilson, to ask Helen to come to her home with the excuse she had a problem with a cake she was preparing. Thankfully, Helen complied. Now Sara stood wide-eyed at the window waiting for the truck with the sign that read "Palm Oasis Party Planners." Four minutes later she heaved a sigh when the truck parked in front of the house.

A sixteen year-old boy wearing jeans and a T-shirt that read "Palm Oasis Party Planners" entered the house with a dozen silver "Happy Birthday" balloons.

"Hurry," Sara said. "Arrange them in the living room."

Marge, the party planner, and mother of Cliff, her teenage helper, came to the door. She wore a bright red clown jumpsuit adorned with gigantic white dots, a ruffled white collar, and pom-pom buttons on the front. On her head was a multi-colored wig. She stepped in with her yellow plastic clown shoes.

"We only have twenty minutes until everyone shows up," Sara said raising her voice.

"You're a nervous wreck," Marge said. "We brought the birthday cake and the ice cream."

Ten minutes later the doorbell rang and the guests poured into the house bringing wrapped gifts. George was the first one to enter. He was dressed in a summer suit, white shirt, and navy tie. He had insisted upon paying for the cost of Palm Oasis Party Planners.

Alice, Helen's twin, who knew that Sara had planned a surprise sixty-sixth birthday party for them, came with her husband Lenny who didn't bother to dress up.

Right after them Elliott, Helen's nephew, showed up with Tracy who was clamped to his arm like glue. Both looked slightly inebriated and were dressed inappropriately with shorts and T-shirts. Sara looked them over and was disgusted, especially with Tracy, who obviously didn't own a bra. Not a word passed between Tracy and Sara.

The bell announced one more person. Sara had invited Alex, the good-looking police officer, whom she had dated a few times. He impressed her as a decent sort, so she had asked him to the birthday party. He brought a bouquet of red roses and a box of White Russian Martini Godiva chocolates that he gave to Sara, kissing her lightly on her cheek. "The bouquet is a gift for the twins, and the chocolates are for you."

Sara blushed. "Thank you, Alex."

Eight people crowded into the living room, which was decorated with balloons, pink streamers, and a banner that read "Happy Sixty-Sixth Birthday, Alice & Helen." Marge's son had brought in folding chairs and everyone seated themselves in a circle.

Five minutes later Ann, the friendly neighbor, showed up with Helen in tow. Helen's mouth was agape with true surprise as Marge played the "Happy Birthday" song. The guests sang it loudly and gleefully with the exception of Lenny and Tracy, who looked bored.

"George," Helen said going over to him. "How did you know about this party?"

"Why Sara e-mailed me. She did a good job keeping it a secret from you, didn't she?"

"Wow, I can't get over it."

"Ready for the entertainment," Marge said as she blew on her squeaker horn.

"We're ready," Sara shouted. "Full speed ahead."

Marge did a bang-up job and it seemed everyone enjoyed her performance singing songs she had written. Elliott volunteered to give one of his humorous speeches from *Hamlet Revised*. Lenny and Tracy, both frowning, stepped out.

*　　*　　*

Tracy used the bathroom to apply another coat of violet bombshell lipstick. *If it wasn't for Elliott's relationship with Helen, I wouldn't have come to this birthday party for those two old maggots.*

After opening the back door and going out onto the porch, Lenny sat down on a plastic chair, lit a cigarette, pursed his lips, and began to blow smoke rings. A minute later Tracy came out and sat down in the chair next to him. Lenny's eyes focused on her great shape. *Wow, that Tracy is sure some hot chick. No bra, and what a build. Think I'll play my cards like I had a few million bucks. That ought to interest her.*

Tracy admired Lenny's huge biceps. *I wonder why that guy married the old crow, Alice, probably for her dough. He's cool, fairly young, and I like that his blond wavy hair hangs down to his shoulders.*

"Hi," Lenny said with a big smile. "I'm tired of this stupid party."

"Me, too," Tracy agreed.

"You attached to the guy you came with?" Lenny asked.

"Naw. I've dated him, but he's a loser. He writes plays and acts in them. He makes nada." *This dude must be rich. He came in a new Mercedes. Think I'll come on to him.*

Lenny tossed his cigarette on the tile and ground it out with his sandal. "It would be fun to put a scare into Helen, don't ya think?"

"Great idea," Tracy said agreeing whole heartedly. "Also, I'd like to see Sara squirm. The bossy cow thinks because she eats so-called healthy that everyone should follow her lead. She goes around preaching like she's Billy Sunday."

Tracy and Lenny pricked up their ears when they heard loud mewing coming from inside the house. A racket with meowing sounds continued unabatedly.

"Are ya thinking what I'm thinking?" Lenny asked.

"You better believe it," Tracy said with an evil grin. "Let's take the cat and hide it. Can you imagine how upset Sara and Helen will be? They'll tear out their hair."

"Ya have a place to hide the cat?" Lenny asked.

"No. I live in the same house with Elliott and he'd bring the cat back."

Lenny mused over his choices. "I got it. I'll take the cat in my car, drive to our home, put the cat in the garage, and drive back. It won't take long. Wanna come with me?"

"Wouldn't miss it for the world."

Lenny scratched his head. "The garage isn't attached to the house. Usually Alice doesn't go to the garage. She won't hear any noise the cat makes. I'll pick you up after I drop Alice off. Then we'll decide what to do with the cat."

"Sounds like a good idea," Tracy said with a big grin.

CHAPTER 20

L ENNY AND TRACY returned to the party after the birthday cake, ice cream sandwiches, and lemonade had been served in the dining room. After the gifts were given to the birthday girls, Tracy piped up, "Time for some booze. Let's toast the twins. Where's the liquor?"

"We haven't any liquor," Helen said. "It isn't healthy."

"You're all stupid health freaks," Tracy shouted. "Let's go." She grabbed Elliott's hand and pulled him to the door.

"I'll take you home, Tracy, drop you off—then I have to go meet a guy."

"We should be leaving too," Lenny said. "Come on, Alice. The party's over."

The crowd dispersed in fifteen minutes after everyone had wished Helen a happy birthday. Then Helen looked in her bedroom for Emeralda. "Here, puss," she said looking in the pet's bed. Not finding the cat, she bent down—blinking—looked under her bed. "Sara," she called, "Emeralda is missing."

Sara and Alex searched the whole house, even looking under the balloons that had fallen from the ceiling to the floor. No Emeralda.

"What could have happened to the cat?" Sara asked rhetorically.

Alex went to the back door. "This door is open. It's possible that someone snuck in and took the cat."

"Why would someone do that?"

"I don't know. Helen," Alex said, "See if anything else is missing."

"Like what?"

"Like your jewelry, money, anything of value."

"I'll help you look," Sara said.

"It was such a nice party. Why did this have to happen?" Helen said sadly as she examined her jewelry drawer. "All my stuff is here."

"Look in your purse," Alex said. "Some burglaries have taken place in this neighborhood."

"All my credit cards and money seem to be here. But where's my cat? Even if someone left the back door open, she'd never go out. She's been a house cat all her life."

"She could've been kidnapped," Alex said. "I've heard of cases like this before. You may even get a ransom note. Do you any money worth mentioning?"

"Why yes, I do. My husband had a big insurance policy, and I was the beneficiary."

"Do you own property?" Alex asked. He sat down at the kitchen table, took out a pad, and began writing.

"Yes, two homes—a house that I rent out, and this house."

"Are they mortgaged?"

"No. They're fully paid up. You're a police officer—what's your advice?"

"Let's wait till tomorrow and see if a ransom note shows up. Usually the kidnapper makes a false move and he or she gets caught. I've experienced this many times. Just don't panic. I'm sure you'll get your cat back."

"I'm so sorry that this happened, and on your birthday too," Sara said as she sat down opposite Alex at the kitchen table.

"Would you like me to drop in tomorrow?" Alex asked.

"Oh, it would relieve my mind if you did," Helen said, her face drained of all color.

"This kind of stuff bugs me," Alex said as he made more notes on his pad.

"You're a kind man."

"You're both wonderful women, and I want to help in any way I can."

"Thanks," Sara said in appreciation. "You know Emeralda and Daisy, my box turtle who died, were friends. In fact Daisy used to follow Emeralda around. We thought it was so cute; a box turtle following a cat."

"That's interesting," Alex said. "I'll drop by tomorrow. Call me at once if you get a ransom note."

"Thank you," Sara said. *Who knows; he may be the one. Being a policeman, however, is a dangerous job, and I'd worry sick about him.*

*   *   *

Lenny drove Alice home and after he gave her a peck on the cheek, he dropped her off. He drove to Tracy's and they went for a drive. Tracy moved so close to Lenny that their bare thighs touched.

"That feels real good," Lenny said as he removed his right hand from the steering wheel and put it on Tracy's thigh. When she put her hand over his, Lenny took a deep satisfying breath, and parked the car in a deserted lot.

"Can you imagine how upset Helen and Sara will be when they find out the cat's missing?" Tracy asked.

"I have an idea," Lenny said with relish as he took a puff from his cigarette. "What do ya think if I take this prank to the next level?"

Tracy tipped her head. "What do you have in mind?"

"I could put a ransom note in Helen's mailbox."

Clapping her hands, Tracy said, "Brilliant. Sara, Helen's peon, wouldn't know what to do. They'll both fall apart."

"Yeah."

"I have a notebook and pen in my purse. Here—start writing."

$$* \quad * \quad *$$

When the cat didn't come home that night, Helen cried herself to sleep. The next morning she looked in the mail box and found a ransom note demanding $150,000. Helen's hands shook as she read the letter repeatedly.

Sara called Alex, and a half-hour later he showed up in his uniform. *I'm so happy he's here. He looks so handsome in his uniform.*

"Let me see the note," Alex said. He took out a magnifying glass and examined the handwritten note.

"Do you want to see your cat again?
Put $150,000 in a suitcass and drop it
off next to the trashbin in front of
Etz Cham syngog at exactly
2 p.m. tomorow.
DO NOT CALL POLISE
or cat is dead."

"One hundred and fifty thousand dollars is not so much," Helen cried. "If I don't give it to him, he'll murder my cat."

"I know you love your cat," Sara said ". . . but the criminal is asking an outrageous sum. Is Emeralda worth it?"

Helen's eyes teared up. "I love that cat with all my heart. Wouldn't you pay that amount to get back Daisy if she was taken?"

Sara was dumbstruck. "I don't have $150,000."

Helen wiped her eyes. "Would you pay $500?"

Sara stammered. "I—I guess so."

"So there," Helen said, "It proves my point. When you love an animal, you're willing to pay what you can to get it back."

"Ladies," Alex said. "I can easily track down this stupid perp. First of all he can't spell for beans. His handwriting will give him away. It looks like he has never done this before because even the place he asks you to drop the money is on a busy street, and I can wait for him to show up."

"Do you have an idea who did this?" Sara asked.

"Let me ask you a question. Was the back door locked during the party?"

"I always make sure both doors are locked before I go to sleep," Sara said without hesitation.

Alex nodded. "I remember seeing Tracy and Lenny leave the living room when the birthday party was in full swing. They were away for approximately twenty minutes. Would either of them have a motive for taking the cat?"

"Yes," Sara cried out. "Both of them would. Tracy is a sleazy, contemptible snake who likes to hurt people, and Lenny is a gambler who's always in debt. It could be someone threatened to break his legs if he didn't come up with $150,000."

"Stealing a cat for ransom is rare but not unheard of," Alex said. "It is true that dognapping is certainly more prevalent; it has been reported since the 1930's. A bill known as the "Dognapping Law" became the Animal Welfare Act of 1966. If we can trace the peculiarities of the misspelled words and the sloppy handwriting, it will be easy to catch the perpetrator."

"I have a notion," Helen said, "that it was Lenny who kidnapped Emeralda."

"Why don't you call Alice," Sara suggested, "and ask her if Lenny is available to help you write Thank You cards. She's busy, and I am too, but Lenny may be free."

"I'll do it," Helen said as she picked up the phone and dialed her sister. "Hi, Alice. I got some gorgeous gifts yesterday, and Sara is too busy to help me write Thank You cards. Maybe Lenny is free. Does he have good handwriting and is his spelling satisfactory?"

"Cut it out. I'm no dope," Alice shrieked. "You don't want Lenny to write Thank You cards. What is it you do want?"

Helen blurted out in a thin voice, "Emeralda was kidnapped and a ransom note for $150,000 was put in my mailbox."

Alice didn't utter a word.

In desperation Helen called out, "Do you think Lenny may have taken my cat?"

Alice spoke in a troubled voice, "I suppose so. I went to the garage after I heard meowing. There's a cat in the garage that looks like Emeralda without its collar. I asked Lenny about it and he said that Tracy found a homeless cat and he wants to keep it. He's been feeding it dry cereal. I'm so sorry."

"Dry cereal?" Helen cried. "She hates cereal. I feed her the best wet canned food, *Delicious Feast.*"

"I guess that Lenny didn't get a chance buy expensive cat food for what he said was a stray cat," Alice said.

"You know it's not a stray cat—it's Emeralda," Helen shouted. "I'm going to have the police arrest both Tracy and Lenny."

"You can't do this. He didn't mean to hurt you. He stole my money but not what I had hidden. He also had a huge gambling debt. Please, Helen, don't do this."

"How could he have taken your money? Didn't you have a prenuptial agreement?"

"Yes, it protected me, but when he kept asking me for money or he'd be murdered, I gave him what he wanted."

"Sara's friend, Alex, the officer from the Ft. Lauderdale Police Department, is here. He's ready to arrest both culprits."

"Please don't have the officer swear out an arrest warrant for Lenny," Alice cried out. "I'll be over in a half-hour. I'm bringing Emeralda back."

Alice showed up at Helen's door twenty minutes later. She had Emeralda in a large cardboard box and handed it to Helen, who gathered the frightened cat in her arms and hugged her. Emeralda meowed her gratitude. Helen ran with the cat to the kitchen where she set down a double cat dish with water and *Delicious Feast*. The cat ate and drank hungrily, and when she was finished lay down in her bed and fell asleep.

Sara, Alex, and Alice sat at the kitchen table and watched Helen as she stood over the sleeping cat. Helen, heaving a sigh of relief, soon sat down on the fourth kitchen chair.

Alex tapped his fingers on the table. "I'm at your service. Do you want the perpetrators brought to justice?"

Alice burst into tears.

"What aren't you telling me?" Helen asked. She stood up, opened a cabinet door, took out a box of tissues, and offered it to her sister. Alice grabbed a bunch of tissues and attempted to dry the fountain of tears.

"It's awful," Alice managed to say. "Lenny has left me. Here's the note he put on my dresser." Alice handed Helen a note with rough edges torn from a notebook.

"Sory. I and Tracy are leaving town.
Do not tri to find us.
Its OK for you to divorse me. Lenny."

"That's wonderful news," Helen said. "Two slimy worms have found each other."

Alice sniffed. "You don't understand. I don't want a divorce. I want Lenny back. I love him."

Sara stiffened. "How can you love a man who is abusing you, running away with a tramp, kidnapping your sister's beloved cat, taking your money? I can't understand you."

"You're impulsive," Helen said. "You were impulsive when you were a teenager, and now in your senior years you're still impulsive. You've been enabling Lenny's misdeeds and it's time to stop. But I love you and I want you to find happiness."

Alice rose and with tears in her eyes said, "I don't want them arrested, officer. I'll go to Reno for a divorce."

CHAPTER 21

SARA'S HEART SWELLED with happiness as she continued dating Alex. *Is he truly interested in me? I'm not really attractive and he's so handsome.* When she looked in the mirror, she saw the chubby woman who lived for years in her parent's home under their critical rule. When Alex declared that she was beautiful, she told him he needed to have his eyes examined. Gradually Alex fell deeply in love with Sara, who joyfully reciprocated his feelings. One night when Alex brought Sara home, he parked the car, leaned over, and took Sara in his arms. Encircling Sara's neck with his hand, he whispered, "I love you." He leaned into Sara's lips and her stomach tightened into a knot. Her lips parted with a slight give when his lips met hers.

So this is what a kiss feels like.

They broke apart—then came together again, their noses meeting at the ideal tilt, their lips moist. Sara's eyes closed. It was an epic kiss.

"I've never been kissed," Sara said as she opened her eyes. "It's the most wonderful feeling in the whole world."

"How did you manage to avoid being kissed?"

"I was overweight until recently and had a poor self-image. I used to think of myself as an ugly duckling. Boys avoided me like I had the plague."

"Let's go," Alex said as he pulled Sara to her feet.

Puzzled Sara said, "No—I want more kissing."

"It's too much right now. Let's take it a step at a time."

*   *   *

After four more months of weekly dates, one Saturday evening Alex brought her to an upscale restaurant. Sara wore a dazzling silver dress and high heels, and he dressed in a light blue suit that fit his athletic frame perfectly. His tanned freckled face had a rosy tint, and he had shaved with a new razor which made a nick on his chin. His ebony hair was carefully combed and parted on the left side. Alex had spritzed Polo cologne on the front and on the sides of his eighteen-inch neck. Sara breathed in the masculine scent with deep pleasure. She was thrilled to be in his company, and somehow she felt prettier than she had ever felt in her entire life.

The *maître d'* led them to a remote corner booth, put the huge tasseled menus on the white tablecloth, said "Bon appetit," and left them alone. They sat opposite each other in the booth, and Sara hoped that the expensive French perfume she had dabbed behind her ears was lightly bewitching and didn't clash with Alex's cologne. She trusted Alex. He was special—steady, truthful, responsible, and refined.

Alex leaned forward, put his hand on hers and smiled. "Marry me, Sara. Not tonight, but soon. I love you. I've been waiting for a wonderful woman, and luckily I've found her."

Sara raised her hand to her mouth—gently nipped her thumb nail. "I don't—know."

"I thought you loved me."

"I do, but…"

When the waiter approached, Sara, embarrassed, stopped talking. They studied the menu and when Sara ordered flounder, Alex said he'd have the same. Meanwhile an Asian busboy brought water and rolls.

"This fish is mushy," Alex complained.

Sara tasted hers. "It's pulpy."

Alex took charge and sent the fish back.

I would've suffered in silence. I like that he stands up for himself.

Alex sipped some water. "What were we talking about?"

"You asked me to marry you. I'm flattered, but I wonder if you'll always be an officer."

"What's wrong with being in the police force? You make it sound like it's the Mafia."

"No—it's kind of scary—you know what I mean."

"So is every other job. I believe in fate. If it is meant for you to be safe, then you'll be safe."

"Let's keep dating. I need time to consider what a life with you entails. I don't have much courage. I get easily upset. I need time."

"Take as much time as you need. I'm a patient guy."

*   *   *

REVA SPIRO LUXENBERG

A month later when they went to the same restaurant for lunch and sat in the same booth, Alex pulled out a maroon velvet box for Sara's inspection. He had wanted to propose at dinner time, but he was on duty and couldn't wait another day.

She opened it and seeing a beautiful marquis diamond engagement ring, with an expression of wonder cried out, "It's gorgeous!"

"Well, will you marry me?"

"I love you."

"That's not the answer I'm looking for."

"Have you thought about changing your job?"

"Oh, are you still worrying about my job?"

"Sort of."

"My father was an officer. When he retired, he became an insurance agent; and he never got hurt, and my mother was supportive of him."

"What will happen to me if you get shot?"

"You'll sympathize and I will heal—but, Sara, it will never happen."

Sara wide-eyed looked with love at the handsome man she had fallen for.

"You're right. It will never happen. I love you so much that now that we're engaged I want to make love with you."

Alex's eyes opened wide. "My parents are on a cruise to Jamaica. Are you willing to come with me to my house?"

"Of course."

A full moon illumined a sky studded with diamond stars as Alex drove into a cul-de-sac with three ranch homes. He pulled up to a house at the end and parked in the driveway. Sara saw a dark ranch house, simple in design, not at all opulent. Alex opened the passenger door and helped Sara step out.

I'm excited and calm at the same time. He's bringing me here to have sex. Today is the first time I'll know what it feels like when a girl becomes a woman.

Sara smelled the fragrance of sweet-smelling flowering bushes that lined the entrance. Alex didn't open the front door—instead he pressed a clicker and the garage door opened. She stepped into a two-car garage filled with all kinds of woodworking equipment and gardening tools hanging on cement walls. A door at the end of the garage led into a kitchen. Alex turned on a light, and pointed to modern art prints of masterpieces hanging on a kitchen wall. "My mother loves modern art.

Here are a Picasso, a Kandinsky, a Dali, and a Matisse. What do you think?"

"Wow. Never in my life have I seen a kitchen like this. I'm impressed."

Alex took her hand in his and led her to the living room. Next to a modern couch was a marble table with a lamp. Alex pulled a cord and the room lit up with a subdued light. "My mother also collects Murano glass bowls."

Sara was surprised when she looked at multi-colored picturesque bowls on the coffee table in front of the couch.

"Would you like to see my room?" Alex asked soothingly.

"Certainly."

Alex led Sara up a staircase to the second floor landing. He stopped at his bedroom where she breathed in the masculine aroma of his favorite scent. Sara's heart swelled with pride when she saw Alex's framed awards for outstanding duty hung on the wall opposite his queen-sized bed. Alex dropped down on his bed and pulled Sara down alongside him. Sara gasped out the words, "Are we alone?"

"Yes. I told you my parents are on a cruise." Alex pulled Sara in his arms and kissed her. *Truly this is heaven.*

"I love you like crazy," he said.

"I feel the same way."

She wanted him to kiss her like before, and he did except when their lips met he started to unbutton her blouse and then removed it. He slid the straps of her bra down her arms, reached around and unhooked it all together. He paused. "Is this all right with you?"

She nodded in answer to his question. He pulled her bra off and cast it onto a dresser.

Bright moonlight filtered through the blinds filling the room. "Oh, Sara," he breathed as he gazed at her in fascination. "You're gorgeous— absolutely flawless."

I should be embarrassed about my nakedness, but all I feel is excited.

Quickly he undressed himself. The moonlight fell on his tightly muscled chest.

He is so handsome he takes my breath away.

Sara leaned against him and felt the delight of his touch on her breast. He teased her with his lips and tongue and awakened a hunger she had never experienced before. She slipped off her slacks. Alex put his hand in the waist band of her panties and removed the last piece of her clothing.

He caressed her as they became entwined on the bed. "Your skin is so soft," he whispered tenderly. His kisses and strokes were all over her naked body arousing her until her breath came out in force. She had never had such an intense feeling. It was magic. After he put on a condom he entered her gently, and then his thrusts became more and more forceful until they climaxed together.

Oh, my God! First fireworks exploded in my mind and then a peaceful feeling of relaxation came over me. We became one person.

Alex kissed Sara with abandon. "My love, you're so responsive—it amazes me."

"I am?"

"Much more than I can describe."

All feelings of loneliness Sara had had were banished. She would never be the same.

CHAPTER 22

IN BED AFTER their lovemaking, Alex said with his arm around Sara's shoulder, "That was fantastic. It's plainly evident how much we love each other. Now I think we should make a decision about our wedding."

Sara perked up. "Let's elope to Las Vegas."

"Not so fast, my dear. My parents will want a catered affair."

"I foresee trouble," Sara said pouting.

"I thought all women look forward to walk down the aisle in a bridal gown with a bouquet of flowers while their families look on with delight. My parents are comfortably well-off; and since my brother is already married, they're waiting for me to have as nice a wedding as he had."

"You don't understand," Sara said with a long face.

Alex's eyebrows rose. "So explain."

"My parents would like me to get married, and they'll be happy that you're Jewish, but— and it's a big but, they want me to marry a doctor, a lawyer, or an accountant, and not a law-enforcement officer. They'll have a fit. They won't help pay for the wedding, and they probably won't even go."

"Don't they love you?"

"Well, they always say they love me, but it's on their terms. They make their own plans and expect me to accommodate their wishes. I have no autonomy as far as they're concerned."

Alex shook his head. "Let's drive to their house and let them get to know me. I'm really a good fellow. I bet they'll change their mind about my being a police officer. Someday I'll be promoted to Detective or maybe even Captain. I have a perfect record—a good reputation in my precinct."

"I know how I'll feel," Sara said with alarm, "when they see us and we tell them we're engaged. I won't be able to keep my food down."

"It sounds like you're afraid of them."

Sara pouted. "I used to be. I think I still am. Why can't we save your parents all that money and elope?"

"I can't do that to my mother and father—kill their dreams of walking me down the aisle."

"My parents won't want to come to a wedding of mine to a police officer."

"Sara, baby, you make it sound like being on the police force is like being a member of the Cosa Nostra or the Russian Organizatsiya."

"Okay. I'll give it a shot. Tomorrow I'll call my parents and arrange for a time when we can meet them." *But I don't have a guarantee that they'll be civil to a policeman. They know the inherent danger of police work.*

*   *   *

The next morning, after Sara had jogged, she downed a glass of tomato juice and called her parents.

"Hi, Mom. How are you and Dad?"

"How can we be at ease waiting for you to come home?"

"I'm engaged."

"To a Jew?"

"Yes. He's a policeman."

"Oooh!"

*   *   *

Alex drove his Ford on the East-West roadway with the menacing name of Alligator Alley while Sara looked out the window at the marshy wetlands, searching for alligators, but finding none. Her mind was troubled with thoughts about what her parents would say once they realized Alex wasn't a doctor or a lawyer. Both might say, "It's out of the question—our daughter can't marry a man in such a dangerous line of work." Or her mother might say, "I had plans for Sara to marry this rich man who manufactures locks." Or her father might say, "You look like a nice guy who wants to make my daughter happy, but have you thought about how she will feel if some gangster riddles you with bullets? I want to make it as clear as possible that I won't contribute to her wedding."

*   *   *

Mr. and Mrs. Solomon, looking perplexed, sat on the front porch sipping root beer from tall glasses. Mr. Solomon opened the conversation. "She's marrying a cop—a cop who earns next to nothing? But then again the way Sara is so stubborn, she's lucky to get a man who will put up with her idiosyncrasies. I thought she'd wind up an old maid."

Mrs. Solomon finished her drink, put the glass down on a plastic side table, and said emphatically, "It's good she's getting married. She'll be someone else's headache—not ours. And you know what the Goldsteins said, 'We're so happy that finally we have grandchildren.' Sara never gave us any pleasure, but grandchildren will. We have to treat the engaged couple nicely."

"I agree."

*   *   *

By the time they reached her parents' home Sara sat in the car absolutely exhausted with worry.

"Come on, hon," Alex said as he opened the car door.

"I think we should elope," Sara said weakly.

"We're not eloping. We're going in to talk to your parents. They won't intimidate me. Take a deep breath and try to relax," Alex said as he reached toward Sara and took her hand in his.

Once in the house, Sara was more than surprised to see that her mother had gone to the trouble of setting the coffee table with all kinds of goodies and a bottle of champagne. She was shocked by her mother's unconventional behavior where she was concerned.

"Let me see your engagement ring," her mother said leaning forward in her armchair in the living room.

She doesn't look angry. What's going on?

"Lovely," her mother said as she took Sara's left hand in hers and examined the ring. "It looks like an antique."

"It is," Alex said proudly. "It belonged to my grandmother, who willed it to me."

"When do you plan to have the wedding?" Mr. Solomon asked as he offered the couple a tray of hors d'oeuvres.

Alex selected a cocktail frank. "We plan to get married six months from now in June."

"That's nice," Mrs. Solomon said. "Sara will make a pretty June bride."

"How many brothers and sisters do you have, Alex?" Mr. Solomon asked.

"I have one brother and I don't have any sisters. My brother is married and is a fireman."

"Sara has one brother who is a bachelor. We're looking forward to having many grandchildren we can spoil," Mrs. Solomon said.

So that's why they're so nice. I should've known. They want me to have a bunch of kids.

*   *   *

Sara sat at her laptop in Helen's house and e-mailed her brother with the good news.

> "Hi, Eric,
> Not only are Mom and Dad happy with my choice
> of a husband but they are paying for half
> the wedding. Can you leave Ireland for a week?
> The wedding is June 10th and I really need you to
> be there."

Eric wrote back,

> "I wouldn't miss your wedding for
> all the shamrocks in Ireland. How come
> Mom and Dad are helping
> financially?"

Sara giggled as she answered her brother.

> "They want grandchildren and since
> you're not married yet,
> they're looking for me to provide them
> with kids to bounce on their knees."

Eric answered immediately,

> "Unbelievable I'm happy that you found
> love. My recipe for love is
> 1 cup Trust
> ½ cup Decency
> ½ cup Humor
> ½ cup Companionship
> Pinch of patience
> Mix well and enjoy for the rest of your lives."

*　　*　　*

Sitting in the car a week later on the way to an art exhibit in downtown Delray Beach, Alex took Sara's hand in his. "My parents suggested Silver Hall Caterers—they prepare the best food ever. It's important to make the reservation as soon as possible since June is a crowded month."

Oh my! It'll cost a fortune. "Why can't we get married in your parents' house? The money they'll save will help us as a down payment for a house."

"My love, we have to invite uncles, aunts, cousins, friends, police buddies, and your family. Hundreds of people will not fit in my parents' ranch house."

"Can't we keep the numbers down?"

"Sure. We'll list all the close relatives and friends who are the most important for us to invite. Let's limit ourselves to first cousins and best friends."

Sara nodded. "I just realized—where will we live after the wedding?"

"No problem. We'll look for an unfurnished condo to rent."

"That's expensive. We'll also need a month's security."

"We'll get gifts."

"What about furniture?"

"The gifts will be cash and kitchen and bathroom supplies. No furniture."

"We could buy used furniture."

Alex looked serious. "We could, except we need a new bed and mattress. I'm not sleeping on someone else's bed."

Bed. He said bed. He wants us to sleep in the same bed. Will I be able to fall asleep with Alex next to me? Maybe he snores. Maybe I snore. Maybe when he finds out I snore, he'll divorce me. I like to make love with him, but sleeping together may be a problem.

*   *   *

Alex, dressed in a white cotton cable-knit sweater, khaki slacks, and moccasins, pressed the doorbell of Helen's house. Sara opened the door, "Hi hon, sorry I didn't call but I just wondered if perhaps you may like to go to a movie with me."

"Come in," Sara said as she led him to the kitchen where Helen was finishing a cup of coffee. "Sorry I can't go now as Helen and I are going to the bridal shop to look for a wedding dress."

"May I come?" Alex asked.

Helen piped up. "It's bad luck to see a bride in her wedding dress."

"That's just a superstition," Alex said frowning, "but all right—tomorrow we'll go shopping for our wedding rings."

Did I hear right? He said wedding rings, which means he intends to wear a wedding ring. My father would never wear a wedding ring. I'm very lucky.

"Well? What do you think about buying the rings tomorrow?"

"I think it's a splendid idea."

*   *   *

When Sara and Helen entered the bridal shop, the scent of roses delighted them both with a feeling of enchantment that intensified with every moment. A slim blonde saleslady rushed over and politely seated them in front of two rows of bridal gowns. "Just in time," she said. "Our model is showing our new line of wedding gowns. They're breathtaking."

Sara and Helen sat next to a teenage bride and her mother. They all gawked with fascination at the pencil-thin model who changed gowns every few minutes.

"I can't afford expensive gowns like these," Sara whispered to Helen.

"I can, and I will pay for whatever gown you choose. It's my wedding gift to you," Helen said in a low voice.

"But I want you to be my maid-of-honor; and you have to buy your own gown," Sara protested.

"Shush. I have the money. Now pay attention, select the gown you love, and try it on."

When Sara came out of the dressing room, Helen's jaw dropped almost to her chest. Sara looked like an angel in a long-sleeved tulle lace gown with a sweetheart neckline, an empire waist, and a chapel train with beaded appliqué lace. Sara spun around and the gown, buttoned in the back, was magnificent. It fit Sara so perfectly she didn't need to have it altered. Helen was the same size as Sara and she wished she were young and could wear that lovely gown.

*　*　*

As soon as Sara got back home she called her mother to tell her the good news.

"Mom, Helen paid for my wedding gown. Isn't that kind of her? I'm lucky to have such a caring friend."

"Your father and I wanted to pay for your gown, but now it's too late. We spoke it over and will pay for the wedding, but our limit is $10,000."

"Thank you," Sara said as a cloud passed over her face. "I don't have enough money to chip in, but Alex will, and he said his parents will help out."

"How much will it cost?"

"I think $10,000 is approximately half the cost."

"I want to talk to your father. Hold on."

Five minutes later Mrs. Solomon got back on the phone. "We'll pay for everything except the liquor, the flowers, and the valet. We've been saving up for your wedding and we're glad you're finally getting married."

*　*　*

Sara, flushed with pleasure, gazed at the wedding gown in her closet. Another day they'd look for the headdress and she'd pay for it. She'd like a rhinestone tiara with a veil just long enough to cover her face during the ceremony as Jewish law requires. They already chose the young rabbi from Alex's Conservative congregation. Alex's brother was an experienced photographer and that would save them some money.

The two of them had to order invitations and send them out six weeks before the wedding. There was so much to do that Sara's mind was spinning in the whirlwind of activity. *I'm so looking forward to seeing Eric. I picture him looking on as I walk down the aisle in my wedding dress. Everything is so wonderful, but why do I have a feeling that an axe may fall?*

CHAPTER 23

I T WAS BREAKFAST time when Sara sat at her laptop in the kitchen, gnawing on a baby carrot. She was working on the thirtieth chapter of her novel and couldn't come up with a synonym for "suggestion." She turned to her *Thesaurus* for help. Ten words were listed, and Sara decided to use "recommendation." Helen was at the sink washing dishes when she turned to Sara who had two books on the kitchen table next to her: a *Thesaurus* and *Webster's Collegiate Dictionary.*

"Your life revolves around books," Helen said.

Sara stopped typing. "I guess."

"I have an idea. How about going to Barnes & Noble? We could eat lunch there and you could browse leisurely for a few hours."

"Good idea."

Barnes & Noble was a huge two-level bookstore with a section for dining. After Helen looked at the cookbooks, she was finished browsing and sat down with a cup of coffee while Sara, her heart light with surveying the myriad books that surrounded her, set off to her favorite section. Sara admired the classics and she chose Charlotte Brontë's *Jane Eyre* and Emily Brontë's *Wuthering Heights.* Then she moved to the autobiography section and selected Bill Clinton's *My Life.* Next she went on to the books on writing and, since she was familiar with Nancy Kress from reading her articles in *Writer's Digest,* she chose *Dynamic Characters* about creating personalities that interest readers. Sara felt that she was coming close to ending her novel, and so she picked the latest *Guide to Literary Agents.* Helen had suggested she buy a book of advice for weddings as Sara's wedding was in a couple of weeks.

Helen insisted on paying for all the books as an additional wedding gift, and they went home. Sara's face was flushed with happiness.

* * *

It rained heavily the next afternoon. Thunder roared and lightning flashed through the blinds as Sara sat at the kitchen table eating a late lunch. Her vegetable soup turned from hot to a distasteful, dull room temperature. She took a sip, and instead of reheating the soup in the microwave, poured it down the sink. *I have no appetite. I'm thinking about the gorgeous three-tiered wedding cake I ordered and how handsome Alex will look in a white tuxedo.*

A forceful knock at the door caused Sara to tremble. Helen had gone to the movies with George, so Sara, nervously, not anticipating a visitor, jumped up and raced to the door. She opened the door and found a rain-drenched UPS man standing at attention in his dark brown shirt-and-shorts uniform, holding a big package. "Something special for you today," he said.

"Thanks," Sara answered as she took it from him. "Have a good day."

"You too. See you again," he answered as he left.

The package was heavy, and Sara was glad she had started to exercise with weights to develop her arm muscles. She gently placed the package on the kitchen table, wondering what kind of wedding present someone had sent. She took a kitchen knife to cut the tape, opened the box, and was disappointed when she saw that the item was hidden by plastic bubble wrap. She cut the wrap and peered inside where there was another box. She turned the larger box upside down and wiggled the inner box carefully so that it came out and landed on the table. The box said "Juicy Juicer," and there was a note for her inside an envelope that read "To my dear sister, with love—Eric."

With enthusiasm Sara read the note that Eric had written to her.

> This gift is for your new life
> As a cherished man's sweet wife,
> May you use this juicer well,
> After the sounding of the wedding bell.

Enclosed was a recipe from Eric, who knew how fond Sara was of ice cream. With deep interest Sara read about how to make nutritious ice cream with this juice machine.

Cut bananas in half and freeze them.
Take a handful of frozen blueberries,
and feed the frozen bananas and
blueberries into the machine.
Mix with a drop of vanilla extract.
Eat and enjoy, and you won't know
the difference between real ice cream
and fruit dessert. Much love, Eric.

Sara's eyes teared when she realized how much her brother meant to her. He was a man who was thoughtful, kind, and supportive. She read the booklet that came with the juicer, washed the many parts, and raced out to Publix to buy bananas, frozen blueberries, and vanilla extract.

That night Helen watched as Sara made the fruit ice cream. When it was finished, they sat down at the table and dug in with spoons. "This is so delicious," Helen said. "I can't believe it's not real ice cream. How thoughtful of your brother to send you this machine two weeks before your wedding."

Sara licked her lips. "He's the best brother in the world. This is not only scrumptious, it's healthy."

They were finishing the frozen fruit dessert when the doorbell rang.

Sara jumped up. "I'll get it." She ran through the living room to the foyer, released the chain, and opened the door. Two police officers stood there—the Captain and the Chaplain. Sara's heart leaped.

"Who is it?" Helen called from the kitchen.

"Police."

Sara recognized the senior officer from a recent party Alex had taken her to. He had unusually large features, and he looked somber— his badge read Captain Luis Mendoza. The other officer was a stout young woman with piercing green eyes. Her badge announced her as *Shelly McCarthy, Chaplain.*

"May we come in?" Shelly asked in a soft voice.

"Of course." Trembling Sara led them to the living room. Helen entered and pointed to a sofa where the officers seated themselves. Sara stood next to an armchair and Helen placed her hand on Sara's shoulder.

Oh, my God! Something terrible has happened to Alex. Why is the chaplain here? There was an accident. Maybe he's hurt—maybe he's unconscious—Please God—let him not be dead.

Sara dropped down to the armchair and grabbed hold of the armrests.

"I'm so sorry," Captain Mendoza said, his wavering voice showing his grief. "Alex shielded his partner in a shootout during a robbery and died instantly. He's a hero. This horrific homicide took one of our finest officers. We don't know the motive of the perpetrator, but we can tell you that he's dead. Alex will be given a police funeral and awarded full honors. I'm so sorry for your loss. The services of our chaplain and a psychologist are immediately available for you."

In slow motion Sara slipped off the chair and fell to the floor. Helen bent down and put her hands on Sara's forehead. It was as cold as ice. Her eyes were closed. Sara was unconscious. She had gone into shock.

CHAPTER 24

"OH, MY GOD," Helen cried as she leaned over Sara's prostrate body.

Slowly Sara's eyes opened and then carefully she sat up. Her eyes darted from Helen, to Captain Mendoza, and then to Chaplain McCarthy. She was puzzled that two of them were wearing uniforms with police emblems. She braced herself leaning with her hands against the armchair, pulled herself up, and dropped down on the chair.

"How do you feel?" Helen asked as her hands shook.

"Who are you?" Sara said her voice quavering.

Helen's face turned ashen. "I'm Helen."

Sara went rigid. "Do I know you?"

"Yes." Helen gnawed on her bottom lip. She paused momentarily. "Who are you?"

Sara shook her head from side to side and hesitated. "I—I—don't know."

"Your name is Sa-ra, Sa-ra Sol-o-mon."

"Sa-ra, Sa-ra, Sol-o-mon," Sara repeated in the same slow cadence that Helen had used. Slowly she looked around the room. "Why are the police here?"

Helen, Captain Mendoza and Chaplain McCarthy looked at each other in bewilderment. The chaplain, with a look of grim resolve, motioned for Helen and the captain to approach her across the room out of earshot of Sara. Chaplain McCarthy spoke softly, "I believe Sara has an acute stress reaction, which has manifested in amnesia. The psychological shock was too much for her mind to handle, and the amnesia is protecting her from the traumatic reality of losing Alex two weeks before their wedding. She'll need treatment. Do you know if she has a psychiatrist?"

"Yes," Helen said as she leaned in closer. "She was seeing a doctor in Tampa when she was living with her parents. I'm trying to remember his name." Helen paused. "I think it's Dr. Stevens—no—it's Dr. Strauss."

"Her parents are her next of kin and need to be notified," the captain said. "Sara is in no shape to go to the funeral. Her mother and father can come here and bring Sara back with them so she can get treatment from her psychiatrist."

"I don't think that's a good idea," Helen said firmly.

"Why not?"

"Sara left Tampa because her parents were too controlling—sending her back there will make her regress to an earlier stage."

"I'm not sure," the captain said trying to be helpful.

Chaplain McCarthy added, "If Sara once had a solid relationship with her psychiatrist, it's more important to let him treat her, and perhaps she really needs to be with her loved ones who raised and nurtured her."

Helen bit down on her lips. "But Sara suffered verbal abuse mainly from her mother. Her mother bullied her and caused her great anxiety. Now you want to send her back to that so-called home she called a "cage" where she will suffer again?"

"She may not remain in her present situation, the chaplain replied, "…and if she does, after she receives the proper treatment, Sara can come back here and continue healing."

$$* \quad * \quad *$$

Dr. Strauss had finished with the last patient of the day when he received a call from Chaplain McCarthy.

"Hello, Dr. Strauss. This is Chaplain Shelly McCarthy from the Ft. Lauderdale Police Department. I'm afraid I have bad news about your former patient, Sara Solomon."

"What about Sara?"

"Sara had been planning to marry one of our finest police officers in a couple of weeks when she learned that he was killed in the line of duty. Her mind couldn't accept the horrendous news, and I believe she protected herself by immediately getting amnesia. I'm familiar with another case of this kind. Sara doesn't remember who she is and is unable to identify people she knows."

"I understand," Dr. Strauss said as he clutched the phone tightly. "I'm so sorry to hear this about such a lovely young woman. I have studied different kinds of amnesia, and since I have treated Sara I certainly would take her on again as a patient. However, I would like to talk with her parents before I see Sara."

"Thank you, Dr. Strauss. I'll call her parents and inform them about the tragedy and Sara's reaction to it. Goodbye."

* * *

The next morning, after Chaplain McCarthy confirmed she had notified Sara's parents, Dr. Strauss called the Solomon household.

Mrs. Solomon answered the phone and when she heard that Dr. Strauss was on the line she said, "Pardon me, but I think it's better that you talk to my husband." She put Mr. Solomon on the line but listened in on an extension in the bedroom.

When Dr. Strauss explained Sara's memory loss to him, Mr. Solomon's knees shook and his eyes widened in shock.

Dr. Strauss continued, "This disorder is usually a brief one, and I would be willing to treat Sara for it."

"Yes, of course," Mr. Solomon said. "We have confidence in your expertise, don't we dear?"

Mrs. Solomon nodded. *I'm not thrilled with Dr. Strauss, but maybe he can help Sara.*

"When Sara comes home," Dr. Strauss said, "and doesn't remember who you are, just try to stay calm knowing that this amnesia will eventually disappear. I would like to see you, Mrs. Solomon, the day before I see Sara. Can you come in tomorrow at 2 p.m.?"

"Yes. Should I tell Sara that I'm meeting with you?"

"No. Meanwhile any questions that Sara asks answer briefly and truthfully."

* * *

After Sara had moved to Palm Oasis, Mrs. Solomon kept her daughter's room exactly the way she had left it. Now the mother and daughter stood in the middle of Sara's bedroom.

"This has been your room since you were born," Mrs. Solomon said. "Do you remember living here?"

"No—I don't remember." Sara moved to a shelf that held six books. She picked one up and read the title *Guide for Turtle Care*. "Mrs. Solomon, why am I interested in turtles?"

"Please call me Mom."

REVA SPIRO LUXENBERG

"Yes, Mom. Did I have a turtle?"

"You had a box turtle named Daisy."

"Daisy? That's a cute name. Where is she?"

"You told me that she died."

"Poor thing."

"Eric told me that you were very upset."

"I was? Who is Eric?"

"He's your older brother."

Sara sat down on the bed. "Where is he?"

"Eric's in Ireland. He's flying here and will arrive in two days. He'll help you get your memory back. Let's go to the kitchen and have lunch."

"All right, Mom. I'm hungry."

"Sara, you have an appointment on Thursday to see Dr. Strauss."

"Am I sick? Why do I have to see a doctor? I really feel fine."

"Dr. Strauss is a psychiatrist."

"Am I crazy?"

"No. Dr. Strauss will help you remember your life."

"Why did I lose my memory? Was I hit in the head?"

Mrs. Solomon pursed her lips. "Dr. Strauss will tell you what he thinks when you see him. Meanwhile our cook has prepared a cheese and spinach soufflé especially for you."

"Do I like soufflé?"

"I don't remember."

Her memory is also not so good, just like mine. I feel so uneasy like I lost part of myself. Why? What happened to me? Why can't I remember my mother? Why can't I remember anyone? I must be crazy.

CHAPTER 25

D R. STRAUSS SAT on a black leather armchair in front of his
desk in an attempt to make Sara's mother more comfortable.
He had seated Mrs. Solomon on a matching chair a few feet away.

"I'm pleased to meet you at last," the doctor said. "Sara made
considerable progress when I treated her before. She's an intelligent,
pleasant, and resourceful young woman who I understand had gone on
to make a wonderful life and was preparing to marry when she suffered
a serious traumatic loss."

"But other people lose loved ones and their memories stay intact.
Why hasn't Sara been grieving like most people?" Mrs. Solomon spoke
with a graveness that showed her concern for her daughter that she had
hidden under a veil of criticism before.

"That's true," Dr. Strauss said. "We keep learning about psychogenic
amnesia, which is what your daughter has."

"This illness frightens me, doctor. Please tell me how I can help my
daughter."

Dr. Strauss crossed his legs. "It's important for you not to criticize
Sara. Her memory will return in due time, and she will get on with her
life; but, meanwhile, since she's living with you, she needs a peaceful
environment. No arguments. No forcing anything on her. No control.
She needs structure. She needs healthy foods, exercise, and plenty of
sleep."

"I have criticized Sara unjustly in the past, and I feel that maybe
this has to do with her present condition." Mrs. Solomon clasped her
hands tightly together as her eyes filled with tears.

"Is there a reason you used to find fault with Sara? What you tell
me will be confidential, but it may help me understand her condition."

"Well—there is something that my husband and I never told
anyone; and perhaps this is the reason I was harsh. Before Eric and
Sara were born, we had a year-old daughter who died from crib death,
and I have always felt it was my fault. I didn't mourn outwardly. I made
my husband promise that we wouldn't tell any future children that they

had had a sibling who died. I felt we had an obligation to protect them. I felt guilty and I was very depressed."

"You suffered considerable trauma. Did you ever seek treatment?"

"No, I felt I had to be strong and overcome the depression by myself."

"What you have just revealed explains a great deal. Thank you for telling me this."

"You're welcome." Mrs. Solomon took a deep breath. "How will you treat Sara? Will you give her medication?"

"There is no medication for psychogenic amnesia. Understand that Sara can't remember personal information about herself. Since at this point without being tested, there is no evidence pointing to structural brain damage or a brain lesion, this memory disorder will resolve itself."

Mrs. Solomon's eyes clouded over. "I thought there might be a pill that would cure Sara, and I'm disappointed there isn't."

The doctor looked at Mrs. Solomon with compassion. "There is a remote possibility of damage to Sara's brain since I understand she fell off a chair, and therefore I am referring her to a neurologist for an examination. He may order a PET scan and an EEG just to rule out brain damage. Meanwhile I intend to counsel her and offer emotional support. Believe me, she will get better. It's frustrating for family members to see a loved one suffer from this disorder, but it's important for you to try to be cheerful and go on with your lives as usual."

*   *   *

The next day Mrs. Solomon drove Sara to her appointment with Dr. Strauss.

"Mother, do I know how to drive?" Sara asked quietly as she sat in the Lincoln's passenger seat.

"Yes—you're a good driver. You have a Mazda and it's parked in the garage. When your memory comes back, you'll remember how to drive—you'll remember everything."

So I knew how to drive. Will I ever drive again?

*   *   *

Mrs. Solomon, fingering a few magazines, and Sara, nervously tapping her foot on the tan carpet, sat in the doctor's reception area for two minutes before the psychiatrist appeared.

"I'm Dr. Strauss," he said with a warm smile. "Sara, please come into my office." He turned to Mrs. Solomon. "Sara will be back in fifty minutes. The small fridge holds drinks. Help yourself."

He escorted Sara into his office and pointed to an armchair for her to sit. Sara knees shook as she sat on the edge of the leather armchair, her face ashen. She didn't remember anything in Dr. Strauss's office as she glanced at the books on the shelves that dealt mainly with psychiatry. Her eyes fixed on Dr. Strauss's diplomas and licenses.

"Sara, I know you don't remember me, but I recall a lovely young lady who came to my office and sat in the chair you're in right now. And the day came that you left and started a brand new life on the east coast of Florida and you were happy there."

"Am I crazy? Please tell me the truth." Sara's palms were moist.

"No—certainly not. You have psychogenic amnesia, a disorder of memory loss which will eventually go away."

"Why—why do I have this disorder?" Sara voice cracked.

"You suffered a loss, and your brain is attempting to protect you from the shock of it. As you regain your memory, you will grieve over your loss; and then you will slowly heal. Meanwhile I'll refer you for some tests that your mother will take you to. I'll continue to see you on a weekly basis. I want you to keep away from all alcoholic drinks. Keep a notebook and jot down any memories that come to you. Look at the photographs that have been taken of you, your friends, and your family."

"I'm so scared, Dr. Strauss. Suppose I never get my memory back, what will I do? What will become of me? Who is Sara Solomon?"

"First of all, you still have the intelligence that you had before the memory loss. You're able to read and write, and you can converse as much as you want with your family. They're in a position to help you. You have awareness, an acceptable attention span, and good judgment.

Secondly, you must take care of your body by exercising, getting enough sleep, and eating nutritious meals. Listen to music, watch funny movies, and keep away from sad TV programs like the news. By the way, do you know who the President is?"

"Of the United States?"

"Yes."

"I don't remember."

"You'll remember eventually."

"What else can I do to bring my memory back?"

"Write down any life changes you can recall. Bring your notebook and a pen to every session. If you have dreams, write them down and we'll analyze them together."

"Is there anything I shouldn't do?"

"If a scary memory returns, don't try to stop your feelings. Accept all feelings of fear, anger, frustration, and sadness, as well as of joy. I'll see you next week on Wednesday at the same time."

I'm not crazy. What loss did I suffer? I don't know who I really am, but the doctor says I will remember. When? Can I trust him?

CHAPTER 26

OUTSIDE THE SOLOMON home a cold black sky promised continuing heavy precipitation. The rain began to pound the windows of the house like fast moving fingers on a keyboard. Inside the tantalizing aroma of baking chocolate chip cookies permeated the living room where Sara and her mother sat close to each other on the sofa holding the family photograph album between them.

Sara's mother pointed to a photo. "Here's the picture of you in your cap and gown when you graduated from college. Your father and I celebrated by taking you and Eric to the best Japanese fish restaurant in Tampa. Do you remember?"

Sara squinted at the photo and frowned. "No, I don't remember. Why was I so chubby?"

"You liked to eat the delicious desserts that our cook made."

I don't know what to say. Not only don't I remember my college graduation, or why I was so fat, but I don't remember my mother, father, or my brother.

"Here's a picture of you and your classmate Rhonda when you went to New York and stood in front of the Statue of Liberty. You had such a nice smile. The dentist had capped your front tooth after you broke it falling off your bicycle."

I have no recollection of being at the Statue of Liberty. Who's Rhonda? I'm bewildered about the unfamiliarity of the house I'm in and the people I don't remember. I'm overwhelmed.

"Well," Sara's mother said as she pointed to another photo of a stout young man with his arm around a young roly-poly woman in a sleeveless dress that displayed her fat arms,

"...do you remember when Stanley took you out on a date?"

I feel dizzy. "I don't feel well, Mom. I have to go lie down."

"It's all right if you don't remember now. Soon you will—the doctor said so."

Sara lay down on her bed, her head swimming. She began to sob. *I'm a freak. Maybe if I sleep, I'll dream and then I can tell something to Dr. Strauss. He may help me remember. I hope when I wake up I can write down my dream.* Sara grabbed a tissue from a box on the night table next to her bed. She wiped her eyes, blew her nose, closed her eyes, and fell into a troubled sleep.

*   *   *

That afternoon Sara opened her notebook in Dr. Strauss's office. "Doctor, I wrote down my dream. I think my real name is Betsy Moss."

"Tell me about your dream, Sara."

Slowly Sara read her notes. "I was in college—frightened that I couldn't pass the English final. I was racing around in a circle in the quadrangle, running as if my life depended upon it. I woke up in bed, a mass of perspiration."

Dr. Strauss nodded. He made a few notes on a pad. "What do you remember about being a student in college?"

"I don't remember anything. I'm straining to recall even a snippet, but I can't. This morning my mother showed me a picture of myself in a cap and gown. I couldn't believe that fat girl was me. Dr. Strauss, I'm scared."

"Right now you're frightened, but that will pass when you relax and are able to wait patiently for your memory to return. Gradually it will return. The tests you took demonstrate there is no physical basis for your amnesia."

"Am I crazy?"

"Certainly not."

"Why do I think I'm Betsy Moss?"

"I don't know. Why don't you ask your brother or your parents if it's someone you knew in your past?"

*   *   *

The heavy rain stopped pounding as Sara, gnawing on her index finger, stood at Eric's bedroom door. She heard him speaking on the phone and waited until he said goodbye. Then she knocked gingerly at his door.

"Come in," he called.

Sara entered the room and found Eric sitting at his desk. He was wearing shorts and his legs were covered with curly black hair. "I don't want to bother you."

"Sit down and we'll talk," Eric said, motioning to a chair next to his bed.

Sara sat down, a troubled expression on her face. "Do you know who Betsy Moss is? Is it me? You can tell me the truth. Am I adopted?"

"No, you and I aren't adopted. We are biologically brother and sister. My name is Eric Solomon and your name is Sara Solomon. You majored in English in college and you were a wonderful writer. When I was in Ireland, you wrote to me about a novel you were working on. The title was *Betsy Moss* and it was about a college student with academic and social problems."

"Did I ever finish the novel?"

"No."

"Why not?"

"Your life was complicated and the trauma you suffered interfered. What I read was good. You will definitely finish the novel, and I believe it will get published."

"What was the trauma?"

"This is something that the psychiatrist told our mother that you have to remember by yourself, and eventually you will."

"I don't believe I'll ever remember my past."

"You will."

"Why was I so fat when I was in college?"

"You ate fattening foods."

Sara pursed her lips. "How come I lost weight afterwards?"

"I sent you a diet." Eric paused looking thoughtful. "I'm not only your loving brother, but I have extensive knowledge about nutrition. You listened to my advice."

"What will become of me if I never regain my memory?"

"You will regain your memory—you will get married and have children. You will become a novelist of repute."

I certainly hope so because now I feel like drinking a whole glass of whiskey and drowning my troubles.

* * *

REVA SPIRO LUXENBERG

Dr. Strauss had just finished another session with Sara. He had been hoping for more progress, but he recognized that things often cannot be rushed. Her memory was completely blocked, and she was depressed at the lack of results.

He rose from his chair, took a deep breath, and went to open the blinds in his office. He looked to the sky for comfort. One of his favorite hobbies was weather prediction and cloud formation. He could identify twenty-three types of clouds. He raised his eyes to the sky noticing straggly lines of Cumulus Humilis clouds that he recognized formed from pockets of warm air. He could predict that a thunderstorm wasn't heading his way.

He closed the blinds, sat down at his desk, and put his head in his hands. What could he do to help Sara get back her memory? A few seconds later the wrinkled face and bald head of his old professor, Dr. Max Adelbrecht, came to mind. Would the professor be able to help him? After all, Adelbrecht means "bright nobility"; and the ninety-year-old doctor was surely a man of brilliance and truthfulness.

Dr. Strauss shrugged his shoulders, glanced through his Rolodex, found the doctor's number, and dialed it.

"Hello, Dr. Adelbrecht. This is Walter Strauss. How are you?"

"Valter, my boy. Gut to hear from you. I'm very vell, dank you. How are you and how is de rest of de family?"

"I'm good. Lenore and the kids are fine, thank you. Richie is on an expedition in Antarctica, and Denise is married and now has a son."

"Yah—den I haven't spoken mit you for at least two years. Okay den, vhy are you calling now? Spill the beans, Valter."

"Doctor, I've been treating a young woman called Sara and I haven't made any progress with her. I'm at a loss what to do."

"Sounds interesting. Vat's her problem?"

"Sara was on the verge of marrying when her financé was shot and killed. As a result she developed psychogenic amnesia."

'Ah ha! Ya—I know about psychogenic amnesia, the dissociative disorder vat is attributable to an instigating event."

"Yes, professor."

Dr. Adelbrecht paused for a few seconds. "De event does not result in injury to de brain."

"How can I help this young woman?"

"Clinical lore holds dat psychogenic amnesia can be reversed by hypnosis or barbiturate sedation, but there is no evidence for de reliability of recollections produced by dees techniques."

"Yes, I know this."

"Vell, the DSM-IV-TR, 294.8 has an umbrella term, Amnestic Disorder Not Othervise Specified. My boy, dere is insufficient evidence to even name psychogenic amnesia in the DSM. You're facing a difficult situation. Tell me, does de patient have an extensive loss of autobiographical memory?"

"Yes. She remembers nothing of her life."

"Ah, ha. Fugue memory. Vat about semantic memory, or her repertoire of procedural knowledge?"

"Semantic memory is adequate. She has forgotten how to drive but otherwise her procedural knowledge is adequate."

"Vat have you done so far?"

"The usual—counseling—notebook keeping—a peaceful home life. No hypnosis. No drugs."

"Is de patient living in de same place vere she vas before?"

"No. She moved to her parent's home."

"I suggest you get her back for a few weeks to vere it happened. Dis may jolt her memory. Time has to take its course. Gut luck. Keep in touch, my boy. Bye for now. Bye. Bye."

CHAPTER 27

E RIC DROVE SARA across the state to Palm Oasis and parked the car in front of Helen's house. Helen, dressed in shorts, was engaged in snipping roses off a bush in the front garden.

As soon as Helen spotted Sara and Eric stepping out of the car, she laid her clippers on the ground, approached Sara with a warm smile, and gave her a big hug.

Sara pulled back and lowered her eyes. "Hello," she said softly.

"Do you remember living here?" Helen asked.

"No."

"What do you remember?" Helen asked, her voice subdued.

"Oh, for God's sake—I told you I remember nothing," Sara shouted. Breathing rapidly, her mind raced to grasp a tidbit of her former life.

"Don't excite yourself. It's all right if you don't remember. Maybe if I show you to your room it'll help with your recollection."

Eric carried Sara's suitcase to her bedroom and placed it on the bed. "I need to get back. You'll stay with Helen for three weeks, and next week I'll pay you a visit and see how you're getting along." Eric kissed Sara on her cheek and left.

"I'm sorry I yelled before. Please forgive me," Sara said.

"It's perfectly okay. I know you've been under great stress," Helen said with a kind tone.

"This is a nice house, and the room is pretty," Sara said as she looked at the light blue wallpaper with tiny flowers, a vase filled with roses on a neat desk, and navy carpeting underfoot. Outside the window were pink flowering bushes. *Sure the house is nice but the morass of emotion that's churning inside me is unpleasant, and more than a little frightening. The lady says I lived here, but everything seems so unfamiliar and strange.*

"Do you remember your room?" Helen asked.

"It seems a little familiar," Sara said as she opened the drawer in the desk and found an assortment of pens and pads and a photo of herself and a handsome man with his arm around her shoulder. *I'm lying to please this woman. Nothing is familiar. Who is this man? I wish I knew.*

"Let's go outside and sit on the front porch," Helen suggested. "You can unpack later."

"All right. I have nothing else to do."

When they were sitting on the porch, Helen turned to Sara and asked in a concerned tone, "How are you really feeling?"

"Depressed. Angry. I'm really sorry I was so rude before."

"You don't have to apologize, Sara. It must be awful not to remember people and things you experienced—laughter, sadness, smells, sounds that once meant much to you."

Ann Wilson's long-haired miniature dachshund bounded out of its garden, raced across the sidewalk, and, wagging her tail, approached Sara who bent down and petted the dog. "I remember you. Your name is Dolly. How are you, Dolly?"

"Sara," Helen cried. "Your memory is returning. I knew it. Time fixes everything."

Ann Wilson walked up the porch stairs. "Naughty dog. I'm sorry she bothered you, Sara."

"Who are you?" Sara asked.

"I'm Helen's neighbor, Ann Wilson. Don't you know me?"

"Yes, of course." *There I go again, lying to please. But at least I remember the dog.*

"I gotta go fix Dolly's dinner. See you girls." Ann put a leash on the dog and led it away.

I think maybe Helen can tell me more about the book I was writing. "Did I ever tell you about the novel I was writing before I lost my memory?"

"I know all about it," Helen said as she stretched out her legs. "Every time you wrote another chapter you read it to me. It was very interesting."

"Do you remember the story?"

"Sure. It was about a college girl by the name of Betsy Moss, a freshman at Fields University. She struggles to overcome her shyness. I remember one scene where poor Betsy gets turned down by the Alpha Omega sorority and she turns to drinking and overeating."

"Did I really write that?"

"Yes. Do you want to know what happens next?"

"I do. But tell me, where is the manuscript? I'd like to read it by myself."

"My nephew, Elliott, came here after you went to your parents. He took the manuscript because he's a playwright and he said he might turn it into a play."

Sara's eyes widened. "Can you please ask your nephew to return it?"

"I will. Right now he's in New York City, but I bet he can mail it."

"Oh."

Helen noticed Sara's disappointed expression. "I can tell you more of the plot, if you want to hear it."

"Sure."

"In the beginning Betsy's mother thought she was a plain-looking baby. She grew up feeling she was a weed, not a rose. So you see, Sara, your character has emotional scars that leave her depressed and lonely."

Sara bit down on her lips. "Why did I write such a sad story?"

"If you wrote about someone without any problems, it wouldn't be interesting. You went on to write that Betsy tries to commit suicide and a young student, Morgan, saved her. He started to date her even though she was very overweight."

"That sounds better."

"Yes, she dated for a year, stopped drinking, and lost weight, but Morgan dropped her in favor of another girl who was much heavier."

"Why?"

"Oh, Morgan only liked heavy girls."

Sara leaned closer to Helen. "Did I write more?"

"Yes. Betsy made friends with a girl name Renee who introduced her to Lester, and eventually Betsy and Lester became engaged and planned a wedding. That's as far as you got with the novel."

"I want to know what happened to Betsy and Lester."

"You never got that far. Something happened and you got amnesia."

"Who is that man in the picture I saw in my room?"

"He was a friend of yours—Alex—he's not around anymore." Helen stood up. "I have some calls to make. What will you do, Sara? Do you want to watch TV?"

"No. I'll lie down. I'm kind of tired."

$*$ $*$ $*$

Sara pulled out all the drawers in her dresser looking for something she may have hidden. Under her lingerie she found another picture of

Alex dressed in a police uniform, the same man who Helen told her used to be her friend.

What happened to me? Was I in jail? How come I knew a police officer? This is so weird. No one is telling me what the trauma was that I had. Could it have been that I tried to commit suicide like Betsy Moss? Was I in a hospital? I remembered the dog; maybe if I go to sleep I'll remember more. But what if I don't?

Sara yawned and lay down on her bed, clutching the photo of Alex in his uniform. She fell into a fitful sleep and woke up after having a nightmare in which she was shot. *I don't think I was ever shot. I don't have any scars on my body. I wish I could remember.*

*   *   *

At 5:30 p.m. Helen knocked at Sara's bedroom door.

"Come in," Sara called out.

Helen carried a small purse, wore high heels, and was dressed in a green dress. "I prepared a light supper for you," she said kindly. "I have a date with a male friend. He's taking me out to dinner. We're going to the movies afterwards, so I'll be back around 11 p.m. Is there anything you need?"

"No, thank you. I'm fine. You're dating a man?"

"Yes. George is nice. I've been going out with him for many months."

Sara's eyes widened. "How did you meet him?"

"From a dating service."

"Really? Is that how I met the man you called Alex?"

Helen hesitated, not knowing how much she could reveal without hurting Sara. "Yes, you met Alex online. I gotta go now. Take it easy. There's a good movie on Channel 5 tonight that you may like. Bye now."

"Goodbye. Have a good time."

I must ask Helen more about this dating service. How come I remembered the dog? I can't remember anything else. This is so frustrating I could scream.

CHAPTER 28

TWO-AND-A-HALF WEEKS LATER, Dr. Strauss began to experience a frustration with Sara's lack of progress. He reached for the phone in his office and called Dr. Adelbrecht. As soon as the phone rang once, the doctor picked it up.

"Hello there."

"It's Walter Strauss again. Do you have time to talk, Doctor?"

"Ya. Plenty of time, Valter. Too much time on mine hands."

I'm worried about Sara. I need his professional advice, but I don't want him to assume that's all I'm calling about. "Dr. Adelbrecht, I was reading about how psychiatry has a terrible business model and how anyone with a business license can become a psycho-therapeutic competitor."

"Ya, I agree. But Valter, please call me Max. Ve are colleagues, not professor and student."

Dr. Strauss touched his earlobe and raised his chin a centimeter. "All right Max. I'm aggravated when I read that 80% of 'psychotropic' medications are prescribed by nonpsychiatric physicians."

"Valter, don't take this so much to heart. It's true health-care plans generally pay psychiatrists only for prescribing medications and dey leave counseling to nonmedical people and destroy a basic guideline of medicine. But Valter, you didn't call me to discuss de problems of psychiatrists. Now tell me vy you really called."

"You are still as sharp as ever, Max. I want to talk about my patient, Sara."

"Ah ha! The girl with functional amnesia. Has she remembered anything?"

Dr. Strauss wiped his brow. "Sara and I talk on the phone. She told me she remembers only a dog, named Dolly, that she once liked. Otherwise, her mind is blank."

"Vat is she doing vit herself?"

"Sara has moved from her parents' house across the state to where she was living before. She walks. She watches TV. She reads."

"Not gut. Ven she vas vit you, did you make sure she took the Vechsler Adult Intelligence Scale?"

"Yes. I sent her to a psychologist who administered it. The Wechsler Adult Intelligence test showed she has an IQ of 140."

"Ah, ha!" Dr. Adelbrecht paused for a few seconds. "Sara has superior intelligence. She needs intellectual stimulation. How did she do on a personality test?"

Dr. Strauss took a deep breath. "She attempted to present herself in the best possible light."

"Gut. She is responding in a defensive manner to preserve her ego. My boy, I think you should persuade her to attend college."

"What? If she does poorly, that will surely damage her ego."

"No— No—No. At first she vil feel lost, but then she vil adjust. She vil meet vibrant young students and carve out a new life for herself. Ve don't know how much of her memory vil return, or ven it vil happen. Good luck, my boy. I have a patient waiting. Keep in touch. Bye. Bye."

*　　*　　*

Sara was sitting in the living room watching a re-run of *Star Trek* on TV when her cell phone played a tune. She pressed the mute button on the remote and answered the phone. It was Dr. Strauss. She nervously laughed when he made the suggestion for her to go back to college.

"I don't remember anything about my college years. I don't even remember reading a textbook."

"Sara, you're a college graduate. You'll adjust. A colleague of mine and I both agree that it would do you a world of good to matriculate toward a Master's Degree in English. You were writing a novel, and— who knows— maybe you could finish your novel and get it published."

Sara's eyes filled with tears. *I'm caught in a real life dilemma, and all this psychiatrist wants to do is push me into a classroom with younger students.* Sara wiped her eyes and blew her nose. "I'll think about it." *Why can't he leave me alone?*

Dr. Strauss made a last ditch appeal to his patient. "Just in case you're wondering who will pay your tuition, your parents are most willing. I spoke with them and they want to do what's good for your health. I advised them that living with your friend Helen is good for your mental stability, and they accepted that."

Helen is nice. I like living with her.

Helen left the kitchen carrying two glasses of iced tea. She sat down on the sofa next to Sara and handed her one glass. "You look upset. What's wrong?"

Sara took a sip of the tea. "I just heard from my psychiatrist. He wants me to go back to school. I can't even remember what a classroom looks like. It's absolutely ridiculous."

Helen put her tea down on the marble-topped table next to the sofa. She knocked Sara off balance with the question, "If your doctor says that it will help you remember, why don't you listen to him?"

"I'm twenty-six years old. I don't know anything about college. How can I sit in a classroom with younger students of twenty-two or twenty-three? They'll laugh at me." *I'll feel like a freak.*

"Your mind will allow you to absorb new information. I see how you're reading books now. Twenty-six year-olds, and even older students, are studying for their Master's. And if the students are younger, so what—big deal? You have to be crazy not to go."

"Right now, I feel I *am* crazy!"

"Stupid, not crazy. Now you have to apply to Fields University, get the application, and send them your college transcript?"

Sara found herself eye-to-eye with Helen who stood in front of her. "I'll go tomorrow."

"You'll go today."

"Slave driver."

"You better believe it."

Sara reached into the pocket of her denim shorts and drew out a silver bracelet. It had charms of elephants with raised trunks. "I found this in my jewelry box. Do you happen to know if I bought this pretty bracelet?"

Helen's green eyes widened. "Well—I know that a friend of yours gave it to you for Valentine's Day."

"What friend?"

"His name was Alex."

"You make it sound like he's dead."

"Excuse me, Sara—I have to go to the bathroom."

*   *   *

Sara went online and looked at the requirements for admittance to Fields University. She studied the classes and was overwhelmed by all the student activities. The seed had been planted by both Dr. Strauss and Helen and it began to grow.

A week later Sara found herself in the Student Services Building. "How do I enroll for a Master's Degree in English?" she asked the thin female clerk behind the counter.

"Fill out this application. Here's another form for you to request that your college transcript be sent here to us."

A month later Sara was accepted as a graduate student in English for the coming fall.

*   *   *

Helen insisted upon taking Sara shopping and paying for new clothes. They went to Chang Boutique at the Palm Oasis mall.

"You'll feel more confident with stylish clothes, Sara," Helen said as they stepped into the store that had the aroma of spice.

"My simple clothes are good enough. I don't want to call attention to myself," Sara said as she spied unusual Asiatic styles.

"Look at these different lightweight pants." Helen put on her reading glasses and peered at the label that read that the washable material was a soft cotton rayon blend. "They come in blue, burgundy, or black. Since there is a graduated elastic waist, the size fits all up to size 14. How nice—they even have side pockets."

"I can't wear a print with elephants all over. Students will laugh at me."

"No one will laugh. You like the elephants on your bracelet. People will admire your good taste."

"It's not *my* good taste. It's *your* good taste. Why don't you go to college instead of me?"

Helen looked annoyed. "You're the student. I'm the buyer. What color do you want?"

"I choose black—under protest."

"Now, what blouse do you like?"

"I guess that one," Sara said pointing to a black short-sleeved top with a mandarin collar and black-and-red trim. "I do like the red looped frog fasteners."

Helen nodded her approval. "You do have good taste, my girl. When students ask you where you bought such unusual clothing, don't tell them I helped you since you want to be independent and special."

Sara ground her teeth together. "Well, special I am—the only student in the whole university who can't remember anything but a dog."

CHAPTER 29

E RIC SHOWED UP on a balmy Sunday morning and presented Sara with the gift of a digital camera.

"Get ready to have fun," he said with a big grin. "I'm taking you to the wetlands. They're not far from here."

Sara looked at her brother with defiant eyes. "Thank you for the camera, but no thank you. Why can't you understand that I don't want pictures of people I don't recognize?"

"But you can take photos of one-hundred-and-forty species of birds."

"I'm as interested in birds as I am in going to college."

"Oh!" Pausing, "I'm sorry."

"I'm sorry, too. I shouldn't be rude. I'll take the camera. It's time I moved on with my life." *I wonder what wetlands means. Is it marshy land? I really don't know what it is to have fun, but Eric doesn't realize how lost I feel not remembering him or any other person from before my amnesia hit me like a wet towel.*

As Eric drove, Sara held on to the camera wondering how she would feel once they were in a new place. *I'm only comfortable sitting in my bedroom in Helen's house.*

Eric drove just a few miles and parked.

My brother is right. The wetlands take only five minutes to reach.

"Come on, little sister—get out of the car and get set to see things you've never seen before."

I don't remember seeing any sights before, and I really don't want to see anything now.

Eric leading and Sara apathetically trailing behind, they climbed a ramp to a twisting warped wooden boardwalk. Eric stopped at a pond and pointed to the water. "Look down among the bulrushes and snap a picture of what's there."

Sara leaned over the fence. "Why that's an alligator," she said with surprising enthusiasm as she shot a photo of the dark green reptile with the ominous staring eyes.

"Keep walking," Eric ordered.

As Sara strolled along, her hand on the worn wooden handrail, she called out, "Ouch, a sliver of wood went into my hand."

"Hold on, Sis. I'll yank it out." Eric gave a big pull and Sara heaved a breath of relief.

"Thanks. I guess I won't touch that again."

As they moved along, Sara noticed many people with professional-looking camera equipment taking pictures of colorful birds she never knew existed. *He was right. This is fun.* They came to an area overlooking a mangrove island dotted with trees. A colony of large heavy-billed birds were settled on branches with green leaves. A bird was feeding its young in a nest. "Isn't that the cutest thing you ever saw?" Sara said.

An older man with a canvas hat and deep wrinkles stood next to them. "I'm the guide here. You're looking at wood storks that have taken over this island. There was a Great Blue Heron who died in the nest, and her mate got another partner in a few days. Both of them built another nest on top."

"How unfeeling," Sara said.

"No," the man contradicted. "This is nature's way. People do the same thing. A mate dies and the remaining one goes on and finds another one."

"I guess," Sara said sadly.

"Did you know that we have raccoons here, a mother and three babies? And then there are three big gators, and many soft-shell turtles. There's an anhinga, the bird who likes to stand by itself with its wings spread wide apart. The otters that live here have razor-sharp teeth. They can rip birds apart. Every tree is loaded with birds at 7 a.m. and they leave regularly at 5:15 p.m. and fly to another location."

"Thanks for the information," Eric said.

The guide nodded and walked away.

"Here's a bench," Eric said to Sara. "Let's rest and talk."

"Okay. What do you want to talk about?"

"I think it's great that at the end of summer you'll be off to college. Are you excited?"

Sara sighed loudly. "No. I'd rather not go. I don't remember any books that I've read. I don't remember anything. I'll fail every course. I know I will. I can't understand why Dr. Strauss suggested I go for a Master's Degree in English."

Eric patted his sister's shoulder. He removed his sunglasses and cleaned them with a handkerchief. "I'm sure the doctor knows what's good for you. I have a suggestion if you want to hear it."

"Okay," Sara said reluctantly.

"You have the whole summer to prepare for college. Get a list of books that the instructor will use and read these books."

"Where can I get this list?"

"Go online."

"I don't know if I am able to read all those books." Sara turned her face away and looked in the dark water. "There, over there," she pointed. "It's a turtle sunning herself on a log."

Eric's eyes widened. "How do you know it's a she?"

Sara shook her head. "I don't know. I just think it's a female. Why do you ask me that?"

"I don't know if I should tell you that you used to be interested in turtles."

"I was? How come?" Sara paused. "Why wasn't I interested in dogs or cats?"

"Because of Mom and Dad."

"What about Mom and Dad?"

"They didn't approve of your having a dog or a cat and as a result you bought a box turtle."

"So that's why I had a turtle," Sara said as she nervously tapped her foot on the boardwalk.

Eric nodded.

"Now I remember I had a turtle the size of my hand and I used to feed it cantaloupe." Sara put her hand to her mouth. "I called it Daisy and it was a female. Mom told me Daisy died."

"I'm very excited," Eric said with a broad smile. "You just remembered something of your past. I knew your memory would return. Somehow I surmised that if I brought you here you would remember Daisy, and you did. Let's go back to Helen's place and tell her. She'll be so happy."

Just as Eric and Sara rose from the bench, a thin young woman, dressed in short shorts that showed her muscular legs, drew near. "Sara," she shouted, "Where the hell have you been all these months?"

Oh, no! Who is she? What shall I say? I'm in a quandary.

Sara gave the girl a weak smile. The girl smiled back.

REVA SPIRO LUXENBERG

Eric replied instead of Sara, "Sara has been staying with our parents in Tampa. I guess you missed seeing her."

"You better believe it. Every morning I had to jog by myself. It's tough when your jogging partner leaves, especially when she leaves without saying goodbye."

"I'm sorry," Sara said.

"Our father was sick," Eric explained, "...and Sara was needed at home in a hurry."

"So that's what happened. You're forgiven. How about jogging again?"

Do I jog? I don't remember her. "Not right now. I've twisted my ankle, but thanks for asking me." *I'm so embarrassed. I don't even remember the names of people I knew. Life sucks.*

∗ ∗ ∗

Helen's grandfather's clock in the foyer struck midnight when Sara awoke screaming. Helen rushed into Sara's bedroom and took her in her arms. She waited until Sara stopped crying, handed her a box of tissues, and asked her what was wrong.

"I had an awful nightmare. It was so real that it made me shake all over. Did this really happen? Don't spare my feelings. I want to know the truth."

"All right. Tell me what you dreamt, and I promise I'll tell you if it's real."

"I saw my turtle, Daisy. She was on an operating table. A knife cut into her. Blood poured out. Daisy died."

"I'm sorry, Sara. That did happen. It did upset you very much at the time."

"Is that why I lost my memory?"

"I don't think so because after a while you went on with your life, and this is what you still have to do. It's good that you're beginning to remember the past. It's a gradual thing. Soon you'll remember people you've known. Actually my nephew, Elliott, who is my husband's brother's son, helped you feel better."

"You spoke about Elliott before. He took my manuscript. Is he sending it back to me?"

"He told me he's waiting for you to finish it, and he thinks he can turn it into a good play. He said it has excellent deep characterization and a decent plot that will appeal to an audience."

"I think I'd like to meet Elliott."

"You will. Now go back to sleep and have pleasant dreams."

Sara was dispirited with her life as it was. *I'm afraid to sleep. My dreams are far from pleasant. Why, oh why, did this have to happen to me? Is God punishing me? Did I do something wrong?*

CHAPTER 30

THE FIRST DAY of the fall semester God opened the floodgates of the heavens wide. At first it was only rain that pounded the Fields campus, but then the rain turned to hail so fierce that it sounded like applause. The hail hit the three buildings that made up the quadrangle, Boston Hall, the science building; Roosevelt Hall Library, with its clock tower; and Wilson Hall in which Sara, clutching Helen's black umbrella, was headed to her graduate Shakespeare class. Next to her a pair of male students wearing yellow ponchos raced ahead of her on the slippery cobblestone walkway.

Sara closed the umbrella and wiped the moisture from her face. *Finally I make it to college and the weather stinks. This must be an omen that I'm doomed to failure.*

Just as Sara was about to step through the door, she changed her mind, turned around and bumped into a male student who dropped the backpack he was carrying. When he stood up, he was her height.

"What do you think you're doing?" he asked as his striking blue eyes shot a look of annoyance at her.

Sara bent down, picked up the soaked backpack, and handed it to him. "I'm sorry. I changed my mind about going to class."

"That's not very smart," the guy said. "You miss the first day of class, you're consigned to death. That's when Professor Grumpy assigns the work for the semester."

"I thought his name was Professor Grossman."

"Yeah, it is—but we call him Grumpy because the man never cracks a smile."

Sara frowned. "I'm going home."

"Do you have the doldrums?"

"Sort of."

"Come on—don't be a scaredy-cat," the male student said as he grabbed Sara's hand and pulled her along the entrance to Room 132, just around the first bend.

"Let go of me."

He dropped Sara's hand and as he opened the door, the professor shouted, "Both of you are late. Come in, close the door, and take a seat." *Already I don't like this professor.*

Ten seats were occupied but two in the front row were empty. Both students dropped down and took out their laptops. Sara looked at the forty-something professor who had thin lips and long straight dark hair that hung down to his shoulders like black drapes. His voice was gritty as he called out the names of the students. Sara trembled when he came to her name. "Sara Solomon."

"Present." *I wish I wasn't here.*

"Rusty Hooper."

"Here," the guy next to her said in a pleasant tone.

So that's his name. He's really a great looking fellow except for his bright red hair. I like his smile, and he has the shiniest pearl-white teeth. I wonder why he's studying English and not going to dental school.

Professor Grossman handed out the syllabus for the semester. "For next Monday you are to read *Othello* and hand in a characterization of two of Shakespeare's characters in five hundred words—no more than five hundred—since I don't want to be up all night reading."

Othello? Why is he starting with Othello? I read it, but for some reason it upset me. I seem to remember I saw the play and hated the actor who played Desdemona. I think Helen was with me at that time. I have to ask her.

Professor Grossman positioned himself at the side of the classroom on a tall chair in front of a stand that had a laptop and a projector that cast some notes on the large screen that faced the students. Hastily Sara copied some of the graduate course offerings. *Major British Authors Approaches to Literature, Literary Merits of Harry Potter.*

"You, in front," Professor Grossman said pointing to Sara, "...stop taking notes and listen. *My hands are shaking. This is so embarrassing.*

"I put these two graduate courses on the screen to encourage you to take these courses that are being offered in the winter semester. I am of the opinion that *Harry Potter* has literary merit and is a significant and far-reaching work. You, young lady, what did you think about *Harry Potter?*

Sara sputtered, "I don't know who Harry Potter is?"

All the students snickered with the exception of Rusty who looked at Sara in amazement.

"Have you inhabited Mars this last decade?" Professor Grossman asked without cracking a smile.

I can't stay here another second. Quickly Sara gathered her belongings and raced out the door, her flushed face contorted with shame.

Rusty called out, "How can you insult someone like this?"

Professor Grossman, his chin raised defiantly, answered, "That young woman is in need of a tougher skin." He continued talking about Shakespeare as if nothing had disturbed him.

*   *   *

Helen was mending a seam in her dress, when Sara flew through the front door and tossed her backpack on the floor.

"I've had it with college," she yelled as her heart pounded. "I'm never going back."

"Okay. What happened? Sit down." Helen patted the spot on the sofa next to her.

"The professor asked me about someone called Harry Potter, and when I said I never heard of him, the professor said I must've been on Mars in the last decade. I ran out the room and came home and I'll never go back."

"Wow! First day of graduate school and you get picked on. I'm sorry you came across an unfeeling misanthrope like him."

Sara took some deep breaths and tried to relax. "Just who is Harry Potter?"

"A woman in England wrote about a boy and a bunch of magic, and her books became best sellers. Even I read the whole series. Kids and adults alike loved the adventures of Harry Potter and the books were even adapted for the movies."

"Since I don't remember the past, I'll never adjust to college. It's a waste of my parents' money."

Helen continued sewing the seam. "You could drop this course with the unfeeling professor and enroll in another course, or you could take fewer credits this semester. If you give up at the first bite of venom, you could stay here and wither away like the last rose of summer."

Sara's eyes welled up in tears. "No one understands how hard it's for me to have no past."

"You have a past. You remember your verbal and writing skills. What's important is not your past, but your present. You must learn to live in the here and now. Was there any memory of school that surfaced?"

Sara hung her head. "No… but I did have an inkling about my seeing a play called Othello. And then—I had the oddest sensation that I was angry with the leading actress. Did this ever happen?"

"Yes—you and I saw Othello, but it wasn't the play Shakespeare wrote. My nephew Elliott made it into a comedy. Desdemona was played by a young woman who used to torment you. I think it's wonderful that your memory is returning, if only in small spurts."

"I guess I shouldn't be so negative. I do remember the dog, my turtle, and now seeing a play with you. Maybe I just need time."

"Of course you do. Now was there anything in school that you liked?"

Sara bit down on her lips. "Yes, there was a guy I thought was kinda cute."

"Really? Tell me about him."

"He sat next to me in class. He has bright red hair, blue eyes like the sea, and a winning smile. I had good vibes about this fellow."

"If you go back to class, you'll meet him again and maybe develop a relationship."

Sara shook her head. "I won't go back to that horrible teacher. I don't care about building a relationship. Anyway he looks too young for me, and maybe he has a girlfriend, or maybe he's married."

"Was he wearing a wedding ring?"

"No."

"So you noticed. I think you should drop the class and look around for this guy. You told me the graduate English department in Fields University is small. You may meet him in another class, or in the library, or the lunchroom. Throw your hat into the ring, Sara."

"If I threw my hat into the ring, it could get very dirty."

I do wish I could meet Rusty again. He seemed so nice and I feel so lonesome. But nobody normal will be interested in a girl like me who has forgotten her past.

REVA SPIRO LUXENBERG

CHAPTER 31

THE CELL PHONE rang and woke Sara from her habit of taking an afternoon nap. She began it when she dropped out of Fields University two weeks previously. "Hello," Sara said in a sleepy voice.

"Did I wake you?"

"Oh, it's you, Dr. Strauss. Yes, I had dozed off."

"That could be a sign of depression. Are you still going to college?"

"No—something happened and I dropped out."

"Are you driving?"

"Yes. I have my car."

"I want you to come to my office tomorrow morning at 9 a.m. It looks like we have much to discuss."

*   *   *

Sara, clasping her hands tightly together, sat uncomfortably on the chair while Dr. Strauss gazed at the clouds in the sky through the window in his office. He turned, looked at his patient, and said with a bright smile, "The sky is clear—I believe we're well out of hurricane season. You and I need to come up with a plan for your future that doesn't involve afternoon naps. I'm not criticizing you. I truly want to help you."

"I know you do, Dr. Strauss, but I expected after six months to have my memory back and it hasn't happened."

Pulling his chair in front of Sara's, he seated himself. "Tell me everything that you remember from the past."

"My memories are kinda hazy. I remember I once had a turtle named Daisy. I remember the dog from next door, and it's nice that she remembers me. There's a faint memory of my being in a wetlands, and then going with Helen to see the play *Othello*. There's a foggy, confused memory of a woman I didn't like who acted in the play. That's about it."

"Good. You remember animals, places, and some people. It's taking time, but definitely the veil will lift. Why aren't you in college?"

Sara tugged at a strand of her wavy dark hair. "I didn't know who Harry Potter was and the professor made a point of it. The students laughed at me, and I ran out of the class. This will happen again and again, and I'm so embarrassed I can't face anyone."

"Do you want to lead a normal life?"

"Of course—but I'm not a normal person."

"Sara, you need to go back to college, mix with students, date a man, sleep at night and not during the day, eat healthful foods, exercise, and stick to a routine. Concentrate on learning new material and meeting new people."

"I'm trying to protect my mind by keeping away from people."

"That's the opposite of what you should be doing. Are you seeing your brother?"

Sara sneezed.

"God bless you."

Sara grabbed a tissue and blew her nose. "Eric flew back to Ireland. He needed to return to work. He e-mails me, but I don't have any news, so I don't answer him."

"Try and write about what you're feeling. You need to communicate. This will help you heal. What about your parents? Are they in touch with you?"

"Yes. They keep calling me to say they would like me to return and live with them."

"What do you think about that?"

"I like living with Helen even though I don't remember much about her from before. She's kind to me. I want to stay with her, but she's dating a man. What will happen if they marry? She won't want me."

"Cross that bridge when you come to it. Now your mind is a clean slate. Learn new things and live in the present."

"I'm scared, but I will go back to college—I just won't take that class with Professor Grossman."

"Sara, I think it's important that you do take the class in which you began to remember the play you saw. Something happened to you then, and you need to face it and conquer your fear."

"All right. I'll do what you say because living like a hermit doesn't really make sense. How should I handle my return to class?"

"The best way is with the truth. Tell your Professor that you have a form of amnesia that will resolve itself in time."

"But suppose he thinks I'm lying? I'd be mortified."

"It makes no difference what he thinks. What's important is that you return to his class."

*   *   *

Helen went shopping with Sara and helped her select a new dress for her return to Fields University. The morning that Sara returned she put the flattering dress on. It was a blue madras print with a full, sweeping skirt and shaped bodice that cast an artful emphasis on Sara's legs, hips, waist, and bust.

She made sure that she arrived before the rest of the class. Professor Grossman was sitting at his desk and when she approached him her knees buckled. Holding on to the side of the desk, a quiver went through her body as she spoke quietly. "Hello, Professor Grossman."

"Good morning young lady. You fled from my classroom. Welcome back."

"I'm sorry I ran out, but I want to come back."

"That's all right with me." Professor Grossman resumed marking a paper.

"I have to tell you something," Sara said, knowing she interrupted his concentration.

Will he listen to my explanation? What will he think?

"Well, what are you waiting for? Spit it out."

"I have a form of amnesia which the doctor says will resolve itself. I don't remember people or places."

"That's news to me. Is that your excuse for not knowing about Harry Potter, or is it for real?"

"It's real. It's called psychogenic amnesia and I got it as a result of a trauma in my life."

"I've never heard of anything like that. Can you memorize new material?"

"Yes, I can. My intelligence is the same as before."

The door opened and the students poured in.

"Sara, take your seat and don't worry, I won't call on you."

Oh boy, it wasn't as bad as I thought it would be. Actually it's a relief!

During the time the professor was lecturing, Rusty was writing in a notebook.

Why isn't Rusty taking notes on his laptop?

It became evident when Rusty tore out a piece of paper and handed it to Sara.

She read, "Meet me in the lunchroom at noon."

Sara bit down on her lip and nodded. *I'm so glad I listened to Dr. Strauss. Now a guy is interested in me. Should I tell him about my amnesia? I'll make up my mind when I met him.*

*   *   *

The noisy lunchroom was filled with students eating, chatting, and fooling around teasing one another. Sara looked for a table with two empty seats on a bench and found one near the entrance. She placed her tray on the table and began to nibble on her raisin-bread peanut butter sandwich. *I don't see him. Maybe he won't come. And what if he does, what should I reveal? If I tell him the truth, he'll lose interest in me.*

"Hi," Rusty said, ". . . I was looking all over for you." Rusty put down his tray next to Sara's. A tuna fish sandwich and a salad were on his plate. "I'm really glad you came back to Grossman's class. He shouldn't have spoken to you like he did. It took courage for you to return and I give you credit for that."

"I almost didn't return," Sara said. "I was so embarrassed." Sara took a sip of her iced coffee.

"The professor is the one who should've been embarrassed. I figured if you didn't know who Harry Potter was then you must've been living on an island in the South Pacific."

"I wasn't."

"Where were you?"

Sara's face turned crimson. "I was living right here in Palm Oasis."

"I don't understand." Rusty's eyes shifted to Sara's face. "If you don't want to tell me, what happened to you, you're not obligated."

Can I trust him? I wish I knew what to say.

Sara felt the beginning of a headache. "Here it goes—I've been suffering from psychogenic amnesia."

Rusty's eyes widened and he whistled. Students sitting at the next table peered at him. "We've finished eating. Let's go outside where we have privacy."

They sat on a bench opposite the lily pond. "Now you can tell me what psychogenic amnesia is."

I don't know what to say. It's humiliating. I don't understand it myself.

CHAPTER 32

SARA PLACED HER hand on her forehead and shut her eyes. *How can I explain my amnesia to Rusty when I don't understand it myself?*

A couple of boisterous students passed the bench near the university's lily pond where Sara and Rusty were sitting. Rusty waited until the students were out of earshot before he asked, "Do you have a headache, Sara?"

Sara opened her eyes and looked at him with pain evident on her face. "Yes. It feels like I have a tumor in my head."

"I carry aspirin and a bottle of water in my backpack. I'll give you two aspirin."

Sara smiled weakly. "Thanks." She swallowed the pills with some sips of water.

Rusty put things back. "I think it's too much stress for you to speak about what you referred to as psychogenic amnesia. You don't owe me an explanation. I'll go to Google and look it up."

"Never mind. I'll tell you what my psychiatrist told me. A trauma occurred involving something quite terrible, and amnesia developed in order for me to deaden my extreme pain."

"I don't understand. You remember how to talk, read, and learn. You know who you are." Rusty looked confused.

"Yes, I can do these things and I can even drive; but I don't remember people or events from my past. I know my name because I was told it."

"Will your memory return?"

"My doctor said it will. I do remember some small things like a dog I knew, a turtle I had that died, and some things from a play *Othello* that I saw. Sometimes I get a hazy picture of when I used to live with my parents."

"You don't live with your parents now?"

"No. They live in Tampa. I'm staying with an older woman, Helen, in her home."

Rusty looked thoughtful. "So I guess your trauma had nothing to do with your parents' death."

"No. My parents are alive and so is my older brother."

"How old are you?"

Sara took a deep breath. "I'm twenty-six. I was told when my birthday is since I didn't remember."

"When is it?"

"Next Tuesday."

"Happy birthday."

"Thanks. How old are you?"

"How old do I look?"

"You look about eighteen, but you must be older because you're in graduate school."

"I'm twenty-three."

Sara chuckled. "Oh, a kid."

"May I take you out on a date for your birthday?"

"I don't date younger guys."

"Do you remember that you don't date younger men?"

"No. I don't really remember."

"Well sometimes I date older women, and I like you. How about going out with me?"

"I'll have to think this over. I'll let you know at the next class."

"I could become a good friend. Who knows? Perhaps even a great one."

*   *   *

On Sara's twenty-seventh birthday Rusty showed up at Helen's house with a gift-wrapped box.

Rusty handed her the box. "Happy Birthday, Sara!"

"You didn't have to do this." Sara held it up to her ear and shook it.

"Watch it," Rusty said pointing to the box. "It's fragile. Guess what it is."

"Thank you. I'm not good at guessing, so I'll open it."

Sara led Rusty into the living room where they sat down in matching arm chairs. Sara tore off the wrapping, folded it into eighths and placed it on the table. After she opened the box, she sighed, "Ah! Why it's beautiful. How thoughtful of you."

"It's nothing."

"I disagree. It's a rose that will never die."

Rusty grinned and shrugged. "It's handcrafted Capodimonte porcelain." He paused and confessed. "Actually my mother helped me pick it out. I told her what a nice girl you are and she said I should buy something special for your birthday."

"Thank you so much, and thank your mother for me."

"Now I'm taking you to a science fiction movie that has great reviews. We can walk the five blocks to the theater."

I guess he doesn't have a car. Poor fellow—he must be poor. But he's generous. I bet that porcelain flower cost him a lot of money.

*   *   *

Sara was turned off by the violence in the movie when the military from Earth used deadly missiles to destroy the aliens from a distant planet. She closed her eyes when it came to the scene of actors exchanging blows and dying.

Then ten minutes into the movie something confusing occurred in the dark theater. Rusty took her hand in his and squeezed it.

Did that ever happen before to me with other guys? Should I let him hold my hand? I wish I knew what to do. I'll have to ask Helen. Meanwhile I don't think there's any harm in letting him hold my hand. Actually it feels kind of good.

When *THE END* was shown on the screen, Sara felt relieved. They rose from their seats, made their way up the aisle, and left the theater. Rusty stopped at the entrance. "There's a luncheonette at the corner. Would you care for something to eat—a snack or a sandwich?"

Sara turned to Rusty. "The movie had so much fighting it took my appetite away, so I'll skip it for now."

"Then I'll walk you home," Rusty said looking disappointed.

"I changed my mind. I do feel like having a dish of ice cream."

They sat in a booth, and ordered dishes with two scoops of chocolate chip ice cream topped with hot fudge, whipped cream, and a cherry.

"I'm sorry I took you to a movie with so much violence," Rusty said apologetically. "I won't do that again. I didn't know you would be so disturbed by the fighting."

"I haven't gone to a movie since I lost my memory. I also didn't know that fighting would upset me. It's not your fault. Do you like science fiction?"

Rusty nodded. "I do—but that movie was silly. I've watched reruns of *Star Trek* on TV at least three times. That series is clever and mature, and the violence in it is minimal."

Sara licked the ice cream from her spoon. "Tell me one character you liked."

"I like all the ones with Dr. Spock. He's from the peaceful planet Vulcan and he uses logic to solve problems. He has pointy ears and not much of a sense of humor."

Sara wiped her mouth with her napkin. "My favorite character is the android, Data, especially when he tries to be funny and fails."

"I want to try something," Rusty said as he reached into his pants pocket and drew out a blank pad of paper and a pencil. He placed the pad next to Sara's dish of ice cream.

"What's this for?" Sara asked pointing to the pad.

"I've studied graphology and I want to illustrate what I know."

"What's graphology?" *This guy is fun and full of surprises.*

"It's the analysis of handwriting that reveals mental characteristics, intellect, and behavior traits."

"It sounds complicated."

"A person's handwriting tells something about his or her personality. The style with which each letter is written is significant. All I want you to do is sign your name and I'll attempt to tell you about yourself." Rusty pushed the pad and pencil across the table.

"I think I'll skip this," Sara said seriously while tapping her finger on the pad.

"Come on—be a good sport. I won't report anything negative about you, I promise—not that I think I'll find anything problematic."

Sara looked doubtful. Slowly she picked up the pencil and wrote her name,

Sara Solomon. "There now what do you make of that?"

"It's easy to interpret your signature at least on a tentative basis. You wrote slowly so you're a deliberate careful person. The pressure of the pencil is light so you're feeling weak. The capital S's are narrow, which means you are extremely shy. The first 'a' in Sara has a well-defined starting stroke which indicates that you are cautious. Your 'r' is simple and that means you have a quick mind and are shrewd. The next 'a' you wrote is open on top which shows happiness and simplicity. Is there anything I said that you disagree with?"

"I don't know if I accept your interpretations. I think you've gotten to know me a little and thus what you came up with was mostly flattery."

"Sara, dear Sara, why don't I take you home and let you study about graphology on Google to see if you can discover whether my technique has any merit."

CHAPTER 33

THE DAY THAT Helen had planned a date with George a violent storm hit the city of Palm Oasis. Frightful gusts of wind, heavy rain, and peals of thunder caused Helen to wonder if he would have to postpone the date. Nevertheless, she hoped he would call and tell her the weather made no difference in their plans.

She had placed the cell phone close by on her dressing table as she waited impatiently for George to call. It rang four times until she answered it, because she had been applying her pink lip liner carefully. They had been dating for seven months and Helen felt completely at ease with him. George usually took her out to dinner at an expensive restaurant, and that's what she expected. *Hopefully the storm will ease up.*

For this occasion Helen had bought a new teal pinstripe dress with a V-neckline, dolman sleeves, and a sash to accent her slim waist. Sara and she had gone shopping, and it was Sara who encouraged her to buy the expensive dress. With every passing day Helen felt closer and closer to Sara, and she wished she could help Sara get her memory back; but she knew that it would take more time and that she had to be patient and understanding.

"Hello George."

"Hi Helen, I have a surprise for you."

"A surprise?" *What's he up to?*

"We're not going to a restaurant. I've been cooking and I want to take you to my condo. I'm preparing a dinner fit for a queen."

"I'm not a queen."

"You are to me."

This is the first time George offered to let me see his home. I wonder what it's like.

*   *   *

The heavy rain, lightning, and thunder continued for the next hour. George arrived with a man's large umbrella under which he could escort Helen to his new silver Cadillac.

George had told her he bought his condo when he moved to Florida. A friend had said that it was a good deal. The condo was called a villa. It had two bedrooms, two bathrooms, a living room, a kitchen, a small dining area, and a porch, eight-hundred-and-fifty square feet in all. One person didn't need any more room than that. In three months George had shopped around and furnished it. He said he didn't need the services of an interior decorator as he knew what he wanted.

By the time they arrived they were soaked to the skin. Helen changed to George's silk bathrobe in one bathroom while George went into his bedroom to change his wet clothes. When he came out wearing jeans and a polo shirt, he took Helen's wet clothes and put them in the dryer on the porch. Meanwhile Helen went into the living room and looked around.

She was astonished to note that it was furnished in Victorian style. She had imagined he liked modern décor like she did, but obviously he didn't. George's taste in interior design was outstanding. She chuckled when she turned to a mahogany bookcase filled with cooking books. An oil landscape of an English countryside hung on the wall of the small dining area next to the kitchen. It had a round table with a formal setting for two. Heavy purple velvet drapes were tied back with gold tassels at the windows. They matched a patterned purple carpet. She seated herself on a graceful sofa in the living room and admired the gilded chairs covered in lavender satin trim and velvet, which was also purple. *I wasn't aware how much George likes that color. Next week I'll buy a purple dress.*

When George entered the living room, Helen exclaimed with enthusiasm, "Your house is delightful. The chandelier over your table is elegant. Are the crystals Swarovski?"

"Yes they are." George walked across the carpet and came to a halt directly in front of Helen. He took her hand in his and led her to one of the dining room chairs. "Are you hungry?"

Helen paused. She was so moved by the unusual furnishings that she didn't answer until it dawned on her that he was waiting for an answer. "I'm starved."

"Then let's eat. I've prepared my own recipe of veal scaloppini with mushroom marsala sauce, sides of spinach with almonds, and glazed sweet potatoes."

George served the food on pristine Lenox bone china banded with gold rim.

I can't believe George has such wonderful taste. I never ate anything like this. I do feel like a queen.

After they finished the meal that ended with delightful confections served in a crystal compote dish, Helen stretched her limbs feeling happily satisfied while George scurried away to load the dishwasher.

"Let's sit on the sofa," he suggested when he returned.

"Sure. Thank you for the most delicious meal I've ever tasted."

"My pleasure. Helen, I have an important question to ask you."

"What is it?"

"I love you from the bottom of my heart. Will you marry me?"

Helen felt the heat rise in her cheeks. She wasn't expecting a proposal. "I don't know. Why can't we go on as always? Marriage complicates a relationship." She was aware that her voice sounded uncharacteristically breathless. *Why did he have to ask me now? Life has gotten so complicated that I don't know what to do or what to say.*

"Then I have another question to ask—do you love me?"

Helen considered the matter closely before answering. "I believe I do love you. You are kind, considerate, and decent. You make me very happy."

"So why aren't you saying yes?"

"There are complications."

"What complications?"

"I have a house and you have a house. Where would we live?"

"Oh, is that all? Yes, I know my villa is tiny, but I would be willing to move to your house. I'd even give up my Victorian style of furnishings. You like modern, and I can get used to that. It would be a nice change for me."

"No, that's not all." Helen's cheeks turned pink.

"Is there something you haven't told me?"

"Not really. It's just Sara."

"Sara? We wouldn't disturb Sara. How is she doing?"

"Sara is doing well in college."

"Glad to hear that."

"Newlyweds need privacy and I would never ask Sara to move out. This is why I can't marry you."

George stiffened. His jaw tightened. "Okay, you can't marry me now, but when Sara leaves on her own, will you marry me then?"

"I'll be happy to," Helen said hastily.

"Now tell me what's really going on with Sara? Is she getting any better?"

"As I said, she's doing well in the university; but her memory is still hazy. She doesn't remember what set her off and for her to really recover she has to recall that right before her wedding her fiancé was shot and killed."

"That's a terrible thing to have happened. I feel really sorry for the girl."

"I do too. So now you understand why I can't marry you now."

George put his arm on Helen's shoulder and drew her close. "This is the September of our lives. We're not kids and I think we shouldn't wait until Sara gets over her amnesia."

"But suppose we marry and let Sara live in my home, and then she is so uncomfortable she moves out, drops out of the university, goes back to live with her parents who don't understand her and treat her like she's handicapped—what will happen to her?"

"Are you telling me you'll feel guilty if this occurs?"

Helen bit down on her teeth. "I will feel guilty. I can't help it. I'm very attached to Sara, and I can't let anything I do interfere with her mental health."

"You just told me you love me, Helen. We shouldn't let Sara's happiness keep us from being happy. There must be another way out of this dilemma. Is Sara dating anyone?"

Helen pulled George's robe tighter around her body. "Yes. Sara has been seeing a guy by the name of Rusty. He's a student, too."

"Do you think they'll get serious?"

"Definitely not. Students can't afford to marry."

"Maybe he has money?"

"Maybe he doesn't."

"I don't pretend to know the answer to this problem, but I'm sure there is one. We just have to find it." George looked out the window. "It's pouring. The lightning is flashing. I have a guest room. Do you want to stay over?"

"What will people think?"

"Do you really care what people think?"

"I guess not."

REVA SPIRO LUXENBERG

CHAPTER 34

R USTY AND SARA dated again the following week. They walked home after seeing a movie and eating ice cream at the luncheonette. Bright stars twinkled in the black sky and the air was filled with the scent of flowers, when Rusty took Sara's hand in his. The movie had been a love story and both were in a good mood.

When they reached Helen's home Sara cast an interested look at Rusty as he had intrigued her with his explanation of the psychology in Shakespeare's *Hamlet*. Hand in hand they climbed the stairs to the front porch and when bidding Sara goodnight Rusty gave her a light peck on her lips.

She had no time to react when suddenly the door opened and her parents, who shouldn't have been there, stood looking alarmed at both of them. Her mother's jaw hung down, and her father looked embarrassed.

"Say goodbye to the boy and come in Sara," her mother snarled as she held the door wide open.

Sara blinked at her parents unable to say a word. Rusty turned on his heel and fled as Sara's complexion lit up like a burning flame.

"Let's all calm down," her father said as he led Sara and his wife through to the living room. "Let's have a serious talk."

Sara sat on a chair and her parents reclined on the sofa. "I didn't know you were coming," Sara whispered.

"We wanted to surprise you for your birthday," her father said as he held out a rectangular velvet box. "Happy Birthday!"

"But my birthday was last week."

"We couldn't make it," her mother said.

Sara opened the box to reveal a necklace of different colored beads. "Thank you very much."

Mrs. Solomon looked stern. "We had no idea you were involved with a boy."

"I'm not involved."

"He kissed you. I'd say that's an involvement," Mrs. Solomon said.

"He's in my class and we're just friends."

Mrs. Solomon spoke slowly and precisely to emphasize their shock at finding Sara in what she thought was a compromised situation. "We've been here for three hours waiting for you to return. Helen said you were out on a date. She rushed out without an apology because she needed to keep an appointment with a gentleman friend. It seems everyone around here is dating, but no one had the courtesy to inform us about this."

Sara's hands balled into fists at her sides.

Her mother continued grumbling. "Now you come home at 10:30 at night, and we learn that you have started kissing boys. I think you should consider coming home with us before you get into trouble."

Sara didn't know what to say.

Mrs. Solomon pressed on. "What do you know about this boy?"

"He's nice." Sara's voice broke. "He gave me a porcelain rose as a gift."

"Is he Jewish?"

"I never asked him."

"Why not?"

"It didn't occur to me. I don't care what religion he is. I don't remember anything about being Jewish."

Mr. Solomon gave a derisive laugh. "Where did he take you?"

"To a movie and then to a luncheonette."

Mr. Solomon's eyes widened. "Did he drive you there?"

"Oh no—we walked."

"So he has no money," Mrs. Solomon said. "He's a student with no money. What is he planning to do with his life?"

"I never got around to asking him. He's majoring in English like me."

"So—he's a poor student with no future. Why are you dating him?"

"I like him." Sara's eyes became haunted.

"Well—like can turn to love and then you'll marry—and be poor the rest of your life."

"How old is the young man?" Mr. Solomon asked.

"He's twenty-three." Sara drummed her fingers on the table.

"He's four years younger than you. I think you'd better not see him anymore for your own good," Mrs. Solomon grumbled.

Mr. Solomon had a harsh expression. "Where does he live?"

"I don't know. I never asked him."

"What does his father do for a living?"

"I don't know."

"How long has he lived in Florida?"

"I don't know."

"Where was he born?"

"I don't know."

"How many brothers and sisters does he have?"

"I don't know." *I feel like I'm a criminal being grilled in court.*

Mrs. Solomon's voice softened. "You've suffered a trauma and your memory and judgment have been affected. We're your parents and we love you and want the best for you. I would like you to get some of your clothes and books and whatever you need and come with us back to Tampa and we'll take good care of you."

Mr. Solomon nodded. "I concur."

"I don't want to leave here," Sara said with tears in her eyes.

Mrs. Solomon continued, "Helen is a changed woman. She is now acting like a young girl, wearing short skirts, too much makeup, and going out with a man. She doesn't have your interests at heart like we do. Actually she's a stranger to you."

"But Mother I'm enrolled in the university here. I can't leave in the middle of a semester."

"Yes, you can. You can go to Tampa University and live at home. You'll be better off where we can supervise you. Eventually your memory will return and you'll be happy again."

I have to put a stop to this. Sara stood up trembling "I don't wish to leave here and go back to Tampa with you. I like the university and I'll see Rusty if I choose."

Mrs. Solomon answered in a peevish tone as she jumped up. "Your father and I are leaving now. It's late and it will take us two-and-a-half hours to get home. We came to wish you a happy birthday, but we never dreamed you would be out on a date with a young student you know nothing about."

"Please call in advance next time," Sara said, her face bathed in tears. *I hope it will be a long time until they come again.*

*　　*　　*

Sara and Rusty sat on the same bench in front of the university's lily pond. "My mother wanted me to go home with them," she said weakly. "But I didn't want to."

"That would be a mistake," Rusty said as he put his hand on Sara's shoulder.

"My parents asked me questions about you. I couldn't answer them as I really know very little about you."

"What kind of questions?"

"Where do you live?"

Rusty smiled. "168 Tulip Lane."

"Oh—and where were you born?"

"In Miami. What else do you want to know?"

Sara hesitated. "How many brothers and sisters do you have?"

"None."

"This is important to my parents—are you Jewish?"

"You better believe it. That's a yes."

"The next question is kind of embarrassing. What does your father do for a living?"

"My father died in an auto accident two years ago. He manufactured and distributed artificial flowers."

"I'm sorry to hear you lost your father."

"Thank you. My mother and I compose greeting cards mainly for a hobby, but there's a publishing house that buys them from us. My father had savings and heavy life insurance. We don't have to work, but my mother and I enjoy creating these cards."

"What do you plan on doing after you graduate?"

Rusty smiled. "I'm going to teach English in a university, write novels, and create greeting cards."

"What are you going to do after you get your Master's?" Rusty asked with a twinkle in his eye.

"I have no idea."

CHAPTER 35

THE STATELY GRANDFATHER clock in Helen's living room ticked minute after minute, hour after hour—while the days, weeks, months and seasons passed uneventfully. Sara continued studying in the university, but her memory lay dormant needing strong prods to bring it back. Her parents kept nagging her to return to their home, but Sara stubbornly resisted. Once a week she dated Rusty against her parent's wishes. Helen's relationship with George strengthened until he decided not to wait any longer and again proposed marriage.

One sunny day at noon George was preparing a spinach quiche in Helen's kitchen when he looked up at Helen with determination in his eyes. "My patience has evaporated," he said hastily.

"Don't fret dear," Helen said. "I'm not hungry. If the quiche takes a long time to bake, I can wait."

George removed his apron and sat down opposite Helen at the kitchen table.

"I don't mean that. I want to marry you now—tomorrow at the latest."

Helen shrugged. "I already told you why it's not a good idea."

"Well, I guess I do accept that. But Helen— why can't we get engaged? At least it's a step in the right direction."

Helen was acutely aware that if she didn't agree, she might lose the man she had come to love. She wasn't being fair to him, but she felt so sorry for Sara that she couldn't ask the young woman to leave. She realized that Sara was very fragile and needed the close friendship and the home that she was providing for her.

As Helen reflected on George's eagerness to become engaged, she brightened. She turned to him and said, "Okay, I'm willing to be engaged if you're willing to wait until Sara's life improves."

George's spirits lifted. "I'll wait and hope for the best." He reached out, embraced and kissed Helen passionately. "I'm turning off the oven. Let's go to the jewelry store right now and I'll buy you an engagement ring."

"But your quiche will be spoiled."

"The heck with the quiche. This is more important."

"No," Helen said firmly. "You worked a long time and you just put the quiche into the oven. It takes forty minutes to bake. We waited so long to be engaged; can't we wait a little while longer?"

"Fine," George said. "Let's kiss for the next forty minutes."

"You know you're a devil."

"You better believe it."

As George and Helen rode down Fifth Street to Louis Hall Jewelers, Helen's spirits lifted exponentially. Soon their relationship would be disclosed to the whole world. Her friends and family would hear of it and they would either be happy or not. If not, she didn't care. Helen's divorced sister was once again dating, and she already had expressed her approval of George. She didn't know what Sara would think, but she imagined she would be satisfied. Helen still had her diamond engagement ring from her late husband—and she didn't want any ring that resembled the last one. She would search for something different.

At the store the dignified-looking owner himself waited on them. He had a smile as wide as the Louis Hall Jewelers sign over the door. He wore a white suit, a black shirt, and a white tie with black dots. When he brought out trays of diamond rings, Helen shook her head in a disapproving way. Finally she spotted a ring in the showcase and pointed to it.

"Just pick a ring you'll be happy with and wear for many years to come," said George.

"I like that one, but it's too expensive."

"Price is no concern," George said in a strong voice.

Mr. Hall took out the ring and placed it on a velvet tray. "This is lovely. It's our oval ruby and diamond halo ring with a split shank. Try it on."

"I like that it has a ruby," Helen said as she placed it on her left ring finger. "It fits perfectly," she exclaimed enthusiastically.

"We'll take it," George said as he pulled an American Express credit card from his wallet.

*   *   *

Sara in her bathrobe sat on the sofa in the living room reading Shakespeare's *A Midsummer Night's Dream* when Helen came home at 9 p.m. She looked up from her book and saw Helen waving her left hand about.

"Oh, my God," Sara said excitedly. "You're engaged. I'm so happy for you. Congratulations!"

"Thanks. We got engaged this afternoon, and we went out for a long drive and dinner."

"When are you getting married Helen?"

"We decided that being engaged is so wonderful that we're not going to get married for a long time. Do you want to see my ring?"

"Sure. Take it off."

Helen slipped the ring off her finger and handed it to the young woman who held it lovingly in her hand. Suddenly Sara stiffened, her jaw tightened, and her complexion turned pale.

"What's wrong?" Helen cried.

With tears in her eyes Sara said, "I remember I had an engagement ring. I remember feeling sad. What happened to me? Was I really engaged?"

"It's good your memory is returning. Soon you'll remember everything without anyone telling you. You should feel glad that something came back to you."

"Where is my engagement ring? I want to see it. Maybe I'll remember more."

Helen hesitated. "I believe that your parents have it and are keeping it safe for you. It's a bit of shock to you that you remember you were engaged—right now I think the best thing for you to do is to go to sleep." Helen led Sara to her room, put her to bed, covered her with a blanket, and kissed her cheek. *I hate to see Sara this upset but when she remembers what happened to Alex she'll feel worse.*

*   *   *

The engagement party was hosted by Helen's twin sister, Alice, in her gated Mediterranean-style home with its vaulted ceiling, spacious living room with a stone fireplace, gourmet kitchen with granite countertops and stainless steel appliances, a three-car garage, and large pool and hot-tub in the rear. Alice had hidden money away from Lenny before the divorce and fortunately the mortgage had been paid up.

George was happy to finance the party and he invited his only child, his son Murray, and daughter-in-law, Shirley. His grandson was in medical school and couldn't come although he said he'd make it for the wedding.

Helen had invited her nephew Elliott who brought Tracy as his date. Sara didn't remember Tracy but she had a persistent feeling that she had been abusive to her. Rusty brought a gift of a large bouquet of glass flowers in a crystal bowl. There were six more couples present—friends of the engaged couple. Alice had hired a cook, two waiters, and a busboy to help with the festive food.

Luckily the sun shone brightly making it conducive for outside dining. The guests on the flagstone deck gathered around the kidney-shaped pool in small groups, some standing at the outdoor bar, some seated at round rattan tables covered by umbrellas, and others strolled around shooting the breeze.

Sara and Rusty were seated at a table when Tracy appeared with Elliott. She approached and looked down at her in her arrogant condescending way. "Do you remember me?"

Rusty saw how Sara shrunk back. "Please go away. You seem to have upset my girlfriend. Please understand."

"I don't remember you," Sara said as she stood up and went to the bar.

In a protective way Rusty followed. Sara acknowledged his presence.

"Two lemonades, please," Sara said to the waiter.

Tracy came up to Sara and laughed in her face. "You're such a phony, telling everyone you can't remember anyone. That's hogwash and you know it."

Rusty frowned. "You don't know anything about Sara's recent history. Please stay away. You're being abusive, and I don't want to make a scene."

"Your red hair shows you have a bad temper, and I heard that both of you are still in school. No kid sends me on my way, Buster."

"I do remember something about you," Sara said. ". . . and it's not nice."

"Let's go," Elliott said. He took Tracy's elbow and led her away. Tracy screamed as she turned her ankle on the flagstone of the deck.

Sara was not sorry about that.

CHAPTER 36

ONE SUNDAY WHEN the sun shone splendidly Sara drove Rusty to his home so she could meet his mother. She had the impression that the mother and son were struggling financially after the father's death, and she expected to see an ordinary house. When Rusty directed her past a winding driveway to an imposing home on two acres of manicured grass, royal palms, and flowering bushes, Sara was overwhelmed.

"This is where you live?" Sara asked.

"Yes, since I was five-years old."

"It looks so big. How large is your house?"

"It's not a mansion. It's only three-thousand-two-hundred square feet. We have a waterfront view and a pool in the back, but so do many other people."

"How come you don't have a car?"

"I do—but it's a Rolls Royce, and I don't like to show it off, but if you want me to drive you around I will. Let's go in. My mother is anxious to meet you."

Rusty led Sara to a massive front door and pressed a bell with chimes that played 'Yankee Doodle.' A butler, dressed like butlers in the movies, opened the door. "Good afternoon, Mr. Rusty." He led them to an aviary where Rusty introduced his mother to Sara.

The aviary was affixed to the ground with a woodwork frame on a concrete base. Mrs. Hooper stood in the middle of the aviary. A small bird was perched on her shoulder snuggling up to her face and kissing her nose. Mrs. Hooper, short and with bright red hair like her son, wore a simple housedress. Sara stood transfixed. Enchanted with the picture of Mrs. Hooper and her loving bird, she watched four or five birds flying around the aviary and others perched on branches and bushes.

"They're cockatiels," Mrs. Hooper said. "The charming bird on my shoulder is Sweetie Pie. She's a very good bird. She never destroys her toys."

"They play with toys?" Sara asked.

"Sure," Rusty said. "I buy them toys all the time. Cockatiels are rated the top ten best pet birds. Did you ever have a bird?"

"No, I didn't want to constrict a bird by putting it in a cage."

"We didn't either," Mrs. Hooper said. "That's why we had a grounded aviary built. It's not suspended like some, but it has a concrete base that prevents mice and an occasional snake from entering. Let's go into the dining room for refreshments. I'm so happy to meet you. Rusty has been raving about you and I see why. I'd love to give you a bird as a present."

"A bird?" Sara said opening her eyes wide. "Thank you—but I live with my landlady and I don't know if she'd approve. I used to have a box turtle, but I wouldn't know how to take care of a bird."

"Ask the woman if you can have a bird," Mrs. Hooper said as she led them into the dining room. "Rusty could teach you how to care for a cockatiel."

On the way home in the car, Sara kept her eyes on the road. *Should I ask Rusty for an explanation? I will ask.* "I thought you were poor, but are you?"

Rusty burst out laughing. "My father left us very well provided for. I have a generous trust fund and so does my mother. By the way my mother whispered to me that she likes you."

"Oh, I like her, too." *I wish she could be my mother.*

*   *   *

Three months later the bright month of June arrived. It was a Wednesday and the sun streamed down between puffy clouds. Sara and Rusty had received A's for their term papers and high grades in all their English subjects. They had decided to spend their vacation together at the library writing novels.

George persuaded Helen to buy a wedding gown just in case they would be able to go ahead with wedding plans. Sara continued reaching for the memories of her past in the corners of her mind. Bits and pieces came back but not enough for her to feel like a normal person who remembers family and friends, places, and occasions.

"It's time to go to Wedding Expressions for my gown," Helen said to Sara, who was standing at the hall mirror applying rose-colored lipstick.

REVA SPIRO LUXENBERG

"I'm ready," Sara said. "Let's go. It should be fun to watch you trying on wedding gowns."

Sara drove Helen in her Mazda to the mall where the wedding gown emporium was located. Helen was now a perfect size ten, the same as Sara, and she knew just what she was looking for.

"I'm looking for a long gown in silver, plenty of lace, embroidery, and all kinds of glitter," Helen told the saleslady who wore a cocktail dress.

"My name is Matilda and I'll be happy to serve you. I'm sorry, Madam. We don't carry anything but white wedding gowns."

"But this will be my second wedding and I can't wear white," Helen explained.

The saleslady stood with one hand on her slim hip. "Nowadays women in a second marriage are comfortable wearing white."

"Helen," Sara said, ". . . you'll make a beautiful bride wearing a white wedding gown. George will be so pleased."

Helen looked thoughtful and hesitated before she said, "All right. Bring some over. I love satin and lace."

"Will you be getting married in the summer?" the saleslady asked. "If so, satin might be too warm."

"We haven't set a date," said Helen. "Just show me what you have. I don't want to be here too long, as my friend and I are planning to go to the new restaurant in the mall."

"Yes, Madam. I'll be right back."

Sara and Helen looked around at the veils, headpieces, fancy garters, and jeweled evening bags waiting for the saleslady.

Matilda didn't keep her word. She returned in a half-hour with three dresses on satin hangers that she hung on a rack. She took out one at a time and with flair displayed each dress.

Helen creased her forehead. "I don't like anyone of them. We'll come back another time. I'm hungry and I've lost my patience."

"Please Helen—we're here now, so let's look at just one more dress and then we can go and eat a leisurely lunch," Sara implored.

"There's one dress in the back that I forgot," Matilda said. "It was returned by the parents of the bride after her wedding was unexpectedly called off. It's just your size. It has long sleeves, and it's covered with seed pearls."

"Are you sure it was never worn?" Helen asked.

"Oh no, we don't carry used merchandise. But it is reduced by twenty per cent since the prospective bride had taken it home."

"Okay, I'll look at it."

Matilda brought out the elegant wedding dress and Helen took one look at it and said with determination, "I don't like it."

Sara, with equal determination, said, "I like it—at least try it on."

Helen and Matilda went into the dressing room and when Helen came out wearing the dress, Sara blinked her eyes repeatedly, unable to focus. Perspiration fell from her forehead. She shoved her chair back, called out "Alex" with a screech, fainted, and fell to the carpeted floor.

CHAPTER 37

"I'M SO STUPID," Helen exclaimed. "I never should've taken Sara to the bridal shop. It's my fault."

"No it isn't, dear," George said. "You didn't know what would happen." He put his arm around Helen's shoulder as they sat on the sofa in the living room. She leaned against him for comfort, but no words or actions on his part could relieve her anxiety.

"I should've realized that Sara might recognize the shop, but I was so selfish that I overlooked that possibility. After I asked to look at a silver wedding gown, the saleslady and Sara talked me into selecting a white gown. It turned out that I tried on the very gown that Sara had chosen, but never actually wore. When Sara saw me in it she collapsed. I had forgotten what her gown looked like, and that makes me the stupidest woman around." Helen had a deathlike paleness.

"The psychiatrist said that one day something might well trigger Sara's memory," George explained. "It's better this way. She was miserable not remembering."

"I know, but I still feel guilty. She's sleeping now from the shot the doctor gave her, but when she wakes up she'll remember how she felt when Alex died two weeks before their wedding. She'll fall apart." Helen wrung her hands.

"No, she'll mourn her loss. This is what most people do when they lose someone they love. She'll cry. She'll carry on, but that's normal."

Helen looked grave. "Do you think I should call her parents?"

"Yes, they would expect you to notify them if there was a change in Sara's life."

"But they may come here and upset her even more. They may even insist upon taking her home. They're intolerably rude and unfeeling—even though they protest that they love their daughter. Sara is in a dreadful state and may not be able to resist."

George squeezed Helen's hand. "You're uneasy now and you may be exaggerating."

Helen hastily replied, "I know I'm agitated but I have had dealings with Sara's parents. They're selfish and unreasonable. Sara has been comfortable staying with me both when she had her full memory and then after she lost it. I want to take care of her during this trying period of her life."

"You know I love you, dear Helen. Take one step at a time—call her parents, and things will work out."

*   *   *

The next afternoon when Sara woke, she couldn't stop keening. After ten minutes she blew her nose, dried her eyes, and grabbed her forehead. "I have a headache. I'm sure it's a tumor."

"Do you remember me?" Rusty asked.

"Yes," Sara said as she started to bawl again. "I remember everything. I wish I were dead."

Helen brought her a glass of water and two aspirin. "Take this. We all love you and want you alive. Stop thinking about dying."

"I can't. I loved Alex and I'll never see him again," Sara said as the tears rolled down her cheeks.

"I notified your parents and told them what happened to you," Helen said. "They wanted to come over, but your mother had a luncheon appointment and your father had a golf game."

"That's all right with me," Sara said. "I don't want to see them anyway. I remember how miserably they used to treat me in the past."

The rest of the week Sara couldn't sleep. She ate only bites of toast and tea and began to drop in weight. Most of the time, she stayed in her room and wept. She wore the same T-shirt and shorts all week. She didn't shower, comb her hair, or put on makeup. Rusty stayed in the living room and was at her beck and call if there was anything she needed. He recognized she had to have time to mourn, and he displayed a tremendous amount of patience.

*   *   *

A week later Mr. and Mrs. Solomon showed up one rainy afternoon when Mr. Solomon couldn't play golf with his buddies.

"Sara is satisfied living here," Helen said to them stiffly. *I hope they don't insist on taking her with them.*

"We don't believe that Sara belongs with you," Mr. Solomon said. "We came to bring her home with us."

Impelled by an irresistible force to defy them, Helen said, "Why don't you leave that decision up to Sara? She's an adult and capable of making her own plans."

"Sara was always a wishy-washy individual," Mrs. Solomon said. "Now that she's in heavy mourning she belongs with blood relatives, not you. I understand you have your own life that includes your engagement to a man. I'm sure you have no room in it for our daughter."

Helen bit down on her lips. Her face reddened. "George and I are attached to Sara and we're happy to take her under our wings. We want to help her. She has suffered greatly."

"She'll get over it," Mrs. Solomon said moving toward Sara's bedroom. "Now we're going to knock at her door and speak to her. We've talked enough with you."

"Suit yourself." Helen strode away.

Mrs. Solomon knocked at Sara's bedroom door. There was no answer. Mr. Solomon called out, "Sara dear, we want to talk to you—open up."

The door remained closed. Mrs. Solomon tried the knob. It didn't turn. Sara had locked herself in. Mr. Solomon banged on the door.

Sara, her face streaked with tears, opened the door. She looked emaciated and wore a soiled nightgown. "I want to be alone. I don't want to talk to anyone at this time. Go away."

"We want to take you home," Mrs. Solomon said. "Your eyes are red and puffy. I have never seen you look so unkempt. Of course before we take you home, you have to take a shower, change to decent clothes, and make yourself presentable."

"I told you to go away." Sara closed her door, threw herself on her bed, and began to weep.

Mr. and Mrs. Solomon approached Helen who was sitting on the sofa in the living room. Mrs. Solomon said stiffly, "My husband and I will not take Sara home against her will. She won't listen to us. She's depressed, and she will depress us. At this time in our lives we don't need to care for a child who is an emotional basket-case."

"Sara isn't a basket-case and she isn't a child," said Helen. "She has great fortitude. She is an adult who has been severely traumatized."

"Whatever," Mrs. Solomon turned to her husband. "Let's go."

For a week Sara remained cloistered in her room. Rusty brought her toast and tea and left her alone. There was nothing he could say to comfort her, and he knew it.

Finally Rusty watched as Sara emerged from her room—her collarbones protruding from a sundress that hung loosely on her thin frame, her eyes still red, and her face pale and haggard. "Is there anything I can do for you?" he asked.

"Yes, please—take me to Zion Memorial Park Cemetery. I want to see Alex's grave."

"Right now?"

"Yes, Rusty. I showered and dressed, and I don't want to wait another minute. You can drive my car, or I'll go in your Rolls."

"I understand, Sara. We'll take my car. Do whatever you feel like doing and know that I'll always be there to help you."

During the drive to Ft. Lauderdale no one spoke. Sara sat stiffly in the passenger seat not looking at the passing scenery. Rusty located the cemetery easily, and Sara went into the office to find the location where Alex was buried. She came out with a mourner's booklet and directions to Alex's grave. She gave the directions to Rusty, and he drove to the gravesite.

"Wait here until I get back," Sara said in a weak voice.

"I'll sit in my car and listen to the radio. Take whatever time you need. I'll wait patiently."

Sara crossed the velvety grass and stopped in front of a black granite grave marker with Alex's name in gold leaf lettering. On the marker was a picture of a police officer and Alex's badge. Sara lowered herself to the grass, put her head in her hands, and bawled. When the tears stopped flowing, she dried her eyes, took out the mourner's booklet and silently read the 23rd Psalm. She closed the booklet. *You were too young to die. I loved you very much. I'm in enormous pain.*

An hour later Sara walked slowly back to the car and climbed in. Rusty turned off the news broadcast he was listening to on the radio. "Are you hungry? he asked.

"No."

"I'm hungry. Will you go to a luncheonette with me?"

Sara looked downcast. "I guess."

*　*　*

Every day Rusty showed up at Helen's door. He sat in the kitchen and worked on his novel on his laptop. Sara stayed in her room most of the time. When she came out, Rusty used to offer to take her to a quiet restaurant "for a bite."

Gradually Sara came to expect him to be there for her. Her heart was breaking, but she understood that if she didn't take care of her body's needs, she would get sick. Every day they showed up at the same restaurant. Sara alternated between two outfits that she changed in order to launder them. She still hadn't put on makeup and was drawn and pale.

One day Rusty sat opposite her in the booth in the restaurant. "I'm a good listener. Why don't you tell me about how you feel? Talk about anything. Tell me about Alex. Tell me about the novel you had been writing."

Sara gave him a weak smile. "I keep thinking about how hard your mother works to clean the aviary in your house. Sometimes I can picture the cockatiels and the parakeets flying around. I smile when I think about that beautiful cockatiel kissing your mother."

"I didn't expect you to say that," Rusty said. "I thought you would tell me about your past or how you expected to lead your life married to a police officer. But birds? I didn't think you remembered the aviary."

"Rusty, I remember my time in the university, how I met you, and how we became friends. I also remember everything about Alex and our plans. I read that there are people who have brain damage whose memories are lost forever. I'm lucky to remember. I hope I never forget. It's when I'm sad that I think about your mother's bird and how it kissed her."

Rusty thought, I'm going to buy Sara a bird—maybe a parrot that talks.

CHAPTER 38

"**M**OM, I'VE FALLEN for Sara."
"I didn't hear you. What did you say?" Mrs. Hooper stood in the middle of the aviary vacuuming the floor. Every morning she cleaned up the poop that had accumulated from her beloved cockatiels and parakeets.

Rusty raised his voice. "I said I love Sara."

"That's nice," his mother answered, as she shut down the vacuum and picked up her mop.

"I want to marry her."

"It's okay with me. She's a fine girl." Mrs. Hooper started to mop the floor in circles.

Rusty took out bird seed from a container and walked around putting a handful in each glass dish. "But if we marry—I'll buy a house—and you'll be lonesome living alone."

"What? Live alone? I'll never live alone. I have my birds. What about Sweetie Pie? She and I are devoted to each other."

"That's not the same as living with a person and you know it."

Mrs. Hooper pursed her lips. "Do you intend to move to Alaska or maybe the Galapagos Islands?"

"Of course not. We'll live near you and see you often."

"I should hope so."

"There's another consideration. Now that Sara's memory has returned she's still in love with the policeman she was going to marry. I'm not sure if she loves me."

"Why wouldn't she love you? You're lovable. You're handsome, smart, educated, good-natured, healthy, young, and financially secure."

"That's a mother talking."

"She needs time to mourn. Be patient. Propose to her later."

Rusty put his hand on his mother's arm, "Good idea."

*   *   *

The last e-mail Eric got from his sister came as a total surprise.

Dear Eric,

I have both good news and bad news. When I saw my chosen wedding gown, I was so shocked that it triggered my memory and now I remember my past life. I also remember the present time, which is good. But Eric, the bad news is that I feel terribly depressed over Alex's death. I wish I could cry on your shoulder.

Love,
Sara

This e-mail concerned Eric so deeply that he decided he must take the month's vacation he had coming to him.

He flew to Palm Beach International Airport and headed straight for Helen's house to see Sara. She was in the living room playing Scrabble with a red-haired young man.

"Eric, I've been waiting for you," Sara shouted, with tears rolling down her cheeks, as she ran to him and threw her arms around her brother's neck.

"You do remember me, don't you?" Eric asked, hugging her back.

Sara wiped her eyes with a tissue. "Yes, I remember when you gave me the set of Shakespeare's plays for my sixteenth birthday. I remember everything now." A cloud passed over Sara's face. "I remember Alex and how we almost got married."

"I'm sorry. Bad things happen to good people," Eric said as he turned and looked with interest at the man sitting at a card table on which there was a half-finished Scrabble game.

"Oh, I'm so sorry," Sara said. "Let me introduce my new friend Rusty Hooper to you. Rusty, this is my brother Eric."

Rusty rose and the two men exchanged greetings and handshakes. Rusty, looking at Sara with adoring eyes said, "I think I should go now. You two have a lot of catching up to do."

"No, don't leave," said Sara politely. "I'll bring in some refreshments, and we can sit around and talk."

"Fine," Eric said.

Sara trotted to the kitchen to prepare a fruit plate and iced coffee.

"Rusty piped up. "I understand you just flew in. How was your flight?"

"It was long," Eric said, "but I slept most of the way. Before 9/11 the security was easy, but now it's a big hassle."

"I understand. Terrorism keeps us on our toes," Rusty remarked. "Where are you staying now that you're in Florida?"

"I rented a car, and I'll drive to Tampa and stay with my parents. I don't know much about the present state of Sara's mental health. You've been seeing her, and I've been a continent away. Can you tell me about any progress she's made with her depression?"

Rusty took a deep breath. "Sara is a remarkable young woman. I like her very much, in fact more than that. We dated, and she didn't remember her past. We created a new present for her. Then suddenly when she went with Helen to a bridal shop, her trauma and forgotten memories came back to her in a flash. To tell you the truth she's since been in heavy mourning for her lost love. I guess it's natural. Perhaps she should go back with you to talk with her psychiatrist. I would like her to stay here with both Helen and me for us to look after her, but I don't want to be selfish. All the time she's been here she has spoken weekly on the phone with the psychiatrist, but maybe she now needs to see him face to face."

Eric looked grim. "In my opinion she needs to see Dr. Strauss. She may need tranquilizers, or maybe not; but she should have some sessions with him so he can evaluate her state of mind. I know our hypercritical parents' home is not the greatest place for her to stay, but I'll be there. I'll run interference."

Sara returned with a tray of various cut fruits and nuts, and tall glasses of iced coffee. She put the tray on a table and turned to Eric. "Did I hear you say you want me to go back to Tampa with you?" Sara asked with a frown.

Eric nodded. "Just for a consultation or two with Dr. Strauss."

"I don't want to be in Mom and Dad's home."

"It won't be for a long time. I'll keep them in check."

"No one can keep our parents in check." Sara sighed, "But I do want to see Dr. Strauss."

*   *   *

REVA SPIRO LUXENBERG

Sara looked around Dr. Strauss's office. She remembered the diplomas and licenses on the walls. She recognized his collection of medical journals and books in the three wooden bookcases with the glass doors. Even the chair she sat on was familiar.

Dr. Strauss removed his reading glasses and waited for Sara to speak. "As I told you on the phone, I remember much more of my life than before," Sara said in a flat voice without any expression on her face.

"How do you feel about your memory returning?" Dr. Strauss asked.

"Ambivalent. I like that I can see in my mind the sights of my childhood and youth—that I remember my family and friends—but I also remember the bad things that happened, like losing Alex, like my parent's criticism of me, like the time I broke my leg, and like other times when I was sick. The worst part was hearing that Alex had died."

"I understand. It was a tragic occurrence. You need time to mourn. Whenever we lose someone very close, it takes a long while to heal. Some people never heal and they don't live life to the fullest."

"Dr. Strauss, my brother and my parents think I should be taking tranquilizers. What is your opinion?" Sara tightly grasped the rests on the armchair. *I don't want a happy pill.*

Dr. Strauss doodled on his pad. "I don't believe in fooling around with your brain. I think psychiatrists and other medical doctors turn too often to pills instead of letting nature heal by itself. Time is your friend. Meanwhile follow the path you have chosen for yourself. Write your novel. Exercise. Get enough sleep. Eat healthy foods. Socialize. Go back to the people who have helped you in the past."

"You mean return to Helen?"

"Why not?"

"I have a new boyfriend. Should I continue to see him?"

"I daresay he's a good person, so dating him will be good for you. Do everything that makes you happy."

"Should I continue seeing you?"

"I do think you need to leave your parent's home and return to the life you built for yourself on the other coast in Florida. If you need to talk with me, I'm available to you on the phone."

*   *   *

Sara left Dr. Strauss's office with more peace of mind than she had before she spoke with him. Eric was waiting for her in his car. "How goes it, Sis?"

Sara climbed into the passenger seat. "Dr. Strauss didn't prescribe tranquilizers for me. He believes I should go back to Palm Oasis, continue to write—and see Rusty."

Eric started driving. "What do you want?"

"I want to go back to Helen's house. I'm not sure about Rusty. He's getting serious, and I don't know what to do."

Eric stopped at a red light. "I'll take you back. I met Rusty, and he adores you. Eventually you'll know what to do. I'm sure he won't rush you."

"I can't be rushed. My mind now focuses all the time on my relationship with Alex and his death." *I feel like a truck ran over me. I can't get involved with anyone right now.*

CHAPTER 39

WHEN LENNY WAS living with Alice, he believed he made a really smart move when he had her sign her Mercedes over to him. Everything was legal. First he bought the car for a buck, and then he went to the Motor Vehicle Bureau for the change of registration. It was easy for him to outsmart the dumb old bag. He even convinced her to pay for the automobile insurance with GEICO, and that was not a small amount. It had been easy to con her into believing that he loved her. She had been enchanted with his looks, bragging to her friends about his abs.

Now he and Tracy were on their way to Las Vegas where he could pick up *muchos dineros*, and start building up a nest egg for their future. He knew his way around the blackjack and poker tables, and if he won big cheating in one casino, he could always move to another casino on The Strip or go to the GOLDEN NUGGET downtown.

He had sold Alice's diamond rings for more than he told her—paid off his gambling debts and kept the rest of the money for the expenses of the trip. He liked to drive the swanky car. It was smooth sailing. Tracy didn't mind sharing the driving for the twenty-five-hundred-mile trip. They started out in the morning, drove through Georgia, and now it was midnight in Alabama. He looked at the passenger seat where Tracy slept with her skirt hiked up all the way, a sight to behold. She wasn't wearing panties, and he had a hard time keeping his mind on driving.

He spotted a motel, pulled off the road, and eased over to the office. He paid with cash and got the key from the spiked-green-haired teen-aged clerk who was fast asleep when he first entered the messy office.

He returned to the car. "Wake up sleepy head," he said as he touched Tracy's shoulder.

Tracy yawned, stretched, and opened her baby-blue eyes. "Are we in Las Vegas yet?"

"Naw, we got a way to go. We're in Alabama. Next stop Mississippi. Come on, I got us a room."

Tracy looked at the rundown motel. "I'm not sleeping in this flea bag."

Lenny bent down and tugged at her corn-colored ponytail.

"Bug off, Lenny. I'm sleeping in the Mercedes."

"Suit yourself," he said as he pulled a suitcase from the back of the car and marched off.

Five minutes later Tracy knocked at the door. "I need the toilet." When she came out of the bathroom with the cracked toilet seat, she dropped on the bed. They were both so exhausted they didn't hear their own heavy snoring. The next day they headed for Mississippi.

As Tracy drove, Lenny began to remember that the last time he had been in Biloxi there were no casinos. The law was so stupid that he had to gamble on a ship that went out ten miles before they opened up the slots and the tables and he came away with a thousand bucks.

But now they had casinos all over the place. They could stay a couple of days—he could make a bundle—and then they could continue their trip through Texas, Oklahoma, New Mexico, Arizona, and finally reach Nevada where he'd clean up.

As Lenny drove to Biloxi, he turned to Tracy who was brushing her hair. "We're checking in at the Hard Rock on the Gulf," Lenny said. "It's a four-star hotel and you'll love it."

"It better be a whole lot better than that dump we stayed at."

"It'll be terrific—you'll see. You deserve the best, baby."

When they checked out and headed toward Ft. Worth, Texas, Lenny had won nine hundred dollars. Tracy was flying high.

They passed through Oklahoma—Tracy looked at the vast empty land. "Miles and miles of nothing," she said in a bored voice.

She took the car over the mountains in New Mexico, and Lenny drove through the desert of Arizona. He had to stop once when a dirt devil enveloped the car and he couldn't see a foot in front of him. They stayed overnight in a Motel Six in Scottsdale, and the next morning headed to Nevada.

It was dark when Lenny drove along the Las Vegas Strip with its bright colored lights. He checked in at Caesars Palace. "You'll love it here, baby. It has so many shops you can buy anything you want. I'll win big here. I can feel it. We're going to celebrate in every one of the eleven restaurants."

That night Lenny lost every cent he brought with him. He turned to Tracy in bed and said, "I ain't got any more dough. I lost what I brought cause I played poker. I'm better at blackjack, but I need more dough. How much did you take with you?"

"Forget it buster," Tracy said. "You're not getting your paws on my money. I put it in the room safe and you don't have the combination."

"I can break into any safe, and I will."

But that night Lenny was so tired he didn't even try. They went to sleep in separate beds since Tracy wouldn't sleep with him.

The next morning Tracy sat at the dressing table. "I've had it with you," she said as she painted her lips a bright red that matched the color of her finger nails and toe nails. Her face was flushed and her eyes flashed as she looked at Lenny who lay spread-eagled on the bed wearing a pair of jockey shorts and nothing else but a gold chain around his neck. It was 115 degrees in the sun and he couldn't play golf. He decided not to answer his girlfriend's comment.

Tracy raised her voice until it was shrill. "You heard me. I've had it with you. You lied about your assets, and I've suffered enough. You're a gambler—a loser—a sleazeball. I'm not using my dough. I'm going down to play the slots. I need five hundred."

Lenny bolted up. "I told you I have no money." No one was going to criticize his gambling ability and get away with it. "You're not worth five cents. Get lost."

Tracy tugged at her mini-skirt, opened the door, and waved goodbye. "I'll get money my way."

Lenny bolted out of the bed, grabbed Tracy by her hair, pulled her away from the door and threw her on the bed. "Once a tramp, always a tramp."

"Let go of me, you loony."

Tracy managed to slap Lenny on his face. He banged her head against the mattress and covered her face with a pillow. Tracy wormed her way out. Lenny planted a kiss on her lips, and Tracy kissed him back. They stayed in bed another hour.

"Now will you give me a few bucks to play around with?" Tracy asked.

"I did lose all the dough. But I know how to get some more."

"How, big shot?"

"I'll call Alice. She always comes across."

Tracy cackled. "Alice? The old witch you married for her money? You're off your trolley if you think she'll part with any more dough— that is if she has any left. I bet you took it all."

"Not every cent. She has more. The old girl thought she had it hidden from me, but I'm smarter than that stupid broad."

Lenny grabbed his cell phone from the drawer in the night table and dialed Alice's number. It rang five times before Alice answered.

"Hi, baby. It's Lenny. I left Tracy and I've been thinking about you and me and how we used to have good times. How are you?"

"Go to hell!"

"Now is that a nice way to talk to your husband?"

"I went to Reno and got a divorce. I never want to see you again, you worm."

"We can get married again. I'm real sorry I left you. I want to fly home, but I need five hundred."

"You're lucky I didn't press charges against you for taking my money."

"We was married when you gave me money. If you pressed charges, you'd look like a lunkhead. The judge would smell a bad rap."

"*Adios muchacho*," Alice said as she hung up.

"I'm hot stuff," Tracy said as she sat down on a chair and crossed her shapely legs. "I can get any man to pay for me. I'm going down to the casino and when I come back up, you'll have a few hundred to gamble with."

"I don't want money from a girl who uses her body. Besides it's illegal to be a ho."

"Ha! This is Nevada in case you forgot. It's legal in Nevada, you jerk."

"Do you have a license?"

"A license is only a piece of worthless paper," Tracy said as she turned to leave the room.

"You're so balled up you don't know nothing," Lenny shouted.

Tracy yelled back, "Barf out. Get a life."

"Stuff a sock in it," Lenny yelled, as Tracy marched out of the room.

REVA SPIRO LUXENBERG

Lenny got dressed and took the elevator down to the casino. As he was playing poker, he moved his hand to the right and grabbed chips from the guy next to him. Cheaters are not tolerated in Las Vegas. He was arrested and subsequently jailed.

Tracy got a job as a warm-up singer in one of the twelve restaurants. She had no interest in bailing Lenny out of jail. She was through with him forever.

CHAPTER 40

SARA AND RUSTY enrolled in graduate classes the following semester. Rusty gave Sara personal space to mourn for her lost love. They continued to eat lunch in the university's cafeteria. Rusty treated Sara like a friend, not like the girl he hoped to marry one day. They studied together in the library, but didn't date. Sara's appetite had diminished, and she looked emaciated and drawn. Her nightmares returned, often interrupting her sleep. Much of the time, she suffered from insomnia.

One night two months later Helen sat down on Sara's bed as Sara sat at her desk working on her laptop. "Oh! I don't want to upset you, but . . ."

"What is it?"

"I understand that you're still in mourning, but you look like a shipwreck in a violent storm. Alex loved you—he wouldn't want to see you looking like moldy cheese. Come with me to the beauty salon tomorrow and get the works."

"Alex isn't here. He doesn't care how I look." Sara's eyes filled with tears.

"I think he's looking down from heaven and wishing you would go on with your life."

"I don't know if there really is a heaven. No one ever came back and told me so." Sara wiped her eyes with her hand.

"It's true that humans don't have certainties about heaven, but in a corner of your soul you do suspect there is one, don't you? If you don't think you are open-minded about heaven, why do you go to his grave and speak to him?"

"How do you know about that?"

"Rusty told me."

Sara took a deep breath. "He shouldn't have said anything—that's private."

Helen stood up, moved closer to Sara, and placed her hand on Sara's head. "At the very least you need a haircut."

"I can't stand your nagging me. Okay, I'll go with you, but I won't have my hair dyed."

*　　*　　*

True to her word Sara had the haircut on Tuesday. On Wednesday when Sara went to class, Bill Kolbe, the ponytailed student built like his Mack truck, sitting next to her whispered, "I like the haircut."

Sara turned her head, "Thanks."

On Thursday Sara put on lipstick. Bill whispered, "You look nice."

On Friday Sara wore a bright blue sundress. On her face she had added pancake makeup and blush and had highlighted her lashes with mascara. *Maybe if I look better, I'll feel better.*

After class Bill approached her. "There's a new movie at the mall. Wanna go?

Should I? What would Rusty think? What would Dr. Strauss say?

"All right, but I want to get home early. I'll go to the movie with you but then I need to go right home."

"Yeah," Bill said. "I'll take you home like you want."

*　　*　　*

On Saturday Rusty and his mother were nibbling on crackers and peanut butter at the kitchen table. Rusty swallowed a mouthful, gulped and said, "Sara is dating a student in our class. I don't know what to do or say."

"That's a good sign that she's getting better." Mrs. Hooper said with a grin. "Now's the time to ask her out, but not on a regular date. Why don't you take her to the golf course?"

"I don't know if she plays golf."

"Teach her. It'll be good for her to go outside, walk on the grass, and be surrounded by the elements of nature."

"I'll have to teach her if she doesn't know the game. Maybe I'll take her to the driving range."

Rusty called Sara and she said she was upset and couldn't go until she calmed down.

"What upset you?" he asked.

"I'd rather not say."

*　　*　　*

In class Bill was a lamb—even in the dark in the movie he behaved like a gentleman—but in the car when Bill drove Sara home, he became a lion. Sara sat in the passenger side of Bill's truck, glad that he was taking her right home after the movie. Meanwhile he reached in the back of his truck and drew out a bottle of whiskey.

"Have some," he offered Sara.

"I don't drink."

"Fine, there's more for me," Bill said as he took a huge gulp.

He waited until he parked in front of Helen's home, and then he pounced.

"What are you doing?" Sara cried.

Bill didn't answer—he put his hand on her left breast and squeezed.

"You're hurting me," Sara yelled. "Let me out."

Sara reached for the door. *It's locked. I can't escape. Why did I agree to go with Bill? Rusty would never act like an animal.*

"You're not leaving," Bill said as he started the motor and spurted ahead. "You act like you're innocent, but I bet you've been around plenty."

"I've been sick and I'm not completely well. Please, please take me home." *I'm so scared. I don't know what to say.*

Bill drove the truck at seventy-five miles an hour up a deserted street with dilapidated houses. Many had broken windows.

He's going to kill us. Sara's heart pounded. Sweat poured down her face.

"Don't put on an act. I'm a good fellow. Just relax and you'll enjoy the rest of the evening." Bill stepped on the gas. The odometer read eight-five miles an hour.

"I don't feel well," Sara cried out.

"You're a phony," Bill said in his raspy voice.

"Stop the car—now."

"We're not there yet, but if you want it right now, I'll give it to you."

"I'm going to be sick."

Bill reached into the seat in the back and pulled out a cardboard box. "Here, if you need to puke do it in this." Bill tore at Sara's dress. He pulled down her panties and opened his fly.

REVA SPIRO LUXENBERG

Sara vomited all over him.

"Shit! Shit! Shit!" Bill zipped up. Speeding like a lunatic, he drove Sara home and dumped her at the front door.

*   *   *

Two nights later the doorbell rang. Helen opened the door to let Rusty in. She led him to the living room where he settled down on the sofa. Helen sat on an armchair with a worried expression.

"Sara hasn't been in class," Rusty said in a low voice as he grabbed a pillow that was next to him.

"I know. She's been hiding in her room except for going to the kitchen to eat like a canary."

"What's wrong?" Rusty clamped down hard on the pillow.

"She won't confide in me. All I surmise is that something bad happened when she went out with that guy from her class. He brought her home. She was covered with vomit, and the louse dumped her at the front door."

"That's awful. I don't trust that fellow. I've seen some of the material he's written and it's weird. I wonder if he assaulted Sara."

Helen's face clouded. "What do you think we should do?"

"I don't know. Let me think." Rusty rose and began to pace the room. "I have it. Sara likes pizza with cheese and anchovies. I'll call and order a pizza."

"Good idea."

When the pizza truck arrived with a steaming pie, Rusty paid the young delivery guy and gave him a generous tip. He brought the pizza to Sara's door and opened the box. The aroma of pizza spread under the door and it caused Sara to peek out. "Rusty, it's you."

"It is I." Rusty bowed trying to affect a royal manner, ". . . and pizza the way you like it."

"How thoughtful! Let me brush my hair and change my clothes and I'll be out in a jiffy."

At the kitchen table Rusty, Sara, and Helen shared the large pizza. "Why are you upset? Please tell us," Helen said.

"It's embarrassing," Sara answered, as she lowered her head.

"Are you pregnant?" Helen asked with a smile.

"Don't be silly," Sara said. "It's the guy I went out with. He had too much to drink and he came on too strong."

"How strong?" Rusty asked.

"Let's just say he wasn't a gentleman. I was terrified and I vomited."

"I'll barbeque him," Rusty said angrily.

"Don't," Sara said. "I want you to drop it. I'll go back to class tomorrow." *I'll change my seat and ignore the animal.*

CHAPTER 41

"DID YOU EVER play golf?" Rusty asked Sara the next day when they were eating lunch in the school cafeteria.

"My brother Eric and I used to play at a public golf course in Tampa. I like golf but I don't have my clubs. I left them at my parents' house."

"I have titanium clubs that you can use—real nice ones. How about playing with me next Sunday?"

Sara took a bite of pizza. She chewed and chewed and chewed and finally swallowed a piece. *Should I go with him? It sounds like he wants to date me.* "I haven't gone golfing for a while. I don't know if I still remember how."

"It'll come back to you. It's like riding a bicycle or driving a car."

"All right—but don't expect too much. I'll be lucky if I can hit the ball."

"I'm a patient teacher," Rusty smiled. "I'll help you."

The following Sunday morning Rusty showed up in his Rolls Royce. Sara was dressed in navy shorts, baby-blue knit shirt, and sneakers. Rusty was wearing golf shoes. He didn't want to damage the rug in the living room with his cleats so he remained standing on the porch until Sara was ready to leave.

"Helen," she called ". . . don't wait up for me. I don't know when we'll be back."

"We'll play the first nine holes today," Rusty said as he drove the Rolls to the public golf course. "If you need help, I'll help you with your form."

"Thanks. I haven't played for so long that I'm sure I've forgotten everything I used to know."

"Today we'll take it easy and walk the course. Next time I'll rent a golf cart. It's a very scenic place we're going to. It'll do you good to breathe in the fresh air."

When they arrived at the golf course, Sara admired the pristine fairways surrounded by stately oaks, pines, and palmettos. "The greens are lush like beautiful carpets," Rusty said as he paid the fee.

He took Sara next to the club house and gave her instructions. "Let me see how you hold the driver before we go to the first hole. I'll put a practice ball down so you can take a strong swing and not hurt anyone."

Sara took the driver in her hands and folded them over it awkwardly. Immediately Rusty corrected her. "You're a righty so you've placed your hands in the right position," he conceded. "But you have to make sure that the angles between your thumbs and index fingers are pointing to your right shoulder. Now move your feet so that they are as wide apart as the distance between your shoulders." Sara complied.

"Now keep your left arm stiff and right arm bent, and swing the driver." Sara took a whack at it and missed the ball.

"You lifted your head. Keep your head down. Try again." Rusty put his hand on Sara's head. This time she made contact.

"I hit the ball," Sara cried out with glee. The practice ball went flying a couple of yards.

By the time they finished the nine holes Sara's complexion had turned from sallow to bright and she felt like a new woman. Rusty hadn't kept score as he wanted to encourage Sara.

They sat at a table in the restaurant next to the clubhouse. Rusty ordered two orange juices and bagels with cream cheese and chives. Sara said, "I had a wonderful time and I want to thank you."

"You can thank me properly by letting me kiss you," Rusty said boldly.

Sara blushed. "I wasn't thinking of expressing my thanks that way."

"Only kidding," Rusty said. "I wouldn't mind kissing you, but we can keep it for another time. You have a very pleasant personality, and I'm much taken with you. Besides you are a very attractive woman."

Tilting her chin to the side Sara said, "When did you last have your eyes examined?"

"There is nothing wrong with my eyes. I see a beautiful woman sitting opposite me."

"Please, let's change the subject," Sara said as her blushing deepened to a scarlet color.

"Okay. I liked the way you hit the ball over the water hazard," Rusty said as he put his hand on Sara's.

Phew! He's coming on to me. I feel tingly all over. I think I really like him.

"Will you go golfing with me again?"

"Sure. You're a much better golfer than I am, but I intend to improve. I wasn't bad in putting, was I?"

"Well—you should actually be able to hit the ball into the cup in two strokes, not four. Putting takes practice. We can work at it together. You can try indoors too on the rug in the living room."

"What do I use for a cup?"

"One of Helen's old cups."

Sara groaned. "Helen doesn't have any old cups."

Rusty took his hand away from Sara's. He picked up his bagel and took a bite. "I'll go to the golf shop and buy you a special plastic cup for indoor practice. I'll get you your own clubs. Women's clubs are smaller, and you'll do much better next time we play."

"Why are you so good to me?"

"I've already indicated how strong my feelings are for you."

"Well, I do like you, but let's talk about something else."

"Politics?"

"No, I don't particularly like politics or politicians."

Rusty sipped his orange juice and finished it. He indicated to the waitress he wanted a refill. "I'm buying two juvenile Amazon grey parrots."

"You are? How come?"

"I'll keep them in my mother's aviary. They make the most wonderful pets."

"Why grey parrots? I like the multicolored ones with bright blue, gold, crimson, and green colors."

Rusty nodded. "Yes, those colorful ones can talk, but grey parrots are the best communicators."

"Why are you getting two? Isn't one enough?"

A thoughtful look came over Rusty's face. "One parrot is socially isolated. A single parrot is less likely to explore and play with toys. Parrots kept in pairs engage with humans. Companions of the same species fill each other's needs."

"You know a lot about parrots and all kinds of birds, don't you?"

"I've always had an interest in birds. I guess I get it from my mother. The best way to teach parrots to talk is not to play a CD with words, but by talking to the bird. You say 'Hello' and 'Good-bye' as you enter and exit the house. You speak enthusiastically and it picks it up."

"Do they really understand what they're saying?"

"Yes. Many experts—though not all—believe that. When you have the bird on a T-stand and feed it food and talk to it, it seems to understand the difference between an apple, a banana, an orange, a seed, and a nut. Eventually it will ask for what it wants. The best way to teach a parrot is to talk to it like a child."

Sara smiled. "Amazing. How many words can it learn?"

"I read that there is a bird who can say 1,770 words, but I'm not aiming to be in *Guinness World Records*. In parrots vocal learning is distributed throughout three brain regions, but it is mostly concentrated in the nidopallium, mesopallium, and arcopallium of the telecephalon."

"Wow!" Sara opened her eyes wide. "You sure have studied parrots. I don't think I need to know all that technical stuff."

"Just trying to impress you," Rusty said with his engaging grin.

"You've succeeded admirably," Sara responded.

CHAPTER 42

TWO WEEKS LATER two juvenile grey parrots in a large cage were making themselves at home in the Hooper residence. "They're beautiful birds," Mrs. Hooper said. "You can keep them in the living room during the day and in the aviary at night."

"Good idea, Ma," Rusty said. "The smaller one I'm calling Stone and the larger one Granite because of their gray color." Rusty addressed the birds singly, "Hello Stone. Hello Granite." The birds looked at him like he came from outer space. They did not utter a single word between them.

"I'll try leaving the room," Rusty said. He looked directly at the birds with their round black eyes and said enthusiastically, "Goodbye." The birds eyed him like he came from the other side of the universe.

"Try it with fruit," Mrs. Hooper suggested.

"Good idea." Rusty went into the kitchen and came out with pieces of apple. He took each bird out of the cage and set them on T-stands. He approached Granite with the apple and held it out as he said "Apple." Granite took the apple without thanking him. He did the same with Stone and got the same result.

This went on for three weeks—five times a day—until Granite said "Apple." Rusty was so thrilled he ran to the refrigerator and pulled out a whole apple.

In a month both parrots were asking for apples by name. By this time Rusty had a photo of Sara that he showed the parrots. To Stone he said, "Sara, I love you. To Granite he said, "Sara, marry me." Rusty kept repeating these phrases whenever he had a chance. The parrots needed another month before responding and repeating in turn over and over "Sara, I love you. Sara, marry me." This was the result Rusty had been waiting for. Now all he needed was to bring both birds to Helen's house. Stone would emphasize his love for Sara, and Granite would propose for him.

*   *   *

Sara sat on her bed and dialed Dr. Strauss. She was in a quandary, not knowing if she should encourage Rusty. She had started to date him on a regular basis, but didn't say a word to her critical parents about him. She could almost hear her mother say, "A redhead. We never had a redhead in our family." Or her father might say, "His mother raises birds? Quack, quack. She must be crackers. Polly want a cracker?"

"Hello, Dr. Strauss."

"How are you, Sara?"

"I need to talk to you."

"That's plainly evident. I have time now. What's bothering you?"

"You know I've been dating this guy in my class and he's getting really serious. It frightens me."

"What frightens you about this relationship?"

Sara wiped perspiration from her forehead. "I guess I'm afraid if I marry him, something will happen and he'll die and I'll lose my memory."

"I believe the chance of that happening is almost nil. Does this fellow make you happy?"

"Yes, he does."

"You want to be happy, don't you?"

"I do."

"Then you have your answer."

*　　*　　*

The temperature was a perfect sixty-eight degrees on the first of January when Sara and Rusty came to the seventh hole. Sara teed up and drove the ball one hundred and fifty yards. "Great shot," Rusty called out. "It flew straight down the fairway. I'll see if I can match you."

"Don't be silly," Sara said. "You'll hit much further. You always do." Sara stood off to the side. An elderly man hit his ball from the middle of the sixth hole. His voice was weak when he cried out "Fore." The ball came at Rusty like a bullet and struck his head.

Sara screamed, "No!" as Rusty collapsed on the grass. She bent down to examine him and felt a huge lump on the right side of his head. She tried to awaken him but Rusty was unconscious. Sara wrung her hands while tears rolled down her face.

*   *   *

Two Emergency Medical Technicians from the Palm Oasis Fire Department put Rusty on a gurney and moved him over the grass to the waiting ambulance. "Let's go easy with this one," the stout EMT said to his partner. "Drive the bus carefully. He has a head injury and a swelling that's ballooning as we talk."

The siren wailed as the ambulance went through the streets with Sara following in Rusty's car. She couldn't stop the flow of tears from her eyes. *Please God, make Rusty all right.*

*   *   *

Rusty remained in the hospital for a week while many tests were administered to diagnose the extent of his injury. The prognosis was positive that the patient would recover. Rusty didn't need an operation, just rest and his brain would heal. Sara and Rusty's mother remained at his side day and night.

At the end of the week Rusty opened his eyes one night at midnight. "My darling," Sara said, "How do you feel?"

"Where am I?" Rusty asked.

"In a hospital. You were hit on the head with a golf ball."

"I was? How long have I been here?"

"A week—but you're all right now. Your mother left an hour ago. I wanted to stay here and I'm glad I did. You had me really worried."

"You do care for me, don't you?"

"You better believe it." Sara took Rusty's hand and kissed it.

"I'd feel much better with your lips on mine," Rusty said as he pointed to his mouth.

Sara leaned over the bed and planted a kiss on Rusty lips. *I do care for him so very much.*

*   *   *

One summer day Rusty told Sara he had an invitation from Winthrop University in Rock Hill, South Carolina to come for an interview for the position of assistant professor of Modern British Literature.

"I'll be gone for four days," Rusty told Sara.

Sara looked sad. "I'll miss you."

"It's only four days—two days driving and two days at the university. They're putting me up in a nice hotel."

The morning that Rusty left Sara decided to skip her shower and she took a bath instead. She sat in the soothing warm water in the tub, closed her eyes, and remembered being in college with Rusty—how many times he was kind to her—and how happy he made her in the past.

Sara stepped out of the tub, dried herself with the bath towel, put on her clothes, and knocked at Helen's bedroom door. "Rusty's been so good to me. I never want to lose him. I love him from the bottom of my heart."

Helen hugged Sara with a bear hug. "I'm so happy for you. Now the both of us can get married."

"He hasn't asked me yet."

"He loves you. He will ask you as soon."

"Are you sure?"

"Of course—I'm as certain as George and I marrying."

"I'm making an appointment for the beauty salon. I want to look good when Rusty returns."

*   *   *

Rusty came back with good news. He was hired by Winthrop University for the period of three years. "Sara, you should see this place. There are so many buildings in this university that I was overwhelmed by the size. I had pictured a much smaller place. Most everything is modern. The people in South Carolina are very friendly and nice."

"I'm glad to hear your good news."

Rusty extended his arms. "Come here and let me kiss you."

The kiss was a long one. When they broke apart, Rusty said, "I'd like to take you home right now."

"Okay, let's go. I'd love to see your mother again," Sara said with a big smile.

Rusty drove Sara to his home but didn't get out of the car. "Ring the bell and go on in," he said. "I promised my mother when I got back

I'd bring her a quart of rum raisin ice cream. It'll take me ten minutes and I'll be back. Meanwhile catch up with my mother."

"All right."

After Sara rang the bell, Mrs. Hooper welcomed her with a smile and a big hug. She led Sara into the living room where Stone and Granite were on T-stands.

Sara looked at the parrots and they looked at her. "Hello," Stone said in Rusty's voice.

"Sara, I love you," the parrot said.

Sara's eyes widened. "Sara, marry me," Granite said.

"I'll marry you," Sara said.

"You'll marry the parrot?" Mrs. Hooper asked.

"No, I'll marry Rusty."

CHAPTER 43

ALICE'S RENEWED TROUBLES started after Lenny left her for Tracy and she had to divorce him. Alice always had a weakness for men who, though liberal with praise and attention, lacked honesty and trustworthiness. When she realized that her twin, Helen, had found true love on a dating service, Alice copied her sister. The initial results were meager and she went on a couple of lackluster dates.

However, one time she found a man who described himself as a financially stable sixty-five-year-old widower in good health. His screen name was mysterious—"TallandHandsome"— and he said he liked anything with chocolate. He lived in Hollywood, Florida, which wasn't too far from her home. The photo showed a good-looking man with salt-and-pepper hair. Alice was intrigued and wrote to him.

Two weeks later he answered: "Thanks for the e-mail. I'm sorry for not answering sooner, but I don't go online often. I like what you wrote about yourself, as you sound like an interesting person who has had the misfortune of getting divorced through no fault of your own. Your photo shows that you are a lovely woman. I'd like to know more about you. Please e-mail more pictures and tell me more about yourself." He gave Alice his e-mail address, Louis@i.cloud.com.

Louis seemed honest. He forwarded an attractive picture of himself. She always liked tall men and he had written he was six feet tall. In his next message he wrote he was a computer programmer and had lived most of his life in Manhattan except for his youth in London, England. Louis suggested meeting at the scenic Morikami Museum and Japanese Gardens, a noted center for Japanese arts and culture, and dining in the open-air Cornell Café on the terrace overlooking the tranquil gardens. She'd be delighted, he said, with their special vegetarian dish of rice, stir-fried vegetables, dumplings, Asian eggplant, noodles, green salad, and egg rolls. This, he wrote, is the ideal meeting place for him and such a nice woman as she appeared to be in her photo. When he had visited the place last month by himself, he said he felt lonely and realized he wanted a woman with whom to share his life.

Alice had never had a man offer to bring her to such an exotic place, and she was thrilled. Obviously as a vegetarian he must be healthy. Sara's brother was a vegetarian, and he had said that meat shortens your life. She wrote, "You seem different from the men I've met. Some men are so dishonest that it angers me."

Louis wrote back, "Dishonesty is a trait I abhor."

For a month they exchanged e-mails. Louis asked probing questions about such matters as her favorite hobbies, quirks, foods, sleeping habits, and financial status. He sounded so very intelligent and he sent her a special stanza that he composed about 'her hair streaked with sunlight, her lips red as flame, her face with a luster that puts gold to shame.' I had a dream he wrote, that our relationship will in time become permanent. We have a lot in common.

Gradually Alice fell in love with Louis over the Internet. When she visited Helen, she told her she was in touch with a man who sounded like a perfect suitor. "You and I are twins," she said, ". . . and twins have similar fates. You found the man of your dreams and I think I did too."

Somehow Helen felt a twinge of suspicion as far as Louis was concerned. He sounded too good to be true. It seemed that he should have met Alice by now, but Alice protested that he was always travelling on business. "You're too gullible," Helen warned her.

"I've spoken to him many times," Alice said. "His voice is soft, and I love his British accent. He keeps e-mailing me and texting too. I told him all about Lenny and how he deserted me and also how he kidnapped your cat. He said that was despicable. He's so empathetic."

When Alice went home, she wondered why he was still working if he was as financially secure as he claimed. He had said he loves to work, but that he feels terrible that he's far away from her.

"Where are you now?" Alice asked on the phone.

"I'm in Malaysia doing programming for a fabrics company."

The fact that Louis loved to travel and to work were positive aspects in Alice's opinion, but she wished she could meet him in person, and especially be with him in the Japanese gardens that sounded so romantic.

One bright morning Alice answered the door to find a messenger holding a glass vase filled with lilies and roses as well as a large box of chocolates. Her jaw dropped. The card read, "I wish I could give this to you in person and see your lovely smiling face. Louis."

An hour later Louis called. "Did you get the flowers?"

"Thank you so much. I was so surprised. You are the kindest man I ever knew. Thank you. Thank you."

"Let me tell you what the flowers are. They are white Asiatic lilies, white roses, and white mini-carnations with lush greens. They represent my deep feelings for you."

Alice went to bed that night with the bouquet next to her. She sat in bed eating some of the delicious chocolates Louis had thoughtfully sent her. She was consumed by love for this unusual man.

She kept e-mailing him about how her twin sister was planning to marry soon and how she wished he could attend the wedding. He wrote that he was in Kuala Lumpur and how awful he found the climate, but that he was thinking about their future meeting in the Japanese gardens in Miami.

When Alice went to visit Helen, she told her sister about how Louis had sent her flowers and how he wants to meet her in the Morikami Museum and Japanese Gardens in Miami.

"Miami?" Helen said suspiciously. "The Morikami is in Delray Beach, not Miami."

"Oh?" Alice said as her brow twitched. "He must've meant Delray Beach."

"Has he asked you for money?"

"Sort of. He said he's planning to retire after this last project, but he's stuck in customs and they are demanding money, and he has a trust fund that he can't liquidate at this point. He did ask me to wire him a thousand dollars and I did. He promised to pay me back as soon as he returns."

"Watch out," Helen warned. "Be careful if he asks you for more."

"The man is so decent. He's not a crook. Relax, Helen. You'll meet him soon."

That night Alice tossed and turned in her queen-sized bed. Even though the air-conditioning was on, her nightgown became soaked with perspiration. She woke the next morning when the phone rang. She rubbed her eyes and picked up the landline on the night table. "It's Helen. Remember you told me that Louis sent you the poetic lines, 'her hair streaked with sunlight, her lips red as flame, her face with a luster that puts gold to shame.'"

Alice stretched. "Yes, aren't those words beautiful? He was alluding to my beauty."

"No," Helen said. "The words aren't his. I recalled hearing them when I saw the show *Camelot*. The words are from the song *If Ever I Would Leave You*. I looked this up online. The words are almost identical, '*Your hair streaked with sunlight, Your lips red as flame, Your face with a luster, That puts gold to shame.*' Now what do you think of this plagiarist?"

"I think you're making too much of a small white lie. You agree the words are beautiful, and so the man thought that also, and he sent them to me. Just because Lenny deceived me, doesn't mean that Louis will too."

∗   ∗   ∗

A day later when Alice went on line with Google and found an e-mail from Louis she was surprised that he was in trouble. He begged her to send him $12,000 because his visa had expired and he needed to bribe officials to let him leave the country.

Alice answered him that she didn't have $12,000 but if she did she would immediately send it to him.

Louis answered that he had set next Sunday for his flight home and he was forwarding his itinerary. "You told me your home without a mortgage is worth over a million dollars. Can't you get a home equity loan from your bank?"

Alice felt she had to do anything she could to get Louis on the plane back to Florida. She applied at her bank and was turned down as her income wasn't enough to cover the loan. She took out the jewelry from her safe deposit box. She had kept this hidden away, so Lenny hadn't known about it. She pawned the biggest diamonds and came away with $15,000. He could probably use an extra $3,000. She wired Louis the whole amount to pay for the bribe and his airline ticket.

Alice called Helen and told her she'd soon be meeting Louis. She was so excited that he was coming home and she'd meet him in person at last.

His next e-mail said he had gotten injured by an automobile and was in the hospital. They wouldn't treat him for internal injuries unless he paid them another $15,000.

By this time doubt crept in and finally Alice showed up in Helen's house and revealed she had sent $16,000 to Louis—$1,000 when he got stuck in customs—$15,000 the next time when his visa expired and he needed bribe money to leave the country. She was upset and finally decided not to send another cent. As a result his phone calls, texts, and e-mails had ended.

When Helen heard this atrocity her face turned ashen. "Something has to be done but I don't know what. I'll call George and ask him."

"Don't call him," Alice cried. "It's too embarrassing."

"I must call and ask his opinion," Helen insisted. She picked up the phone and told George the sad news while Alice stood by with a handkerchief dabbing at her moist eyes.

"Take your sister to the FBI office and tell them everything," George advised.

"Alice is afraid to report this crime. She thinks it's her fault for falling for a man she never even met." Helen clutched the phone tightly.

"If Alice doesn't report this criminal, he'll go on stealing money from other women. She has a duty to impart whatever information she has about this crook."

Helen finally convinced Alice to accompany her to the regional FBI office. A special agent took down Alice's report. The man told her that the FBI receives close to 13,000 complaints a year related to online-dating fraud. Victims have lost as much as two million dollars.

"You're lucky," he said, "...that you lost only $16,000. The last woman I interviewed lost $600,000. The duplicity of these clever tricksters is astounding. Eventually criminals in such places as Malaysia and Nigeria are arrested, but the chance of arresting the offender in your case is slim. You are left with psychological trauma. I recommend that you seek out a support group for victims."

Alice blew her nose. "I don't need a support group."

The agent continued, "It can help you. As a result of this crime you have to cope with the end of a serious relationship, and you will probably blame yourself, but you have to remember that you're a victim."

"He sent me pictures of himself," Alice wailed.

The agent nodded. "The bastard got it from the Internet. You'll never know what he really looks like."

"Let's go out to eat," Helen said as she took her sister by the arm and guided her out the office. "Life goes on, and the next man you meet may be the right one."

"I never want to see another man," Alice said sadly.

REVA SPIRO LUXENBERG

CHAPTER 44

I N THE EARLY evening Helen and Sara sat on the sofa in the living room conversing in soft tones that belied their alarm at Alice's behavior. "The special agent from the FBI said that Alice is a victim of a crime," Helen said, ". . . but he doesn't know that my sister has always been naïve where men are concerned."

"Are you afraid she'll repeat this self-destructive pattern?" Sara asked.

"Of course I'm concerned. She said she'll avoid men, but I don't believe her. Once she stops mourning for this phony lost love, she'll be on the hunt again."

"You told me the special agent did suggest that Alice could benefit from attending a support group for victims," Sara said.

"How can we find such a group?" Helen asked.

"I bet the special agent knows of one."

Helen frowned. "It sounds like a good idea, but I don't think Alice would go. She can be very oppositional."

"You never know unless you try," Sara said with optimism.

*   *   *

A day later Helen called her sister. "How are you?"

Alice groaned. "I feel like a dish towel. I have no appetite and all I think about is the man I lost."

"You lost a fantasy, not a man. I called the special agent and found there's a support group in the next town from where you live. I believe you'll feel better sharing your experience with other people who are also suffering."

"I'm in no shape to go where there are people. My hair is a mess. My face broke out with a rash and I have no energy to drive."

"I'll take you to the beauty salon. I'll drive you to the support group. I love you and I want you to feel better." *I hope my sister will listen to me. Not only is her hair a mess, she's a psychological mess.*

"I don't think so."

"Please, Alice. I want you to be in good shape when I get married."

"I don't feel like going to a wedding."

"I expect you to go. I'm choosing you as my maid of honor."

"You can pick Sara."

"No, I can't select Sara as she and I have decided to have double weddings."

"Really? How quaint. Thank you, Helen. I always wanted to be a maid of honor. Okay, I'll go to the beauty salon by myself. I'll cover the rash with makeup, and I'll drive myself to the support group—but I won't cry in front of people."

"That's good. Call me if you need anything. Bye now. I love you."

*   *   *

The support group met at 6 p.m. in the austere basement of the Episcopalian church. When Alice entered the room fifteen minutes late, she was dressed in navy slacks with a bold flowery ruffled blouse and long strands of multicolored beads that matched her earrings and bracelets. She gazed in wonder at the five women and one man seated in a circle and her face reddened with embarrassment. They were all dressed informally and she mistakenly had overdressed. Every woman had short unadorned hair and hers was dyed and groomed like she was ready to be photographed for *Cosmopolitan.*

The woman in the center stood up and moved over to her in an extended handshake. "Welcome," she said warmly. "I'm Stephanie, the social worker, and you must be Alice."

"I *am* Alice," she said as she shook Stephanie's hand.

"We made room for you in the chair next to Ivy. Please take a seat and we'll introduce ourselves. Everyone, this is Alice. Let's go around the circle and tell her your first names."

"Welcome, Alice. My name is Ivy."

Alice looked at the young woman next to her who was obviously obese and plain- looking. *I can understand why she was taken in by the crook.*

The next woman had tears running down her thin cheeks. "Welcome, Alice. I'm Rachel."

The small man dressed in shorts looked her in the eye. "Welcome, Alice. My name is Ralph."

"I'm Betty—welcome Alice," the next woman said with a stern expression.

Alice nodded to Betty. *They sound like they've been well rehearsed.*

The last woman looked like she was in her eighties. "Welcome, Alice. I'm Dixie."

Everyone had their eyes on Stephanie. "What we say here is confidential. You are not to repeat anything to anyone. In this way everyone's privacy is protected. All of you are free to express yourselves. At the end of the session we gather together, hold hands, and say a silent prayer. Then in the next room there are refreshments laid out for you. You may socialize or leave—however you feel. Anyway we have to be out of the building by 8:30 p.m."

Alice felt awkward. She wasn't going to be the first one to speak. Dixie held up her hand and was recognized by Stephanie.

"I'm a retired university professor and that means I'm intelligent, doesn't it? But still and all I was duped by a criminal and lost all my savings. I'm glad I have my social security and pension. Otherwise I'd be in the poor house."

Betty spoke up, "You think you're intelligent? What about me? I'm a civil lawyer and I should've known better. My whole family has come down hard on me. You should hear the names they're calling me."

Stephanie looked at both women. "Your intelligence has nothing to do with what happened to you. Did the criminal reach out to you first, or did you e-mail him or her, and then he or she answered? Raise your hand if this was the procedure."

Every hand in the room went up.

Stephanie said, "Look around. Everyone's hand is raised. These perpetrators are sharpies. They wait for their victims to come to them. Stop blaming yourselves, and tell your friends and family to lay off. Let's hear from Rachel."

Rachel wiped off her tear-streaked face. "I'm too depressed to talk. Please skip me today."

"All right," Stephanie said. "What about Ivy?"

"I'm doing better," Ivy said. "This week I didn't have any ice cream. I'm proud of myself."

"We're proud of you too," Stephanie responded. "You're very quiet today, Ralph."

"Just thinking," Ralph said. "After I lost my wife, I was so lonesome that when I went online and found a woman who showed interest in me, I was hooked. She was very sympathetic. When she said she had also lost her husband to malaria, I should've realized that no one in Florida dies from malaria. I should've known that the e-mail was coming from Nigeria."

"You're still blaming yourself," Stephanie said, ". . . and that's not helping you heal. Alice, do you feel like talking tonight?"

"My sister says I'm naïve and I guess she's right. I sent $16,000 on a promise from a stranger."

Rachel piped up. "That's nothing. I wired $60,000 and I'll never see it again."

Stephanie closed by saying, "Your money has been stolen by a crook in an elaborate scam operation. Say goodbye to it, but keep on with your lives and look to tomorrow. See you all next week. Have a good week."

Stephanie left the building bidding everyone goodbye. Ivy, Rachel, Betty, Dixie, Alice, and Ralph filed into the next room where plates had been left piled high with pound cake, chocolate chip cookies, and baby carrots. An urn with hot water had been placed on a metal table next to a china bowl filled with various organic tea bags, a jar of Folger's decaf coffee, and a pitcher of lemonade. Ivy took a small paper plate and filled her paper plate with baby carrots and a slice of pound cake. The others ignored the carrots and went for the cookies and lemonade. They made their way back to the room where they sat with their plates and paper cups.

Alice sat next to Ralph and spoke in low tones to him. "I had no idea that women were involved in scamming men."

"It's a terrible shame. They should be punished for all the damage they cause. We older people are really vulnerable, but younger ones like Ivy are susceptible too. Did you lose your husband?"

"I did, but not to death. He was a scoundrel who deserted me for a younger woman."

"That's too bad." Ralph's voice was sympathetic. "I lost $25,000, but that's not what's bothering me. I'm a retired engineer and I'm comfortable. What gets me is that I fell for this scheme."

"Stephanie said not to blame yourself."

"I can't help it."

"I keep thinking about the crook telling me he'd take me to Morikami Japanese Gardens and about how I was looking forward to going."

"Were you? There's no reason you can't go. How about going with me?"

Should I? He's not my type. He's short and kind of plain looking with that big nose, but what the hell. "Thank you. I'd love to go with you."

CHAPTER 45

ON A BRIGHT sunny Sunday in February Alice and her new friend Ralph sat at a table on the terrace of the Cornell Café at the Morikami Museum and Japanese Gardens.

"It's so peaceful here," Alice said as she put down her half-eaten egg roll. She took a deep breath and sighed, "I wish I could forget how Lenny and that other despicable crook stole my money."

Ralph took his last sip of Japanese tea and wiped his mouth with the napkin. "I've been trying to forget too. If we wouldn't talk about our horrible experience, it would help. Just look around at these lovely gardens. The Japanese were sorely defeated in World War II and yet they rebuilt their country afterwards, and went on with their lives. We should do the same. What do you think?"

"You're absolutely right. Here, ironically, I need to forget, whereas a young friend of my sister suffered a terrible trauma and forgot her whole life until her memory returned."

"Now you're talking sensibly."

Alice bit into the last of the egg rolls with relish.

"We've seen the museum and all the gardens," Ralph said, "but we missed the gift shop. Would you like to go there?"

"Sure, I love shopping. It's one of my favorite hobbies. Oh—that's what I told the crook Louis when he wanted to know my hobbies."

"Now Alice—try to forget Louis. You're with me, and I'm happy to be with you. So let's go and see what's in the shop."

He just said he's happy to be with me. How nice. Alice smiled and stood up—ready to go to the Japanese gift shop.

They browsed there, and Ralph bought her a kimono that appealed to her.

*   *   *

After Ralph took her home, the first thing Alice did was to call her sister.

"Hi, Helen. I just had the most fabulous time and I called to tell you all about it."

"I just stepped out of the shower and I'm still drying off." Helen held the phone to her ear and dried her body while she stood next to the bed.

"I'll wait. You just have to hear what happened today."

Alice, smiling all the while, held the phone in her hand until Helen, dressed in a cotton robe, picked up two minutes later.

"All right, I'm ready. "What happened?"

Alice in a chipper voice said, "There's a new man in my life and his name is Ralph."

Helen dropped down on her bed and cried out, "Oh, my God— you've gone online again. Just when will you learn to be cautious?"

"No, no, it's not like that."

"Were you so desperate you got fixed up by someone?"

In a disgusted voice Alice said, "I went to the support group and met Ralph there. We got to talking and he asked me to go to the Morikami with him. He's my height and not handsome like Lenny, but he is nice."

"You met another victim and right away you went on a date with him?"

"He asked me out. He was pleasant, and I didn't want to refuse."

"Why didn't you call me before you agreed to go on a date with a stranger?"

"Do I need your permission? I'm not a child—As a matter of fact I'm fifteen minutes older than you."

"Oh my goodness! Big deal—fifteen minutes is a really long time. You think he's nice? You know nothing about this man and yet you think he's nice."

"He *is* nice," Alice protested. "He bought me the loveliest kimono. He said he couldn't resist buying it for me because I'm such a beautiful woman."

"You'll never learn. The man is a flatterer. You said you wouldn't be attracted to another man—that you wanted to stay away from men, and now you've gone back on your word."

"Don't you think I've suffered enough? How could I let this opportunity slip by? Now you've aggravated me. I can't talk anymore. Goodbye."

*　　*　　*

Sara was sitting on the sofa filing her nails when Helen walked in with a long face. "What's the matter?" Sara asked as she patted the spot next to her.

Helen sat down and pursed her lips.

"Is something wrong with George?" Sara asked.

"No—it's Alice. She's at it again."

"Oh," Sara said. "She's despondent and hasn't gone to the support group."

"No, that's the problem—she went to the support group. She's not depressed. She's elated. She met a man and already went out with him, and he bought her a kimono which means he wants to see her take it off. She'll wind up like a geisha girl."

Sara chuckled. "I think you're making far-fetched assumptions. I know you love your sister and want to protect her, but she's your age and has to make her own decisions. For all you know this man may be decent."

"I don't think so. On a first date you don't buy a gift for a woman unless your intentions aren't pure."

Sara frowned. "How come he bought her a kimono—that's an unusual gift?"

"They went to Morikami and my sister loves clothes. She must've seen this kimono and raved about it, and so he bought it for her."

"That's so sweet."

Helen balled her hands into fists. "Alice has always been taken in by a man's flattery, and if we knew something about this man's background, it would be different—but he could be married, or have a prison record, or just be looking for a woman to con."

Sara arched her back and took a deep breath. "It takes time to get to know a person. I'm sure that Alice has some judgment; after all she's had a certain amount of experience with men."

"I have thought of that also. She does have experience, but hasn't benefitted enough from it."

*　　*　　*

The next time that Ralph took Alice out on a date he took her to downtown Delray Beach where there were restaurants galore. He selected a cozy elegant seafood restaurant. Even though it was dinner time they were the only customers in the room. The waiter came to their booth and recited the entire menu. There were no written menus so Alice concluded that the restaurant was an expensive one and that Ralph didn't concern himself with price.

"Drinks?" the waiter asked.

"I'd like lemonade please," Alice said.

"I'll have a martini." Ralph looked up at the waiter who was dressed in a T-shirt designed like a tuxedo and in black shorts which displayed his hairy legs.

"Order whatever dish you like," Ralph encouraged her.

After the final order had been given, they waited a half-hour until the salmon with sweet potato fries came. Meanwhile Alice had time to question Ralph about his life.

"This is a fine restaurant," Alice remarked casually. "Did you used to come here with your wife?"

"Yes, we came here occasionally. I shouldn't have brought you here, except that I know that this restaurant serves good food, and I'm not that familiar with other Delray places. Mainly we ate at home. I'd rather not talk about my life with my wife if you don't mind."

"I understand," Alice said. "But I would like to know if you had children with her?"

"Oh, I see. Yes, we had two boys. They have taken over my business. I retired when I turned sixty-five last March."

I don't like that he's two years younger than I. Of course Lenny was twenty years younger. Two years isn't so much.

"Do you have children?" Ralph asked.

"No. My husband didn't like children so we never had any. What business did you retire from?"

"I was a manufacturer of women's brassieres of all sizes and styles."

"How unusual." *I guess someone has to make bras for women.*

"Someone must do it, and since there was a market for it after I got out of the Army, I went into my own business with money saved up. Gradually it expanded and I was able to export my wares all over the world. After all many millions of women need brassieres."

What will Helen say when she asks if I've gone out again with Ralph—and especially what should I say when she asks me how he made his living? It's not easy to have a twin who pries into your life.

CHAPTER 46

ALICE AND RALPH continued dating despite Helen's objection. They attended the support group without revealing to Helen or to the members of the group their developing relationship. "Let's not tell anyone of our friendship," Alice said to Ralph, and he agreed, wanting to please her.

A couple of months passed as they explored various restaurants, went to movies, and took a cruise to the Bahamas. When Helen called, Alice was cool to her and, resenting her sister's attitude toward Ralph, she reported only that she was all right and busy with friends.

One early morning Helen showed up unannounced at Alice's home. Helen was concerned about her and she hoped she would find her sister in satisfactory health and good spirits. She missed their former closeness and thought a visit could produce reconciliation and return them to their previous friendly state.

Helen had a premonition that Ralph had moved into Alice's house and that was her reason for the early visit. She had to find out the truth even at the expense of Alice's anger. Sisters had an obligation to protect each other—and that held doubly for twins.

Helen pressed the bell and was greeted with the ringing of chimes playing *Dixie*. She waited a minute before she rang the bell a second time, and this time she heard someone approaching the door. It was Alice with her hair in curlers and without makeup. To Helen's dismay she was dressed in a lovely Japanese kimono with the print of peonies.

"You woke me up," Alice said, squinting from the harsh morning light. "I hope you have had a good reason for not calling for such a long while."

"Are you going to ask me in?" Helen stood tapping her foot on the porch, an angry expression on her face.

"Follow me to my bedroom," Alice said. "I'll talk to you right after I go to the bathroom."

Helen marched after Alice. *If she's taking me to her bedroom, it probably means Ralph isn't there.*

They walked through the modern well-furnished black and white living room past the sewing room which was next to the guest bedroom. Helen looked through the open door of the guest bedroom wondering if Ralph was sleeping there. The unoccupied queen-sized bed was covered in a flowered bedspread. Helen moved to Alice's master bedroom and was aghast when she saw dozens of bras piled up on a chaise lounge. Quickly she picked one up. It was covered with a pretty pink satin material. She opened her purse and removed her reading glasses. The label read '34B' which was both their sizes. *But why did Alice need so many bras?*

Helen looked at the name of the manufacturer—'Esposito'. *Never heard of that name.* The label read 'Made in U.S.'

When Alice came in, she saw her sister looking at the label on one of the bras. "They're our size. Help yourself to as many as you want."

"Well, I can't pick one right now."

"You can't use a new bra?"

"Not now."

"How are you?" Alice asked, as she dropped down on the unmade bed.

"I'm fine, but I'm concerned about you."

"I'm alive. Why haven't you called?"

Helen pushed aside the pile of bras and sat down on the chaise lounge. "The last time we spoke you were upset with me, and it was you who never called me back."

"I was angry that you're putting your nose where it shouldn't be. I'm now asking you the same question—why haven't you called me?"

"I thought you wouldn't talk to me. Finally I decided to come over."

Alice's eye twitched. "Why did you show up on my doorstep so early? And don't tell me that you wanted to find me home."

"I am concerned about your physical and emotional health."

Alice raised her voice. "Why don't you tell the truth? It's my relationship with a new man isn't it?"

What should I say? I don't want to get her angry but I am afraid that she doesn't know what she's doing. "I do think you started dating too fast after the last escapade."

"So, you call what happened to me an escapade? I was a victim and now that I've met another man you're worried that he's going to take advantage of me. Isn't that right?"

Helen nodded. "In short, yes, I am worried about you. For instance, what's this man's full name?"

"You think I don't know it? His name is Ralph Simon Esposito."

"Esposito? That's not a Jewish name."

"You're right. It's an Italian name."

"You're going with a non-Jew? Dad would roll over in his grave if he knew you were dating an Italian."

"First of all, Dad is not here. Secondly, Ralph is not an Italian. He was born in Brooklyn. Third, his father was Italian, but his mother was Jewish, so according to Jewish law he's Jewish."

Helen decided to change the subject. "So where did you get all these bras?"

"Ralph gave them to me."

"Ah, ha! He wants you to model them so he can take advantage of you."

"Once again, you're coming to the wrong conclusion. After Ralph was discharged from the Army where he received a medal for bravery, he had $4,800 dollars to invest. His neighbor's wife was a dressmaker and she was sewing bras for larger women. Ralph took his money and with the help of this dressmaker went into manufacturing bras for all sizes and all ages."

"I hate bras with underwires," Helen said.

"That's the precise reason his company was so successful. He never made bras with underwires. He named the company Esposito and they expanded with improvements in fabrics, colors, styles, padding, and elasticity. He even introduced new types of training bras. He went international and became rich. He just retired and now his two sons are running the business. So you think you're so smart. You know everything. But Helen you are wrong about Ralph and you owe me an apology."

Helen's face reddened. "I'm sorry."

"I accept your apology. Here take a handful of bras and make me happy. Give a few to Sara."

* * *

That afternoon when Ralph came over to take Alice to the beach, they spoke in the living room before going out.

REVA SPIRO LUXENBERG

"My sister showed up unexpectedly this morning," Alice said as she sat close to Ralph on the black leather love seat.

"What did you talk about?" Ralph asked as he put his arm around Alice's shoulder.

"Naturally, you were the subject of our conversation."

"Did you tell her my last name?"

"I did and she almost hit the ceiling."

Ralph grinned. "Did you add that I'm a member of the Reform temple?"

Alice smiled. "She doesn't have to know everything."

"How are you coming along with the new pattern for the Alice bra?"

Alice rose and went to the sewing room bringing back an Alice pattern and a finished bra that she had designed. It was created with flamingo pink polyester material shaped with heart-shaped cups. One side had an inside pocket inserted with a rose sachet that would release a pleasant aroma when the woman wore the bra. She handed it to Ralph who turned it over and over in his hands.

"It's a beauty. I'll give the pattern and the sample to my sons and they'll begin production for the coming season."

"That's wonderful. My sister never had anything named after her."

"Did you tell her we're engaged?"

"Are we? I didn't know that," Alice said as she gave Ralph a kiss on his lips.

*   *   *

Helen could hardly wait until Sara came home to tell her about what had happened at her sister's home.

"She's still going with that guy, but she seems happier than I've ever seen her."

Sara and Helen sat at the kitchen table drinking iced coffee. "That's great," Sara said. "I couldn't have imagined such a fine outcome."

"Do you know," Helen asked, ". . . Alice has loads of bras given to her by Ralph. He was in the bra manufacturing business, and now his sons have taken over."

"Bras?"

"Yes. I have a large bunch of bras. I'll give you a few. I'm sure there will be more for both of us whenever we might need them. They're beautiful. You can take them with you on your honeymoon."

"Thank you," Sara said. *If you would have told me that I would get bras from Helen's sister, I would've said that's impossible. Life is truly unpredictable!*

CHAPTER 47

WHEN SARA ENTERED the kitchen, she saw Helen seated at the table drinking her morning orange juice. "I'm so happy about being engaged to Rusty that I wish I didn't have to let my parents know about it now. In fact, I'd like to tell them after we're married."

Helen looked up. "Bite the bullet and call them right now."

"Do I have to?"

"You sound like a teenager afraid of her parents' wrath."

"I'll get my cell phone and call them in front of you. I'm sure they'll be angry with me."

"You don't know—maybe they'll be pleased." Helen went to the sink and rinsed her glass.

Sara returned with the phone, sat opposite Helen at the table, and dialed her parents.

"Hello," her mother said with a surprising lilt in her voice.

"Hi, Mom."

"I'm so glad you called, Sara. I have good news. Your father's blood pressure is down to normal as a result of the medicine he's been taking. He's been on it only a month."

Sara bit down on her lips. Helen, eating an English muffin, pointed to Sara and the phone in her hand as a sign of encouragement for her to confront her mother with her news.

Sara sighed. "Remember I told you about the guy in my class who I've been dating? Well, he and . . ."

"Oh, the one who is a young student with no prospects?"

"He has prospects. He's been hired as an assistant professor at Winthrop University in Rock Hill, South Carolina."

"So that means he's going away and you feel bad that you won't see him again."

"No. I'll continue to see him. We plan on getting married and living in South Carolina."

Helen smiled her approval at Sara's forthrightness and silently clapped her hands.

"Mom? Are you there? Say something—anything. Wish me luck. Or say you're happy for me. Or say that you're surprised."

"Sara. Your father and I are leaving the house and driving to Palm Oasis to talk to you. We'll be there in three hours. Make sure you're home. Goodbye."

Sara, with an expression of sadness, put down the phone on the kitchen table. "They're coming here right now. I knew it. They don't know about his inheritance, and they think that a college professor makes a poor living and that I'll struggle financially the rest of my life."

"That won't be a problem when you fully explain the situation."

"But suppose they complain about my moving to another state? What can I say?"

"Tell them you're an adult and it's normal for a husband and wife to live together."

Sara put her head in her hands. "My parents put me in a cage before and they'll try to do it again."

"So don't let them."

"It's not as easy as all that. My mother will say that Eric is in Ireland, and I'll be in another state—and their grandchildren will be far away. She'll tell me about my father's high blood pressure and that I'll be the death of him. They won't pay a cent for the wedding."

Helen rose and went to the refrigerator. She brought back four slices of low-fat swiss cheese on a plate, took two slices, and offered the rest to Sara. "I've been thinking," she said. "George and I don't want a big wedding. We've had that before and don't need a fuss. It's a pain in the neck to plan for a wedding, and we thought we'd go to Las Vegas and get married in a simple ceremony. You can do the same. In fact, we could all go together. We'd have fun and skip the aggravation of sending out invitations, hiring a rabbi and a hall, planning all the minute details of meal service, receiving gifts that we don't need and have to write thank you notes."

"I never considered that option. I'm calling Rusty right now. He should be here when my parents arrive."

* * *

Mr. Solomon clamped down on the car's steering wheel like he was squeezing the neck of a chicken. "Try to relax," Mrs. Solomon said.

REVA SPIRO LUXENBERG

"Your face is bright red. The doctor warned you not to get excited. I'm sure your blood pressure is rising every mile you're driving."

"She's such a fool," he said. "A college professor earns next to nothing. When she has children she'll learn the hard way how much money diapers cost. Then she'll turn to us for help and I won't give her a penny."

"When we talk sense to her, she may come around and drop the loser." Mrs. Solomon looked out the window and saw a blur, as her mind was on the destructive path her daughter was bent on taking.

"If she doesn't listen to us and this would be the second time," Mr. Solomon said, ". . . we'll have to travel by plane for hours to see her and the grandkids."

"I'm afraid of planes. The TV is always announcing how many planes crash. And if a plane doesn't crash, the germs from all the passengers circulate and older people like us get pneumonia."

*   *   *

Rusty came to Helen's house an hour before Sara's parents arrived. He brought three large cheese pizzas to share. Sara had informed him that George was coming over and her parents might be hungry after their trip from Tampa. He put the pizza boxes in the kitchen and the two couples made themselves comfortable in the large living room.

The furniture was arranged with a sofa against the wall, and two love seats at right angles to the sofa. Helen had an interior decorator design the living room because she liked her company to be comfortable. With the exception of Helen's lavender bedroom and Sara's blue bedroom, the house was done in earth colors. Sara and Rusty sat on the sofa—Helen and George were in the left love seat.

"What do you think about Helen and me and you and Sara skipping a catered affair, flying to Vegas, and getting hitched there?" George asked Rusty.

Rusty pushed his cowlick back with his hand. "I like the idea, but it's up to Sara. Whatever she wants is fine with me."

"I'd love to go to Las Vegas. We could stay at a five-star hotel for the wedding and then visit the Hoover Dam," Sara said. "I read that Las Vegas has many interesting museums. It's an exciting idea."

Rusty took hold of Sara's hand and squeezed it with approval and love.

∗ ∗ ∗

Sara kissed her parents on their cheeks and ushered them into the living room where she introduced George and Rusty. Mr. and Mrs. Solomon sat down in the love seat to the right. They looked so uncomfortable that Sara suggested they might want to have something to drink and eat.

"No, thank you," Mrs. Solomon said.

"We wanted to talk to you privately," Mr. Solomon said in a brusque way.

"These are my best friends," Sara said pointing to Helen and George. "And this is the man I'm going to marry—and anything we have to say I wish everyone to hear."

"You didn't listen to us when we warned you not to marry a policeman and look what happened," Mr. Solomon said.

Rusty's eyes widened. "That could have happened to anyone. What objection do you have to me?"

Mrs. Solomon put her hand on her husband's arm to silence him. "We are sure you're a very nice young man, but our daughter needs security and college professors can't provide the security Sara needs. She's been very ill and needs continuing care."

"Mrs. Solomon," Rusty said, "I love your daughter. She is presently very healthy in both body and mind. My father left me well provided for, and I have a generous trust fund that will take care of both of us for the rest of our lives."

"I didn't know that," Mrs. Solomon said. "The strongest objection we have is that Sara will move away from Florida and we won't see her. We are getting older and more frail and we want our daughter to live near us."

"Mom," Sara said. "I will call you and visit. A plane from Charlotte, North Carolina, to Tampa will take me to you in a couple of hours. You won't be losing a daughter. You'll be gaining a son."

"We won't pay for the wedding," Mr. Solomon said gravely.

REVA SPIRO LUXENBERG

"We decided not to make a big wedding. We'll get married in Las Vegas. I hope you'll come," Sara said.

"I hate flying in an airplane," Mrs. Solomon said.

Helen was thoroughly disgusted. *If you won't go by plane, fly on your broomstick.*

CHAPTER 48

TRACY SHOWED UP an hour late at her singing job at one of the restaurants in Caesar's Palace. She had gone to lunch with a man she met, thinking that because he had a diamond stud in his ear, he was wealthy. When he revealed he was a bus driver from Denver and was on vacation, she left him after she finished her entrée and went back to her room where she took a nap. She woke up too late to do her hair and makeup and she had to dress hurriedly in a red evening gown with revealing décolleté.

When Tracy with an expression of disgust got to the employee's dressing room, her boss was standing in the center of the room. His hairy muscular arms were crossed.

"Hi, Phi," Tracy said. "My alarm didn't go off."

"This is the third time you've showed up late. You may have a gorgeous voice and a striking body, but you don't come on time. You're fired."

"You have the face of a horse and the body of a gorilla. You can keep your lousy job. I'm worth ten times what you're paying me."

*   *   *

It took a month for Tracy to find another gig at a restaurant in downtown Las Vegas. She would have liked to sing at the noted Bellagio Hotel, but her agent had dropped her and she had to take what she could get on her own. Some of the best shows were at the Bellagio's like Cirque Du Soleil that had an aquatic theme combined with surrealism. She often passed the Bellagio's magnificent fountains. If only she could meet a millionaire and stay there as a guest, it would be paradise. Meanwhile Tracy missed Elliott's body. He had been the best lover she ever had. If she called him, she might be able to persuade him to come to Las Vegas. She had heard about a playhouse that needed a new play. He might be interested.

Tracy sat at her desk in her tiny room. She dialed Elliott's number in Florida.

Elliott answered the ring, "You've reached the morgue. We're closed today."

"Elliott," Tracy said. "It's me. How are you?"

Elliott hung up as soon as he recognized Tracy's voice.

Tracy dialed his number again. The phone rang seven times before Elliott picked it up.

"Don't hang up," Tracy said. "I have good news."

"You're in jail," Elliott quipped.

"I know you're angry at me. You have a perfect right to be. You were an angel, and Lenny was a monster."

"Did he hit you?"

That's an idea. He never laid a hand on me but I'll lie.

"Yes, only once. He gave me a black eye—so I left him. We went to Las Vegas and he gambled all his money away. I'm still in Las Vegas and I'm singing in a restaurant and making good money." *It's barely enough to pay for this flea bag room.*

"I see. What's the real reason you're calling me?"

"It's about the Bent's Las Vegas Playhouse. They're looking to stage a comedy. I spoke to the manager about your wonderful plays, and he's interested. He wants to meet you and read your most recent play."

"I don't know. Right now I'm busy writing a newer one."

"You'd be foolish to miss this opportunity. Besides I miss you terribly."

"Give me your number and I'll get back to you."

*   *   *

Elliott hopped in his car and drove over to his Aunt Helen's house. He could have walked the two blocks, but it was muggy and hot and driving was easier. Helen was kind to him after her husband, his uncle, died when he was fifteen years old. He knocked at the door and Sara, dressed in short shorts and a knit top, opened the door.

"Hi, Sara. Is my aunt in?"

"Hello, Elliott. Your aunt is in the shower. You can wait for her in the living room."

Elliott walked to the living room and sat down on the sofa. "I haven't seen you for a while. I'd like to talk to you."

Sara sat on the love seat. "Okay, talk away."

"How are you? You look fabulous. What's new?"

"Thanks for the compliment. I'm fine. I'm getting married."

Elliott stared at Sara for a few moments. "You're engaged?"

"Yes."

"Who is the lucky fellow?"

"Someone I met in school. His name is Rusty. He's going to teach at Winthrop University in South Carolina."

"So you'll be moving to South Carolina?"

"Of course. I finished my novel, and Rusty is editing it."

"That's such good news. Congratulations." Elliott jumped up as his aunt entered the room. He moved over to her and gave her a big hug. "You smell like a rose, Aunt Helen."

"And you smell like you need a shower. Why haven't I heard from you for almost a month?"

"I'm just lazy, Aunt Helen."

Sara rose and walked toward the dining room door. "Nice seeing you," she said. "I'll give you privacy."

Helen tied the sash of her terry robe tighter before she sat on the sofa. "What's up?"

"I need your advice," Elliott said forthrightly.

"Why now? You never took my advice before."

"This is different. I'm pulled in two directions. Tracy is in Las Vegas, and she called me and said that there's a playhouse that's interested in a play of mine. I'd like to keep my distance from her. She is unreliable, but I would like to get work."

Helen, with stern eyes, said, "I'd say keep away from that woman, but you won't listen to me, so I say do whatever you want."

"Thanks, aunt. What's doing with you?"

"It looks like George and I will get married in Las Vegas, and so will Sara and Rusty."

"Then it's all settled. I want to be at your wedding and by going to Las Vegas I'll kill two birds with one stone."

"Watch what you do with that stone," Helen warned her nephew.

After Elliott left, Sara joined Helen in the living room. "My nephew is a fool," Helen said.

"Why do you say that? You used to praise him to the heavens," Sara said.

"He's planning to go to Las Vegas because Tracy called him and told him that there's a playhouse interested in one of his plays. Tracy is poison for Elliott and he knows it, but when she beckons with her finger, he comes running."

"I know you want to protect him but he's a grown man and he'll do whatever he pleases."

"Sara, we'll be in Vegas at the same time as Elliott. Maybe I can pick up the pieces," Helen said with trembling hands.

"We'll be having weddings and honeymoons and you will want to take time to help your nephew deal with Tracy's shenanigans? Does that make sense?"

"I guess not."

"What hotels are George and Rusty researching for our affairs?"

"George hasn't gotten back to me, but I'm pretty sure we'll approve what they suggest."

"I'm so nervous I can't wait to make final plans. If I know Rusty, we'll have the time of our lives."

CHAPTER 49

G EORGE AND RUSTY sat opposite each other in a booth in Tom's Diner enjoying apple pie. The men were engrossed in planning for their double weddings. The girls insisted on them, and they had no choice but to acquiesce.

"Have you ever been to Las Vegas," Rusty asked.

George took a sip of hot coffee. He licked his burnt lips. "Ten years ago. It's a fun place in which to get married."

"I like the idea of going there, but I don't know how to make the arrangements. Are there any hotels you'd recommend?"

George looked like he was deep in thought. "I don't know. The Strip has many hotels. They are torn down very often, and new ones are built before you can say *cash in my chips.*"

Rusty's eyes brightened. "I just thought of someone who could help us."

"A travel agent?"

"No. Let's pay the bill and go to my house. My mother knows everything."

*   *   *

Rusty led George into the aviary where his mother stood feeding the cockatiels. George was startled when he heard voices call, "Sara, I love you. Sara, will you marry me?"

Mrs. Hooper laughed heartily. "Don't let the parrots knock you for a loop. They've been trained by Rusty to repeat those words."

Rusty made the introductions. "George, this is my mother, Mrs. Hooper."

Mrs. Hooper wiped her hand and held it out for George to shake. "Pleased to meet you," she said as they left the aviary and sat on the back patio.

"Ma," Rusty said. "Do you know of a nice hotel in Las Vegas where George and Helen, and Sara and I can get married and spend our honeymoons?"

"What a great plan! A fabulous place is the Bellagio Hotel-Casino. My friend Myra raved about her stay there. There's a sculptured ceiling of hand-blown glass blossoms in the lobby that impressed her so much she sat on a chair and gazed up with admiration at it for an hour. She told me that every morning before dawn a team of engineers cleans and maintains it. I'll look forward to seeing it."

"Sounds wonderful," Rusty said.

"I'd like to see that," George said. "How about looking at the Bellagio site online?"

"Fine," Rusty said. "I'll get my computer." He walked to his bedroom, returned with a large laptop, pressed the ON button and eagerly waited for it to activate. He went on Google and typed *Bellagio*, and the site yielded a great deal of information. "Look," he said, "they have a gallery of fine art."

"Oh, I forgot to mention that Myra raved about its collection. The holdings range from the Rembrandts to Picassos."

"I love to see good art," George said, ". . . and so does Helen."

"What about birds?" Mrs. Hooper asked.

"It doesn't mention birds, but the hotel has a conservatory and a botanic garden," Rusty said.

"How many people are you inviting?" Mrs. Hooper asked George. "We have fifteen between Sara's family and our family and friends, but one first cousin can't come as she's bedridden."

"Helen has her sister, her nephew, and three cousins, and I have a small family—my sons and their wives. That makes about ten. I also have two close friends—twelve all together. I think we've forgotten some people so we should figure on about thirty or so."

"Look what I found," Rusty exclaimed. "The hotel has a place for weddings called the Terrazza Di Sogno, a magnificent terrace that accommodates up to thirty-four guests. Also they say they have a technical team that can broadcast the ceremony in a live webcast so that Rusty's bedridden cousin can see it."

"It sounds perfect," George said happily.

"The website describes a restaurant with the French cuisine that I like," Rusty said. "Look at this picture. There are red-cushioned armchairs around tables covered with white linens. On the ceiling is a canopy of materials in purple, yellow, crimson, and bronze. Too bad that Sara's friend Joan is traveling in China. She won't return until after the wedding, but we'll take photos. I wish I were at the hotel right now."

"Before we know it, the four of us will be happily married," George said with a big smile.

CHAPTER 50

BOTH WEDDINGS SOARED like a rocket to the moon. All the guests were delighted with the exception of Tracy, who accompanied Elliott even though she hadn't been invited. The morning after the wedding diverse conversations took place in the Bellagio hotel rooms occupied by the wedding parties.

Mrs. Solomon, with a stern expression, looked out the eleventh floor window at the almost empty streets. The few people who ambled along looked like toys. She wore an olive cotton nightgown and had her hair in curlers. Mr. Solomon, in boxer shorts stood at the coffee machine trying to figure out how it worked.

He grunted, "Where does the coffee filter go?"

"Forget that. We'll get dressed and go down for a full breakfast," his grumpy wife said.

"But I need my cup of coffee now," Mr. Solomon protested.

"I've been thinking that when Sara has children, they'll all have red hair like their father. I hate red hair. It is associated with a terrible temper."

"Isn't it time you stopped being so critical? I'm sick and tired of your always finding fault. You should be dancing with joy that Sara married someone who is rich."

Mrs. Solomon turned her back on her husband. *That man thinks he knows everything. Red hair is repulsive.*

*   *   *

Eric knocked at his mother's door. Mrs. Solomon put on a terry robe and opened the door. "Good morning, Ma. How did you sleep?"

"How do you expect me to sleep when my son works in Ireland and my daughter is moving to South Carolina? I tossed all night. The bed was hard. It was like sleeping on stone."

Eric moved over to where his father was fussing with the coffee machine. "Here let me help you with that." In a moment he had set the coffee to brew. "I have good news. I didn't want to tell you before because I wanted Sara to have the attention she deserves. I'm engaged to an Irish lass—yes, she's Jewish. I had a promotion and we'll be living in Dublin."

Mrs. Solomon dropped down on a chair. "Pooh! We'll never see you."

Eric patted his mother's shoulder. "When I get my vacation, we'll visit. We expect to get married in March. We want you at our wedding."

Mrs. Solomon's forehead wrinkled. "You know I hate to fly. The plane can get hijacked and we can be killed. Get married in Tampa."

Eric answered calmly, "That's not possible. Lucy has a large family and her parents want to make the wedding in Ireland."

"You've always been a rebellious child," Mrs. Solomon shouted.

And you, my mother, have always been a difficult mother.

*　　*　　*

Rusty's mother and her first cousin, Dennis, sat at the round cherrywood table in Mrs. Hooper's room. She had taken the wedding centerpiece of pink, yellow, and red roses and placed it on the table in her room. The sweet aroma of the flowers filled the air.

"I was so sorry I couldn't bring doves to the weddings," she said.

"The weddings were beautiful without birds, although they would've added an extra touch of romance," Dennis said. He had changed from his tuxedo to a yellow shirt and shorts. He was a man with a head that looked too small for his stout frame. "How do you feel about your new daughter-in-law?"

"Wonderful. She's a really good person, and you can tell that she and Rusty are very much in love."

"That's fine. My wife was unfaithful and I was forced to divorce her. I'm happy we didn't have children. Tell me, who is taking care of your birds for the week you are staying here?"

"I have a male friend I can trust. He's getting serious. He's teaching one of the grey parrots to say 'I love you sweetheart. Marry me.'"

"Will you marry him?"

"Who knows? It's too early to tell. I think I'll wait until the bird learns the new phrases."

*　　*　　*

"I love this room," Tracy said to Elliott. She was naked under the satin comforter and he was shaving in the bathroom.

"What did you say?" Elliott asked, as he came into the room and sat down on the bed. "I didn't hear you?"

"I said I love this room. I would like to remain in this hotel forever. I hate to work. Here I would have a full staff of maids and cooks. I wish I could shop in all the boutiques. This is the life I want to lead."

"Forget it, Tracy. The director turned down my play. I've decided that it's better for me to get an English certification for teaching in high school. I don't like living from hand to mouth."

"Teachers earn pennies. I couldn't live on a teacher's salary."

"I never asked you to. I never proposed to you."

"I'd never marry you even if you asked me." Tracy smoothed down her long hair with her hand. "Sara is a fool for marrying a teacher. She always was a stupid person. I think she was acting when she said she couldn't remember anyone. And did you see the midget she picked? He's her height, a shrimp."

"Get dressed and get out. I'm tired of your selfish ways. I never want to see you again."

"You and your aunt Helen are dogs. I'm sorry I asked you to take me to the worst wedding I ever attended."

How could I ever have had anything to do with Tracy? My eyes must've been closed.

*   *   *

The waiter knocked at the door of room 715. George opened it and the waiter with slicked-back ebony hair entered carrying a breakfast tray packed with delicacies for the bride and groom. He placed the food at each setting on the table and put one large rose in a crystal vase in the center. George took his wallet out of the pocket of his navy bathrobe and gave him a generous tip. George was feeling like a king, and the world was rosy.

"Thank you, sir. Much appreciated. Hope you and your wife enjoy the meal and the rest of your stay."

Helen came out of the bathroom with a big smile on her face and bridal lingerie on her body.

"You smell delicious," George said as he pulled the chair out for her to sit.

"That's not me. It's the eggs with the onions. I'm starved. How about you?"

"I'm starved for more loving," George said as he lifted a glass filled with freshly squeezed orange juice. "I feel so lucky that I found the nicest woman I ever knew. And a real beauty too."

"You're making me blush," Helen said as she put her hand on his.

George got up and circled the table. "Ain't love grand?" he said, as he bent down and planted a kiss on his bride's soft lips.

When he moved away, Helen said, "I think we should give a present to whoever is in charge of Matchmaking for Love."

"Agreed," George said with a big grin.

*   *   *

Alice, dressed in a peach nylon brief and a matching peach Alice bra that she had designed, slid open the drapes in room 414. She looked out the window at a cloudless sky. *Wow, I miss the pretty Florida sky dotted with all kinds of clouds. Too bad Ralph couldn't come. I really miss him.*

*   *   *

Rusty had his arm around Sara as they stood in robes on the balcony of room 828. "I couldn't have asked for a more perfect wedding and a lovelier bride."

"It was fantastic," Sara said. ". . . especially last night."

"You naughty girl."

"Naughty? You call me naughty? I think you were just as naughty as me."

"Sara, my love, you're a perfect pearl. A pearl is made from the irritation of sand, and you have overcome a sandy past and come through exquisitely. You went to college where we met—you kept writing and now you have an agent and your first novel has a good chance of being published. I'm so proud."

"I did what I had to do. And what about you? You got your degree and a wonderful position in a university. If anyone is proud, it's certainly me."

"Let's have breakfast," Rusty said as he took hold of Sara's hand and led her to the table in the room. A fruit basket was laid out on it.

"And after breakfast will we go back to bed?"

"You bet."

When they sat at the table Sara spotted a blueberry that called out to her. She picked it up and found it was firm and plump. The color was deep and she anticipated that it would taste delicious. The texture of the berry's skin looked smooth and she wanted to feel it in her mouth. She knew it would be juicy, even though it was firm inside it would have the right softness. As lover's bodies show their readiness for each other, tasting the fruit brought a rush of sensations. The scent of the berry was sweet with a distinct flavor. She bit into it and she could feel the juice as it spread in her mouth like an intoxicating wine.

After they ate their fill, Rusty took Sara by her hand and led her to the bed that was still mussed up after last night's lovemaking.

"I love you like crazy," he said stroking her face.

"I love you, too. I never thought I would ever love anyone again, but I was wrong."

"If a mother has ten children, she loves them all. Love isn't a one-time feeling," Rusty said as he slipped off his robe.

"But what about romantic love? How many times can one person love?"

"One thousand and twenty-two times," Rusty joked, "and now I'm going to show you just how much I love you. Stretch out and relax." Rusty took Sara's feet and began massaging her arches.

"Oh, that feels good. Please don't look at my toes."

"Why not?"

"One of my nails is discolored."

"Silly girl—as if that would upset me. I love every single part of your gorgeous body." Rusty gently pulled each toe. When he finished with Sara's feet, he moved up her legs and continued massaging. "Now I'm going to pull your negligee over your head."

"I'm your slave. Do what you want with me," Sara said giggling.

Rusty let out a low whistle as he looked at her up and down. "Your body is very beautiful." He planted soft kisses on her face, her breasts, and round and round in circles on her stomach. "Your skin is as smooth as a baby's."

Sara moaned with pleasure.

When Rusty entered her, Sara with her arms around his back, held him tight and planted kisses on his face and neck. She heard music like angels singing. As the tempo increased, Sara drowned in timeless eternity. Her breathing increased and pounded in her ears. "I love you," she called out.

"I adore you," Rusty replied. Spent, they lay flat on the bed holding hands.

"I never thought such joy existed," Sara said.

"It'll be like this for the rest of our married life." Rusty leaned over and gave Sara a kiss.

"You kiss well," Sara said. "By the way now the parrots say, 'Sara I love you. Sara will you marry me?' When we go home will you teach them, 'I'll always love you?'"

"What a question? As soon as I carry you over the threshold I'll drop you and run and talk to the parrots and in a few weeks they'll be saying that."

Life has its hills and valleys, but now I'm on the crest of the mountain and I never want to descend.

REVA SPIRO LUXENBERG

Printed in the United States
By Bookmasters